The Wizard by the Sea

ANNA WINEHEART

Copyright © 2017 Anna Wineheart

All rights reserved. This is a work of fiction. Names, characters, businesses, places, events and incidents are either the products of the author's imagination or used in a fictitious manner. Any resemblance to actual persons, living or dead, or actual events is purely coincidental.

No part of this book may be reproduced or transmitted in any form or by any means whatsoever without express written permission from the author, except in the case of brief quotations embodied in critical articles and reviews.

This novel contains graphic sexual content between two men. Intended for mature readers only.

Warnings: Alcoholism, themes of death, some gore

ISBN: 154462994X
ISBN-13: 978-1544629940

For the two loveliest guys ever.

As always, a huge thank-you to my mentor, Jessica Mueller, who is wise and incredible, and my husband, David, who shakes his head when I come up with a million new storybook ideas.

CONTENTS

1	Ten	1
2	Eleven	6
3	Twelve	9
4	Thirteen (Part I)	15
5	Thirteen (Part II)	23
6	Thirteen (Part III)	30
7	Fourteen	41
8	Fifteen	53
9	Sixteen	64
10	Seventeen	74
11	Eighteen (Part I)	80
12	Eighteen (Part II)	89
13	Eighteen (Part III)	98
14	Nineteen (Part I)	107
15	Nineteen (Part II)	126
16	Twenty	134
17	Twenty-One	145
18	Twenty-Two	153
19	Twenty-Three (Part I)	162
20	Twenty-Three (Part II)	172

21	Twenty-Three (Part III)	182
22	Twenty-Three (Part IV)	190
23	Twenty-Three (Part V)	200
24	Twenty-Three (Part VI)	209
25	Twenty-Three (Part VII)	220
26	Twenty-Three (Part VIII)	228
27	Twenty-Three (Part IX)	236
28	Twenty-Three (Part X)	242
29	Twenty-Three (Part XI)	253
	Epilogue	262

1
Ten

ON HIS tenth birthday, Connor trips over a sleeping wizard.

The shores of Fort Bragg lie. They shroud the rumbling waves with gray fog, make him think the brine-darkened sand stretches flat when in reality, it rises and dips, clumps of seaweed hiding bits of too-straight driftwood.

The wood splits into two just as his foot passes over it. Connor's heart lodges in his throat. *The kraken!* He flails. His toes hook onto the driftwood and it *jerks* beneath him. He lurches forward into the sand. In the last moments before he's eaten by a monster, Connor scrambles up, breath ragged, and whips around.

A man sits up straight in front of him, eyes flying open. "Suck my dick!" he yelps.

Connor stares. The driftwood is actually a thin, pale man, fire-red hair a mess on his head, smart white shirt hugging his lean torso. His trousers had looked so much like rough bark. *Not a kraken.* "What?"

The man gapes. "What are you doing here?"

"What are *you* doing here?" Connor asks. He's

been walking the shores of Fort Bragg for years, and he's never seen anyone with hair this red. "You tripped me and then you said, 'Suck my dick.'"

The man slaps a sandy hand to his forehead, scowling as though he's just let a secret slip. "Oh, suc—Neptune's mercy. Pretend you didn't hear that."

"Why not?" Connor asks. "You just said it!"

"It's not polite," the man says. He claps the sand off his palms and looks up at the angry clouds. The wind picks up, icy and crisp, sighing through Connor's hair. Yet the man gives off a strange, flickering heat, noticeable even from two feet away. "Nothing I should be saying to a child."

"I'm not a—"

"What time is it?" The man scrunches up his face. "There's a storm coming in."

Yards away, the wind whips the sea up into a froth. Connor thinks about the crash of thunder, the deafening patter of raindrops on the roof, and winces. He wants to walk the beach, but he can't go home with a cold. "It's two," he says, because that's when his mom goes for a nap, after she's gutted his dad's harvest and Connor's salted the fish. "Three soon."

"That's late. I shouldn't have fallen asleep." The man rocks forward and stands, dusting off his pants.

"You're short," Connor blurts. The men in town are taller than him by at least two heads; he's as tall as this man's shoulder.

The man laughs. "Well. Nothing I can do about it." But he pauses, rubbing his thumb over his other hand. "Or maybe I can, but it isn't worth the effort."

"How can you get taller?" Connor watches, expecting the man to straighten his shoulders like Connor does in front of his grandma.

Sea-blue eyes linger contemplatively on him, and a kind smile tugs on the man's mouth. "Would you like to see?"

Connor nods. The man wriggles his fingers, beckoning him to follow. They walk ten yards down the shore. Amidst long, shallow ruts extending from the sea, deep swirls have been carved into wet sand: roses, whirls, crosses. The man pauses at a drawing of a clover leaf, where seawater has smudged the lowest curve away. He crouches, redrawing it when the wave retreats. When brine roars back along the shore, it rushes along the lines of the leaf, filling the drawing up to the top.

The lines glow blue.

Connor blinks. The lines shimmer merrily. The man dips his sandy toes into the clover leaf and breathes in.

And right in front of him, the man grows taller. His legs stretch. So does his torso. He grows like a beanstalk, until he stands three heads above Connor, pale shins peeking from the hems of his now-short trousers. "See?" he says, and exhales. With the breath goes his height. He shrinks again so he doesn't seem all drawn-out, and his trouser legs fit perfectly once more. The glow in the clover fades. Before Connor can ask to try it, the wizard says, "It's better that you don't learn."

"Did you just read my mind?" Connor asks, wary. They've only just met. He can't know what

Connor wants.

The wizard shakes his head. "You're not the first to ask. But you aren't old enough to understand the weight of magic yet."

Connor ducks his head to hide his disappointment. He's never seen a wizard. Sure, he's heard stories, but no one in town knows for certain that there's one out here. So he studies the drawings in the sand, and the wizard and the dunes watch him. The shore sprawls empty around them, littered with abandoned cutlery, wallets, and ragged clothing. On the horizon, a jagged shipwreck sits in the sea, and the cliffs yawn craggy and misty further away.

The wizard turns toward the cliffs. "Go home," he says over his shoulder. "Maybe we'll meet again."

"Really?" Connor memorizes the crosses and roses on the shore, so he can describe them to his mom later. He wants to see more magic!

"Really," the wizard says, brushing his fingers through Connor's hair. Warmth trickles down into Connor's body, coating his limbs like the heat from a hearth.

When he trudges through the pouring rain, his clothes catch a bit of damp instead of plastering against his skin. Connor knows in his gut that he won't catch a cold. He turns around on the shore, but all he sees are the roiling waves.

"SAVING ALL My Love for You" plays on the radio that night. As his mom ladles fish soup into a wide bowl, Connor says, "I saw a wizard by the sea. He said I'm too young to do magic."

"Really?" His mother meets his eyes, before glancing surreptitiously at his dad across the tiny kitchen.

Dad stops singing along with Whitney Houston. "Magic," he scoffs, his face twisting into a scowl. "You'll do better helping me with the boat."

"I already did." Connor traces a clover leaf in the dusting of flour on the granite counter, blowing lightly on it. But it doesn't light up like the wizard's. He wonders if he'll learn the wizard's secrets. Maybe if he asks nicely, like how he asks Mom when he wants another cookie.

Later, Mom pulls him aside and asks what sort of magic the wizard did. Her eyes crinkle when he tells her, and warmth surges through his chest.

No matter when he visits the shore after that, the sand remains smooth and untouched. Connor wishes he could see the wizard and his drawings again, but neither return.

2
Eleven

ON HIS eleventh birthday, he follows his dad to Mack's. Shadows lurk in the corners between aisles of ropes and nails and planks. The scent of wood polish, sardines, and tomato sauce curls up into his nose, and he sniffs, looking around. A plate of sandwiches sits abandoned at the counter. Connor stares after it, trailing behind his dad, wishing they'd hurry home for lunch. But Dad says the boat transmission is handling like crap, and so they're at the store, searching for parts.

"I promise we'll head back after this," his dad says, catching his longing gaze. "But first, tell me: which are the shaft bearings?"

Connor perks up. He scans the products on the shelves — tins of oil, drums of paint, great propellers on the floor — and finds the thin polymer slats in a box at shoulder-level. He points them out.

"Right on, kid," Dad says, his eyes twinkling. He claps Connor on the shoulder. "Gonna teach you how to fix the transmission tomorrow. You learn this stuff quick!"

Connor swells with pride. "You bet!"

"I wasn't aware that they sell bearings made of

lignum vitae," another voice murmurs.

Two feet away, a man reaches into the depths of the shelves. He's a head taller than Connor, and Connor's heart leaps at his shock of fiery hair. No one in Fort Bragg has hair that red. "It's y—"

"Have you heard of it? Wood of Life," the wizard says, looking between Connor and his father. His eyes are a startling crystal-blue, and his hand cradles a slender piece of wood: fine-grained, tan like his dad. "I've heard rumors that submarines used these in the war."

Connor frowns. Wood bearings for the shaft? But wood swells and warps in water. More importantly, where did the wizard disappear to? He peers into blue eyes. The wizard smiles, slow and knowing.

"I've heard of it," Dad says. He checks the bearings, then the price, and whistles lowly. "Here, Connor. Look at this."

Connor hefts the wood in his hand. Unlike the airy lightness of balsa, or the hearty substance of mahogany, this shaft bearing weighs heavy in his fingers, denser than water, smooth as though oiled.

Quietly, the wizard says, "They insist Merlin's wand was made of this very wood." He's acknowledging magic, right in front of Connor's dad, but Dad's distracted, inspecting the bearings for cracks. "I've never seen it outside the tropics."

"You've been to the tropics?" Connor asks. The furthest he's gone is out west, when Dad heads over the deeper Pacific for the rockfish migration. "I never saw you again on the shore."

The wizard winks. "I haven't fallen asleep there since. It was nice meeting you; we had a good conversation. Perhaps you'll see the world someday."

A bubble floats up inside Connor's chest. "Can you teach—"

"Connor," his father says, snapping his fingers. "Are you hungry? 'Cause I am." To the wizard, he raises his handful of bearings. "Thanks for pointing these out. Don't see wood of this quality around at all."

"Anytime, good sir." The wizard dips his chin and sets his hand on Connor's head. Warmth flows from Connor's hair through his body, to his toes, banishing his hunger, and all the weariness from the morning dissipates from his limbs. He gapes. The wizard winks and turns, black coat hiding the length of his frame.

Connor looks between his father, who's chatting with the brunette at the counter, and the wizard, stepping forward. If he can cast a spell without blinking, then surely he can teach Connor to do this, too. His pulse thrums. The wizard raises a finger to his lips and holds Connor's gaze. "Maybe next time."

Hope flares in his chest. "Really?"

"Perhaps." The wizard turns away, twirling a wooden stick between his fingers. His coat swishes behind another aisle, and he's gone again, just like that.

Connor sets a hand on his sternum. Energy thrums in his veins like electricity, making his limbs coil tight, a delightful sizzle that makes him want to run and shout and play.

It feels like a secret.

3
Twelve

ON HIS twelfth birthday, Connor bakes a cake with his mother. In a corner of the kitchen, next to cross-stitched pictures of the sea, the radio plays "No More Lonely Nights". Mom hums along to it. She drags her flour-dusted finger down the recipe book, tapping on the ingredients list, and flour sprinkles onto the page. "Be a dear and get me the vanilla extract, will you?"

Connor wanders over to the pantry, bowl of icing cradled in one arm. The glass bottles sit patiently in the shadows—lemon, almond, mint. No vanilla. "It's not here."

"Can't have grown two legs and run away," Mom says, clucking her tongue.

He peers harder into the shadows. And there, right in the corner, the bottle cowers, shallow brown extract quivering inside. Connor reaches for it. It topples, as though playing dead. When he grabs it, the bottle radiates warmth in his palm. *Magic?* He whips around, expecting to see a wizard in the window, but there's no wizard, only the pastel-blue siding of their neighbor's house.

He sets the vanilla extract on the counter,

keeping a hand around it in case it bolts. The bottle doesn't twitch at all. "I could've sworn it moved," he says. "It was in a corner of the pantry."

"My boy's grown up fierce." Amusement twinkles in Mom's eyes. "Scaring away vanilla bottles instead of girls."

Connor makes a face. He doesn't like girls, but his mom is okay. "I think it's magic."

"Oh?" Mom leans in, unscrewing the metal cap on the essence. "Why do you say that?"

He tells her about wizards and impossible things, about Merlin's wand and drawings on the beach. She never gets tired of hearing it.

"I'm sorry we aren't magic," she says wistfully, her eyes dark with regret. "I'm sure you'd be great with it."

Instead of agreeing, Connor steps forward, hugging her with his icing-flecked arms. She smells like fish and home and *Mom*. "You're better than magic," he says.

She beams and kisses his forehead.

After dinner, Mom and Dad sing his birthday song. Mom's voice soars high, his dad's dipping low, and Connor loves how his parents' faces are lit by candlelight.

"Make a wish," Dad rumbles, lifting his beer bottle. Connor clinks his glass of apple juice against it.

He sucks a deep breath. *I want to see the wizard again. I want him and Dad to think I'm clever, so they'll teach me lots of things. I want Mom and Dad to be safe.* He blows out his candles.

"That's a very long wish," Mom says, chuckling as she slices up the green-frosted cake, crowned with maraschino cherries and shaved chocolate curls. The toppings are from the bakery down the street; he visits it sometimes with her, but she must have sneaked this in while he was out with Dad.

"It's a lot of wishes," Connor says.

"You shouldn't be greedy," Dad says, but he's grinning and ruffling Connor's hair. Connor sits down to the best birthday ever, when his mom hands over a lumpy, newspaper-wrapped present tied up with cotton twine.

It's a wooden sailboat, tiny cloth sails billowing from tall masts, like something from an aged painting. He wants his own sailboat, wants to travel the world in a towering, sturdy ship, canvas sails bulging in the wind. With old textbooks from school, Connor props it up by his narrow bed, pretending it'll sail off to exotic, faraway lands.

"I want to live on a ship," he tells his parents later that night.

Dad grins, and Mom hugs him.

THE NEXT day, when he's done salting fish with Mom, Connor sneaks into the kitchen. He pulls the cake out of the fridge, cuts a thick slice, and sets it on a plate, green icing a smear on ceramic.

Deep gray clouds roll along the edges of the sky. He steps into his shoes, dashing through the town. Midway to the shore, fat raindrops patter down onto his birthday cake. Connor swears. He covers it with his hand, but the raindrops slip around his fingers. The cake turns soggy twenty yards down, and sand squishes up around his feet.

The waves crash along the shore.

He finds the wizard. He wasn't expecting to, when all his walks by the sea have yielded an empty shoreline. Long, shoulder-wide ruts carve across the beach, stretching from the waves to the grass-strewn dunes. The wizard straightens from behind a tall mound of sand, and his mouth falls open when he catches sight of Connor.

"Suck m—No, never mind that," the wizard says, eyes wide. "I wasn't expecting you!"

He rounds the dune, dusts off his drenched clothes. When he draws closer, Connor feels that familiar not-quite-heat again, the flicker of *something*, something *safe* that dances in the wizard.

Connor thrusts the cake at him, uncertain. He should have checked the weather forecast. No one gives a wizard soggy cake. "You were at my house yesterday, weren't you? I thought you should have a slice, but it started raining halfway here. Sorry."

The wizard's face lights up. "Thank you. That's very kind of you, Connor."

He remembers my name! Connor grins. "Sure."

Rain patters on their heads, streaming down their faces. Connor's bangs are plastered over his eyes, and he realizes he's forgotten to bring a fork. Before he can apologize, the wizard wades into the waves. He washes his hands in the brine and wipes them off on his sandy pants. Then he accepts the plate from Connor, grasps the cake between his fingers, and shovels it into his mouth.

Connor doesn't know what sandy-salty-soggy cake tastes like, but when the wizard finishes it, he beams and licks his fingers clean, sand and all. Connor matches his smile. "You have frosting around your mouth."

"Oh." The wizard wipes his lips with the pads of his fingers, rain dripping down his nose. His eyes sparkle. "Happy birthday. I'm glad you remembered me."

"Of course I remember you," Connor says. "You promised to teach me."

"I might have." The wizard pats him on the head, and a thin, warm layer of air envelops his skin. Connor stops shivering, glancing hopefully up at him. The wizard shivers, himself. Then, he presses his lips together and looks away. "Not today, though. I'm sorry."

Connor droops. Dad said not to be greedy, so he quells the urge to pester the wizard for more. "I'll see you again?"

"Sooner than you think," the wizard says, smiling. He hands the plate back to Connor, and Connor hugs it to his chest. He wants to know more about magic. The wizard waves him off, brine crashing at his back. "Maybe when it isn't raining so hard. Go home for now. Thank you for the cake."

The wizard never appears again on the beach, but now that he knows they'll meet again, Connor waits for him with a smile on his face.

YATES STARES after the boy's retreating figure, cake crumbs and sand in his mouth. It's been years since someone remembered him on a birthday. The boy has so much potential. His energy flickers like a growing flame on firewood, warm and bright, and he doesn't seem to realize it at all.

How often does he find an aura that draws him in? It's been decades. More than that, perhaps, but there's been nothing so peaceful, nothing that meshes so well with his own, comforting like a warm hand on his neck.

Someone should mentor the boy. He'll learn the basics of magic quickly, judging by how well he knows his boat parts, and Yates would love to see him blossom under careful tutelage. It won't be from him, though. Someone more qualified can do it. Someone who will take the boy to great heights and coax him to shine brighter than sunlight. He would have a promising future.

Yates wipes his hands off, hugs himself, and heads for home.

4
Thirteen (Part I)

MOM DIES on Connor's thirteenth birthday.

The birds twitter on the rooftops. The sun rises bright and gold, stretching in through the wood-framed windows, and Mom sucks in every breath with a slow, sickening rattle. She lies in bed, pallid, sweating. Her cheeks are gaunt, her eyes sunken. Where it was once smooth and silky, her blond hair is now matted and dull.

Connor can't stand to see her in pain. But he's afraid of what might happen if he leaves, so he stays by her bed, stamping his feet. Dad holds her hand on her other side, his mouth drawn thin, his eyes tight. She's been bedridden for two weeks.

She coughs now, reaching out for him with a bony hand. The doctor says it's a lung cancer, that it's not contagious, but it's too late to save her. Connor hates the doctor. Doctors heal, don't they? Anxious, he sets his hand in Mom's. He crawls onto the bed and looks out the window. The sky is an iridescent blue, vivid like a wizard's eyes —

"I know a wizard," he gasps, full of horror and hope. He should have thought of this sooner, not now, not on his birthday while Mom struggles through her next wheezing breath. How could he have forgotten?

"The hell?" Dad says, his mouth twisting like he's tasted something bad. "No damned wizard is stepping in this house."

"But he'll help! I know he will," Connor says, his ribs tight.

Dad snorts.

"I'll ask him to cure her," Connor says, scrambling to his feet. Why wouldn't Dad want magic when it can solve so many problems? He glares. Mom always cheers up when they discuss magic.

"Connor," Dad says sharply, shaking his head. "Magic won't cure this."

"What do you know about magic?" he yells, indignant. Magic can cure this. Surely it can. The wizard has performed wonders in front of Connor's eyes. He's given Connor strength and protection from the rain. Surely he can cure Mom. Surely if he taught Connor... "The wizard can fix this!"

His father runs a hand across his face, shoulders tight. "Sit down."

"No!" Connor eases off the bed and dashes to the door, nails scraping on the peeling doorjamb.

"Connor!" Dad snaps, glass in his voice. Connor doesn't want to listen, is too afraid to listen. But Dad's never used that tone before, and it roots him to the floorboards, his heart pounding in his ears. Dad's voice breaks. "Stay here. Tell Mom how much you love her."

His blood freezes. Obeying his dad means he is right, that mom will die, and Connor refuses to let that happen. He's talked to his friends at school, Judy Brown with a dog that died in a car accident, Thomas Hills with his dad drowned at sea. Muffin never returned, and neither did Mr. Hills. Death doesn't wait for anyone. Death doesn't wait for you to say your goodbyes. Connor doesn't even know if he'll find the wizard today.

Mom coughs again, more raggedly, and Dad snaps for him. He stumbles back into the room, fear clawing up his throat. Sunlight scatters across the walls, and Mom's still sick in bed, her eyes tiny wrinkles on her face.

She should be covering his eyes while Dad brings the birthday cake in. She should be dishing out creamy fish soup, full of potatoes and carrots, telling him to eat and grow up strong. She should be watching while he unwraps his birthday present. Not lying sick in bed, struggling to breathe.

Connor climbs onto the mattress, holding her hand gingerly, his heart heavy with dread. "I love you, Mom," he whispers in her ear, then louder, when she stares at the far wall. Her dark eyes flicker over to him, and she smiles wanly. Hope flutters in his ribs. "Mom," Connor says. He wants more birthdays with her. He wants to see her laugh with Dad. "Don't go."

But she shakes her head and squeezes his hand. Her fingers are cold. Dad isn't even looking at Connor. He tucks Mom's hair behind her ear and presses a kiss to her forehead, a tear trickling down his cheek. Connor's never seen his dad cry before. Dad's the bravest man he knows.

Mom sucks in a shuddering breath, and her

coughs grow frail, until she's barely gasping. Her forehead pinches. Her chest stills. Light winks out of her eyes, leaving them open and glassy, and Dad leans forward, running his hand through her hair. "Mags? Magda."

He flattens his ear against her chest, and his face goes completely blank. He sits back in his chair, staring at Mom, brushing his thumb over her hand. Then, he closes her eyes.

"Mom?" Connor whispers. When she doesn't turn, he tries again. "Mom?"

Dad sucks in a shuddering breath. "She's gone, Connor."

Connor pushes his ear against her chest, too, straining for a sound, but all he hears are the birds chirping, the kids yelling outside. Mom's hand lies limply in his, still warm. "She can't be dead."

Dad just looks at her, his mouth a thin line.

Connor's not staying here. He can't. He pauses by the bedroom door, glancing at the wedding photo on the bedside table. He looks at Mom lying in bed, and Dad hunched over, his hand wrapped around hers.

He turns and runs.

THE TOWN passes in a blur: teenagers with boomboxes, businessmen in blocky cars, buses trundling down the roads. Connor takes the back streets, gasping, but he doesn't stop. He can't stop. If he does, it's real, and it can't be. Mom's still in bed. He'll find the wizard who will cure her, and she'll wake up and sing his birthday song. Dad will laugh again.

He doesn't slow until his feet plow through soft sand. The waves break along the beach, and the sapphire sky stretches all the way to the horizon. It's eight in the morning, the town is bustling, and back at home, Dad's crying silently by Mom's side.

Connor should be home. He should be helping Mom with the laundry, going out to sea with Dad. He shouldn't be racing across the shore, sand spraying behind him like tears. But the wizard can help. He can make the impossible happen. Surely he can make Mom get out of bed again.

He finds the wizard waist-deep in the surf. Connor yells, "Hey! Hey, wizard!"

The wizard turns, red hair ruffling in the wind. He hefts something up in his arms, dark and bulky. "What are you doing he—Oh, it's your birthday, isn't it?"

"My mom's dying," Connor blurts, because she *isn't dead*. He splashes into the sea, brine and sand swirling into his shoes, then further, until the waves sweep by his knees and thighs. He has to get the wizard out of the sea, get him home to Mom's side.

The wizard's smile falters. He heaves the bulk in his arms, walking backward to the shore. "I can't work miracles, Connor. Not when it comes to death."

Connor remembers *heat* and *joy* and *life*. If the wizard has cast spells on him, surely...

The wizard heaves on his burden. Long golden hair glimmers at the wizard's waist, dark fabric wrinkling, and an arm juts awkwardly out. It's not the wizard's.

He's pulling a corpse out of the ocean.

"Who's that?" Connor croaks, staring at the woman. She looks like his mom, except her face is swollen and blue, and she's too heavy, and *Mom's still alive.* She's at home with his dad, not sick and dead like this, and, and, and...

He's seen the wizard here, seen the lines dragging across the beach. It's never occurred to him just *why* they were there. Horror floods his lungs. He's come to the worst person for help. Maybe the wizard is a killer in secret.

When the wizard steps closer, Connor backs away. "Did you murder them?"

Blue eyes widen. "I found them in the sea. They're victims of shipwreck." The wizard lowers the woman back into the surf, his shoulders sagging. The waves wash over her face, rippling through her hair. Connor's stomach roils. "There are things magic cannot solve, Connor," the wizard says, turning to him. The woman sinks further down. "I'm afraid I can't—"

"Don't leave her in the waves!" he shouts, unease slithering through his stomach. "Take her out!"

The wizard grits his teeth, grasps under her arms, and hauls her out of the sea, leaving a rut in the beach all the way to the dunes. He disappears with the body behind the sand, and Connor keeps his distance.

Further out to sea, the carcass of a ship juts above the horizon, broken by the jagged cliffs. Connor has seen crates and bowls and clothes washed up on the shore, but not people. *He's been burying them. That's what those lines on the sand are from. He drags them out of the sea.* When the wizard emerges from the dunes, Connor inches toward him. "You have to save my mom."

"There are limits to magic, Connor." The wizard looks around, washes his hands, and heads back through the dunes. He's leaving. In a panic, Connor darts after him, past rows of heaped dirt.

The woman lies next to a half-dug hole, three feet deep, and she's starting to reek. Connor turns away, retching. He needs the wizard to save his mom.

When he grabs the wizard's arm, his fingers close easily around his wrist. The wizard turns, gaze locking onto him. Steady heat thrums under Connor's fingers, coupled with a different sort of warmth, bright and flaring, that Connor realizes is magic. "My mom's important! You can't just let her die!"

"I can't create miracles, you know. If I could, I would have saved all these people." The wizard waves at the deserted land around them, his gaze faraway.

A sea of tombs sprawls out behind the grass-shrouded dunes, wedged between the shore and a rolling forest. Mounds of dirt rise up in even lines, each marked by a round stone or a rotting plank of wood. Connor stares. Bodies lie in this land, and he's never thought to walk *behind* the dunes, only along the shore. That's why he's never seen the wizard. Because while he's been walking, the wizard has been digging graves.

"My mom's different," he says, desperate. "The doctor said she has cancer."

"Oh, suck—What did your father say?"

Connor thinks about Dad in the sunlit room, his tears splashing on Mom's face. He thinks about the silence of his mother's chest, the blue of her lips, his father hiding his face with his hand. He swallows past the lump in his throat. "Dad says she's gone. I- I didn't hear her heart. But she can't—can't be dead. She can't."

The wizard's face crumples. "Oh, Connor. Neptune's mercy. I wish I could help, maybe visit, but I don't think your father would want me around. I'm sorry. At least your mother isn't hurting anymore."

"She's not dead!" Connor yells, pounding at him with his fists. The wizard leans in, pulling him into a tight hug, his clothes dragging wet against Connor's arms. "She was still talking to Dad this morning!"

"I've met your father, Connor," the wizard whispers. "He doesn't lie, does he?"

He doesn't. Dad is the most honest man Connor knows, and if he says Mom's gone, if he says Mom's dead... The kitchen will be empty and there will be no cake, no warm hugs, no one Connor can share his secrets with. His chest hurts like someone's torn a hole in it, and he curls his fingers into the wizard's shirt, an inhuman sound ripping from his throat.

Connor breaks, and Mom isn't there to put him back together again.

5
Thirteen (Part II)

YATES DOESN'T know what it's like to lose a parent at thirteen. He does know the loss of a loved one, though, and it hurts no matter your age. So he holds the boy through his wailing, through the flurry of halfhearted punches, and sends his kindest thoughts to the boy's mother.

He's seen Connor and his family before, in town. Connor's dad, towering and rugged and dashing, and his mom, an amiable, gentle woman who once asked him to repair her shoes. They seem like decent people, and Connor doesn't deserve this pain.

He keeps his arms around the boy and listens to the waves.

After a while, the boy quiets. Yates holds him for a minute longer, then guides him to sit on a worn wooden bench. While he sniffles and wipes his tears away, Yates digs the rest of the grave, wraps the woman in a bundle of cloth, and lowers her into the earth. He says a quiet prayer and shovels sand over her body.

Behind, the boy clears his throat. His voice grates when he says, "You're not using magic."

Yates bites down his wry chuckle; he shouldn't be doing spellwork around bodies. "Some things are best done from the heart. The dead deserve respect. And a burial, too. Unless you're on a battlefield, I suppose, and there's simply no time."

He continues to shovel, the firework-crackle of gunfire echoing in his mind. The boy watches him blankly. When his limbs ache with strain and earth piles high on the grave, Yates crouches, patting the dirt into place. He adds a rounded stone from a stack some yards away, then turns back to the boy. Connor's face is blotchy, his gaze stuck on a mess of sticks on the ground.

Yates wants him to feel better. But there's no easy way out of dealing with grief, and he shouldn't teach a child unhealthy methods to escape his thoughts. Shouldn't even make the offer, but... "Do you want to forget all this pain?"

Connor glances up, his eyes dull. "How?"

"I can erase your memories. The painful ones." He dusts off his hands and crouches in front of the boy, meeting his eyes. Yates shouldn't be offering this to a thirteen-year-old. But Connor hurts so much, and he doesn't know how else to help. He had thought about erasing his own memories, years back, when things had gone wrong. "You won't remember your mom passing away. Do you want that?"

Tears well up in Connor's eyes again. He bites his trembling lip and looks at his hands. Twice, he tries to speak. On his third attempt, he says, "I don't run from my problems. It's not the right way."

Yates smiles wanly. Connor is a child, yet he

possesses more courage than Yates ever did. He wishes he could be more like the boy. Brave when facing death. "Shouldn't you be going home, at least? Your father must be searching for you."

Connor swipes at his nose. "Don't wanna."

"Surely you need to eat."

He shakes his head.

Yates glances around. There's nothing for them out here but sand and sea and air. He could bring the boy home and make lunch for him. It would be better than leaving him alone on the shore. "Would you some food? I could bring you some cookies and hot chocolate. How does that sound?"

Connor shrugs, kicking at the ground. "Fine. But... I want you to show me magic."

Yates pauses. He doesn't want Connor to think magic can do the impossible, because it can't. It results in tearing flesh and bodies falling apart, things he cannot banish from his mind. But the child before him is broken, hurting, and Yates doesn't want to leave him in pain, even if he has to learn to recover from it himself. So he says, "Just a little."

He sits on the ground in front of Connor. Traces a circle around himself to form a barrier. The magic in him burns like a pyre, and Yates teases a lick of energy out, pushing it into his breath. He blows lightly to his left, inducing an air current that rushes faster and faster around him. The wind ruffles his clothes, sweeping dirt up in a helix above his head. Connor's eyes flicker up, following the whirlwind, but his mouth remains a thin line.

Simple wind manipulation won't cheer him up, so Yates asks, "What do you like to eat? I'll make you some food."

"Sardine sandwiches," Connor says. "But I'm not hungry."

"Sardines, hmm? I have plenty of those." Yates rises to his feet, extending a hand. "I have a home in the woods. We could eat there, if you'd like. I swear I'm not a monster."

The boy considers his invitation. Slowly, he pushes himself to his feet, keeping his hands tucked in his pockets. "Fine."

Yates leads him on a worn path through the forest, where birds chirp in the shadows of the firs. When they reach his home, Connor's eyes widen. Yates smiles gently. "It's not often that you see one of these, is it?"

"You live in a goddamned ship," Connor says, his gaze drifting from the heavy props at the bottom of the aging merchant ship, up its velvet-blue hull, to the long nose of its prow and the low cabin on the deck. The ship stands regally on its struts amidst the sprawling garden, a beauty in the sunlit forest. "You never told me."

"Perhaps I've never had the chance to." Yates perks up at the spark of life in Connor's eyes, the way his footsteps quicken. Connor scales the rope ladder like a monkey. He disappears onto the deck before Yates even sets his shoe on the first rung, and his footfalls echo through the stillness of the forest.

By the time Yates reaches the messy flowerpot garden on his deck, Connor has wandered past the spinach and parsley, to the locked doorway of the cabin. Yates lifts the geranium pot, snags the keys sitting on the rack below, and unlocks the door.

"Who still hides keys under flower pots?" Connor asks. He pushes into the shadowy cabin. Yates thinks to chide him for his manners, but refrains. There's no need to dwell on the past.

Instead, he lifts the trapdoor that leads to the rest of his living space. Vegetables crowd the deck in painted pots, crammed from railing to cabin, vying for space. Inside the cabin, little glass jars sit by the windows, catching the light when the sun shines through the forest. The cargo hold, though, is where Yates spends most of his time.

He grabs a lantern, draws a spiral onto it for light, and thrusts it at the boy before he ventures too far down the ladder.

In private, Yates' ship is his favorite place in the world. Hardwood floors stretch from one end of the cargo hold to the other, complemented by wood-panel walls and porthole windows. The kitchen vents into a chimney at the bow: forty square feet of bottled spices, pans hanging on walls, and a wood stove. His sleeping area consists of a double bed in the corner, complete with a secretary desk and heaps of yellowed scrolls. Neat shelves of jars line the lab at the other end of the cargo hold. In between, there's an open bathroom, a library, and a section of tiled floor for larger-scale experiments.

"You don't have walls around the bathroom," Connor says.

Yates shrugs. "I live alone. But if you need to use it, I'll go upstairs."

The boy wanders to the rows of laboratory shelves, inspecting neat glass jars of deer antlers, moth feelers, and poison oak leaves.

"What do you like with your sardine sandwiches?" Yates asks from the kitchen, light from the wall sconces warming the cherry-wood counters.

"Cucumber slices. And salted fish."

"Snapper?" Yates reaches for one of the dried fillets dangling from the ceiling. "I have some of that."

The boy looks over, and his mouth falls open. "You're salting the fish wrong."

"Salting?" All his twine-strung fish have turned out fine, left out to dry in the cool sea breeze. "I've never salted these."

Connor wanders over with a grimace. "Never?"

After all these years... "You would think, but no. I've just dried them out in the open."

The boy shakes his head. "Dried fish is tasteless. Where's your salt?"

And so Yates finds himself pulling out a tub of salt, bought in bulk when it was cheap. Connor pours the salt liberally into a pot, lays the drying fish in it, and sprinkles more salt down. "It didn't occur to me to salt them," Yates says. "You must be very good at this."

"I salt the fish after my Mom—" Tears glisten in Connor's eyes, and he wipes them off with his forearms. *I shouldn't have mentioned this at all,* Yates thinks. Connor looks down. "I salt the fish at home. My dad goes out to sea in the mornings."

"And I'm sure your salted fish will turn out delicious. Now, I can show you simple magic," Yates says to distract the boy from his minefield of memories. Despite his age, he still doesn't know what to do with crying children, and he's developed a fondness for this boy. Surely he can teach him something easy. Something safe. "What about making plants grow?"

"Don't like plants," Connor says thickly. "Can we make something explode?"

Yates purses his lips. There's no one in the forest, and he has the herbs to make little flower bombs. "Just the one," he says, thinking about potpourri and fireworks. "Do you want to try?"

A tiny smile twitches at Connor's mouth. "Yeah."

They make so many flower bombs.

6
Thirteen (Part III)

THE WINDOWS are dark when Connor trudges home that evening. He hesitates, then pushes the door open, easing quietly into the shadows. Silence shrouds the house. He creeps to his parents' bedroom and holds his breath, preparing to see a bloated blonde woman on the sheets. His eyes prickle again.

The bedroom is empty. There's an indent on the mattress where his mom lay this morning, but she's not there. He turns back into the living room, wondering if Dad has gone out to sea.

A noise comes from the kitchen, low, rasping, halfway between a groan and a sob. Connor tenses, inching to the empty doorway. Beer bottles surround a silhouette hunched at the kitchen table.

Dad lurches forward, burying his face in his arm. The sound that comes from him isn't human. Connor takes a step forward, then another, and sets a wary hand on his father's back. Dad doesn't turn. Instead, he snags a dark bottle with his hand, drains the last of the liquor, and slams glass onto wood like a thunderclap. Connor jumps.

"Dad?" he asks. But Dad doesn't answer, and

Connor swallows. He doesn't know how to tell his father that he feels the same, but maybe Dad already knows anyway.

Connor turns, leaves the kitchen, and when his dad begins to sob, he tucks himself into bed, pulling the covers over his ears.

DAD'S STILL slumped over the table the next day. Connor shakes him to remind him of the day's harvest. He snores, and Connor eats his cereal with empty beer bottles between them, nudging at his father's legs with his feet. Dad continues to sleep. Connor figures they'll be fine without fishing for a day.

He ignores the school bell and returns to the sea.

The shore is empty. Connor clenches his teeth when he passes through the graveyard, wind whispering behind him. He follows the dirt path through the forest and finds the wizard on his knees in the garden, weeding. Connor stops beside him. The wizard looks up. For a long moment, they stare at each other, sky-blue eyes darting over Connor's face. "You're back."

"Teach me magic," Connor says. "You promised."

The wizard winces. Looks away. He takes so long to decide that Connor starts to itch, needing to do something. Then, the wizard smiles crookedly. "Okay."

Relief unfurls through his chest.

THE WIZARD has a name. Unlike Mr. Jones or Ms. Sarah, he says, "Call me Yates."

"But you're teaching me magic," Connor says. "All the teachers at school want to be known as Mr. So-and-so. Even Jones is uptight, and Judy Brown says he's only twenty-two."

Yates' mouth twists into a wry grin. He scans the deck, where they've pushed the pot racks to the railings to make space. Then he sits in front of Connor. "I've never had a student before. I might not be the best teacher."

His cheeks are flushed, his lips pink, and the skin by his eyes is smooth, unlike the crow's feet by Dad's eyes. The wizard mustn't be very old at all. "Fine."

"What do you know about magic?" Yates asks.

Connor has never seen magic from another wizard, so it's not like he knows. "It does all the impossible things."

"Not all the impossible things, no."

"But it's *magic*." Connor frowns. "Of course it can."

"There are limits to everything, Connor," the wizard says kindly. "Try again. What have you seen magic do?"

Connor thinks hard, back to last year and the year before. "You cast spells on me. So I didn't get sick from the rain, and so I wasn't tired anymore. And you made yourself grow taller."

"Very good. Now, there are two kinds of magic: energy magic and shape magic. Which have you seen?"

"The lines on the shore were shape magic," Connor says. It's a little easier to smile now. "And all the other spells were energy magic."

The wizard claps his hands, beaming. "Good. We'll start with energy magic. Energy exists in different things: wind, waves, and lightning. We can harness and mold these for our spells. But! There's another kind of energy, and that's life magic. Living things have energy in them. For example, wood. Even though it's been severed from its roots, you have to think of it as a living material." The wizard runs his hands over the deck. "There's life in it. Life in the entire ship. If you close your eyes, you'll feel it."

Connor closes his eyes. He hears the lilting melodies of birds in the forest, the rustle of wind playing in the leaves. In the distance, waves crash against the shore. He presses his hands to smooth, sun-warmed wood.

"That's right," the wizard says, his voice gentle. "Feel the age of the timber, the breeze sweeping through its forest."

Connor imagines a forest different from this one—towering giants with clumps of leaves at their tops, broad trees with timber as yellow as clay, and large cats prowling on their branches, their claws scraping on bark. He imagines thunderclouds rolling over them, the patter of warm rain, a mist creeping between their trunks. He opens his eyes and says, "This timber was from far away. Further to the south."

The wizard beams. "I thought you might be magic."

Him? Magic? "I'm not. No one in my family is magic."

"Really?" the wizard asks, surprised.

"My dad hates it." Connor thinks back to his tenth birthday and *You'll do better helping me with the boat*. "My... my mom liked—" He pauses when his throat tightens up, swallowing. "My mom liked hearing about it. But she didn't know any more than I did."

"I'm sorry." The wizard's mouth pulls down, as though in regret. "I didn't mean to bring it up again. Let's focus on magic for a minute." He takes Connor's hand, turns it up, and traces a circle in his palm. "Now, think about a fire in your hand. Make it as real as you can."

Connor thinks about a fire. He thinks about burning coals and an old wood stove, the smoky scent of a fireplace. It makes the ache in his heart recede a little. Heat sparks above his hand, a lick of warmth.

When he opens his eyes, a tiny orange flame flickers in his palm, big as a fingernail. "Holy shit!"

Yates releases him. The flame sends heat curling into his hand, and he doesn't want to close his fingers over it, in case it goes out. "That's your magic right there," Yates says, his eyes shining. "Sometimes it takes a bit of coaxing to present itself."

Connor stares at the fire, disbelieving. Aside from the times he spent with the wizard, he's never seen magic. Except for when the vanilla essence fled. He looks up. "You were at my house, weren't you? When my—my mom and I baked the cake. I gave you a slice the next day."

Yates shakes his head. "I've seen your family around town, Connor, but I don't know where you live."

In his hand, the flame dances like it's alive. The vanilla bottle moved. If it wasn't Yates enchanting it, then it had to be him. He's *magic*. He's special and he has powers, and he wants to run home and show this to — to his mom. She would cheer and be happy for him. She liked hearing about the wizard. And if Connor's been magic all along, he should have saved her. The hollow in his chest tears open again, and his vision blurs.

"Connor?"

He shakes his head, his voice lodging in his throat. He clears it. "My magic. My mom. If I have magic, I could've cured her. I can bring her back."

"No. No, don't even think that," the wizard says sharply, his hand snaring Connor's wrist. "Listen. This is important. Magic isn't for bringing the dead back to life. It isn't possible. Magic doesn't even cure most ailments."

Connor yanks his arm away, grief swelling in his chest. The wizard has done amazing things with his powers. "There has to be a way."

"No." The wizard looks into the trees, their shadows mirrored in his eyes. "There isn't."

"DAD," CONNOR gasps, feet thumping in the silent house. The walls don't seem quite as suffocating anymore. *Dad, I'm magic,* he almost says, but the memory of his father's sullen glares quells those words.

The kitchen rings with quiet, light fading from the window. Connor stops by the doorway and searches out his father, disappointment swimming in his stomach when his dad lifts his head, bleary eyes flickering. Day-old stubble darkens his jaw. "C'nnor?"

"I'm magic," he says, pride trumpeting in his chest.

Dad's face collapses. He squeezes his eyes shut, baring his teeth, and Connor freezes. He's never seen his father like this. Slowly, he concentrates on his hand, on fire, and the dancing flame bursts to life in his palm. He shows it to his father, certain that he will change his mind, but Dad slaps his hand away. "No," he snarls. "No magic."

"But why?" Connor clenches his fist around the fire. "Did you know?"

His father groans and rubs his temple, his shoulders taut with the weight of ghosts. "Shut up about magic."

"Magic can do anything!"

"Magic does shit-all for us!" His father reaches out, grips Connor's shoulder so hard it hurts. His breath stinks of liquor. "Don't you dare bring magic into this house, you hear?"

Connor flinches, bewildered. Dad has never lashed out at him. But he's magic, and he can't set it aside like it isn't part of himself.

He shakes off his father's hand and storms to his room, thinking about his mother. He doesn't ask where she is. He'll ask Yates tomorrow, and Yates will tell him how to bring her back to life, somehow.

"I'VE TOLD you, and I will tell you again. No."

The wizard crouches in front of him, both hands firm on his shoulders, unlike his father's painful grip. Sea-blue eyes bore into his. "There was a reason I didn't teach you to use your magic, all those years ago."

Connor glares at him through the shadows of the cargo hold, swearing all the foulest words he knows. Yates settles on the floor with a sigh. "Do you know how old I am, Connor?"

He shakes his head. He's not interested. What does age have to do with anything?

"I'm two-hundred and forty-three." There's no laughter in the wizard's gaze. Yates shows him the back of his hand. It's smoother than Mom's was, unblemished, his skin pale.

Connor shakes his head. "I don't believe you."

"You don't have to," the wizard says. "But it's important for you to understand this: I've seen a lot more than you have. Made more mistakes than you can imagine. I don't wish for you to do the same."

Connor glowers. The wizard doesn't get it. He wants his mom laughing in the kitchen with him again. He'll find a way, somehow. "Whatever."

Yates narrows his eyes, studying him. "Have you been to her wake?"

His vision blurs. Connor dashes his tears off with his hands, angry that they're betraying him now. He wants to intimidate the wizard, not cry in front of him. "No."

"I can take you there, if you'd rather not go alone," Yates says. Connor shrugs. The wizard leans in, wrapping his arms around Connor's back. "Magic cannot solve everything, child. Trust me."

Connor doesn't, and he tells the wizard exactly

that. Yates looks away, saying nothing.

HE DOESN'T attend his mom's wake. Instead, he hides at home, pulling his blankets over his head. At the cremation, he holds on tight to Yates, trying not to cry.

His father returns from the funeral parlor with a pastel-blue urn the next day. He places it on the mantle next to the cheerful wedding portraits, and the kitchen rings with loss.

Connor spends longer hours in Yates' ship.

YATES STARES first into the horizon, scanning for the carcasses of new ships. When he doesn't find any, he turns his sights closer, to the waves churning along the shore. It's been quiet lately — no shipwrecks, no bodies. Little to do except watch the waves, so he picks his way across the pebble-strewn beach, mulling over his decisions.

"I'm a mentor," he says, trying out the title. He's never been a teacher. Never had young lives depend on him. But he's willing to take on this mantle; Connor needs more than a father who isn't there, and Yates can't leave the boy without guidance. Besides, Yates needs someone to give him perspective, someone who has problems greater than his own.

Yates wonders if Quagmuth ever felt inadequate when he took on his first student. Wizened, powerful Quagmuth, who had split a mountain with a curse, who had taught Yates the intricacies of spell-casting. Would he shake his shaggy head if he knew that Yates has become a mentor? Yates isn't prepared for it. He clearly hadn't learned the rules of magic well enough, but here he is.

"I'll do my best," he says. He'll help mold Connor into someone capable, someone who will use his magic wisely. "I'll make you proud."

The sky stares disapprovingly down at him, and Yates wraps his arms around himself, bowing his head.

He drags his feet back along the shore, picking up little tools and steel bowls as he walks. They would be helpful to have around his home. When he reaches the ship, Yates lets himself in quietly through the cabin door. He sinks to a crouch in front of his carved ebony bookshelves, his heart as heavy as the forgotten tome from his past. He trails his fingers over the books on the bottom shelf, pausing on a worn title: *Death to Life*.

He is a mentor now, and he will give Connor access to these books. It is how the boy will learn, and Yates will let him read all he wants. Except this. Resurrection is impossible. People will always die, no matter the century or their age or how much someone wishes to bring them to life. Connor will have to accept this.

Yates slides the book out. The years have ironed its wrinkled pages flat, and its cloth bindings have faded with age. He brushes his fingers over the dusty cover, cracking the book open. Its spine creaks in protest. Inside, the pages have yellowed, his writing crammed between large, black-inked text.

The energy required for a resurrection can be drawn from various sources. A medley of shapes to harness life magic and runes to direct the flow of power. For a rabbit, drawing a thousand clover leaves should, theoretically, bring it to life.

Bile rises up his throat. Yates snaps the book shut, standing up so fast that he grows dizzy. He doesn't want those memories surging up again, doesn't want Connor getting ideas from the tome. He climbs onto a stool next to the bookcase, drawing an adhesive rune on the uppermost shelf. Then, he presses the book down on it and sends magic through the rune. With his height, Connor won't see the book at all, and Yates will guide him away from the taint of revival spells.

There's more to magic than waking the dead. They should both remember that.

7
Fourteen

ON HIS fourteenth birthday, Connor carries a parcel of salted fish to the forest. School is an afterthought now—he attends classes when the wizard has errands in town.

To save time, he follows his father out to sea, knife and salt bucket in hand. While his dad nurses a beer, Connor guts and salts the fish, and by the time they return, he's cleaned two-thirds of the harvest. When they're done selling fish, Connor sets out for the shore.

Memories of his mother sit like an empty cavern in his chest. He resents the wizard for withholding knowledge on how to bring her back, but Yates is unbending. He's taught Connor so much more: how to coax his flame into a roaring fire, how to make plants grow lush leaves, how to make the waves dance and part around him.

When he doesn't see the wizard on the shore or in the cemetery, Connor weaves through the forest, past the flowering garden, and climbs onto the ship. He finds the key under a pot of daffodils this time, unlocks the door, and slips into the cargo hold.

"Yates?" he calls on the way down the ladder, breathing in the familiar notes of rosemary and mint.

"In the lab," the wizard answers.

Connor finds him hunched over on a tall stool, his feet dangling a foot above the floor. "I brought you stuff."

Yates looks up from his magnifying glass. At the sight of Connor's parcel, he beams, the years falling away from his face. "Really?"

Connor snorts. "It's not like I don't bring you things once in a while."

"It's salted fish, isn't it?" Yates hops off his stool, hurrying over to the kitchen to wash his hands. "No one salts fish like you do."

"I learned it from my mom." It still hurts to say it. Yates glances at him sideways, concern dulling the edges of his smile. Connor sets the package on the island counter, and the wizard pulls its wrappings off with care. The salt crystals on the snapper glitter in the golden lamplight. While the wizard stashes the fish in a plastic bin, Connor grabs a chocolate chip cookie from a jar. He returns to the library to shelf the book he borrowed, tucked discreetly under his arm.

"*Life Magic in Remains*, hmm?" Yates says, stopping next to him. His eyes linger on the worn spine, then flit over to Connor, unsurprised. It feels as though he's seeing right into Connor's secrets. "That's some very advanced magic."

"Just reading." Connor shrugs, a flush sweeping into his cheeks. But he wasn't just reading, when he was trying to find a way to restore life to ashes. He's still trying. And he knows it's advanced magic. Most of the words don't make sense.

From the shrewd way Yates' eyes bore into his, the wizard knows that, too. Connor looks away. "Anyhow," Yates says, "we'll go through shape magic today. We'll practice the spirals from last week, and then I'll take you down to the shore to try it with the waves."

Connor perks up. An hour later, at the shore, the spiral he draws comes out lopsided. The waves rumble over it, surging into his lines, and his spiral glows faintly blue, its trapped energy just enough to knock a toy boat over. He wants more, wants to collect enough magic to topple a tree. "I can't do this," he mumbles.

Yates glances at the spiral and reaches out for Connor's branch. A yard away, he leans over and draws a spiral around himself, graceful sweeps that carve through wet sand. When the wave roars in again, it curls into perfect arcs and compact curves barely an inch apart, and the lines glow a brilliant blue. Connor gasps. The wizard smiles wryly. "I've had two hundred years to practice, Connor. What about you?"

But Connor can't help staring at Yates' spiral, the glow that imprints into his retinas. Yates is amazing like Connor's dad, but in a different way. "That's awesome," he breathes. He wants to draw shapes as powerful as Yates', right now. "Teach me."

Yates' mouth twitches as he returns the twig. "Trace the circles I drew. Be careful to follow the lines; you'll learn to anticipate the curves better."

"Okay."

"And tomorrow, we'll learn about the stones," Yates says. "They have personalities, you know."

Connor stares at his wide grin, trying to decide if he's joking. The wizard cracks jokes every other day, and sometimes his punchlines involve singers from thirty years ago. In the end, Connor says, "Bullshit."

Yates laughs. "What language."

"I don't want to learn about stones," he says.

"You'll have to. Those are the basics." Warmth gleams in the wizard's eyes. He picks up another piece of driftwood, drawing intricate crosses by his feet. "Someday, you'll love the rocks just as I do."

Connor scoffs, but he traces the spirals anyway.

WHEN HE gets home, Connor sets a package of cookies on top of the fridge, counting the beer bottles scattered across the table. He drops those in the trashcan, checks on his dad sprawled out on the couch, and returns to the kitchen, scanning the recipes covering the walls. They're all written in a looping script, the scent of rosemary and mint still fresh on them: creamy fish soup, dill and chicken stew, baked acorn squash. There's tuna in the fridge, some leftover buns, and red bell peppers.

"You hungry, Dad?" he asks. Dad snores.

Connor glances at the cookies and gets to work.

SOMETIMES, YATES wonders about life after death. Whether his family watches him from afar, whether they know he's doing what he can to compensate for his mistakes. He thinks about lives winking out when he wades into the ocean, thinks about the bodies people leave behind, whether they know someone in this world is here to give them a burial. Heaven knows he needs a reminder—that people will not return, that people cannot be brought back.

On one such afternoon, while he's studying a ship's carcass in the horizon, Connor taps his arm.

"Why do the shipwrecks keep happening?" Connor asks, his forehead crinkled. "Even the kids at school know you should avoid the northern coast."

Yates walks over, his feet dragging over tiny sea-glass pebbles. He thinks about giving the boy the answer, but he's discovered the joy of watching Connor figure things out. When he lets the boy mull over his theories, Connor remembers them for months longer. "Do you know why the ships sink?"

"I think it's the rocks in the sea. There's plenty of them around."

"But the ships don't always crash in the same places, do they?"

The boy chews on his lip. "Guess not. Seems like there's rocks everywhere."

Yates crouches down and grabs a handful of translucent pebbles. It intrigues him how frosty brown glass turns a coppery hue when seawater wets its surface, how pale green deepens into vibrant jade. "Why do you think that is?"

Connor wanders a few feet away, messy chestnut hair hiding his eyes. "The other fishermen say it's the kraken. My dad says that's bullshit. But we avoid the northern coast."

Yates grins encouragingly. He lets the pebbles fall back to the beach, listens to the clear *tap-tap-tap* of scattering glass. "You don't believe the fishermen, and yet you follow their ways."

"It's safer like that."

"What if I told you that the kraken lives in these waters?"

Connor's mahogany eyes flicker up to meet his. "No way."

"Once upon a time," Yates says, enjoying the way his face scrunches up, "there was a monster who lived under the sea. It hated boats that sailed too close, so it grabbed them and flung them deep into the ocean."

"Bullshit."

"How else do you think my ship ended up in the forest?" He pauses for a moment, trailing a spiral in the pebbles. With a pulse of magic from his fingertips, the beads beneath the spiral glow a soft white. "The other ships aren't so lucky. They're smashed to pieces, and the people in them wash ashore."

"Is that why you pull the bodies out?"

Yates glances up, unable to help his wan smile. If that were the only reason he buried the dead, he'd be a saint. "Perhaps. But that's how this beach was formed. The glassware from the ships pours out, and they grind down into pebbles in the ocean. Aren't they beautiful?"

Connor nods begrudgingly.

"Now, I want you to sit down with me, and listen to the water."

The boy pouts. "We did that yesterday!"

Yates ruffles his hair. "Practice will grant you many abilities, Connor. You'll be able to sense things further out than you can now."

"But I want to make more flower bombs." Connor kicks at the pebbles, stomping around Yates' glowing spiral. "Those are fun."

"Maybe later," Yates says. "For now, we practice."

The boy huffs, then flops down next to him. Yates still isn't used to Connor obeying his instructions, isn't used to being a teacher. But every time the boy listens, it settles the unease in his chest, makes him a little more confident in himself. He is a mentor. He will not fail Quagmuth's teachings.

So he grins at Connor, nodding to the waves. "Close your eyes and listen to the sea. It'll always be a friend you can count on."

THEY SIT cross-legged on the forest floor one summer afternoon, light shining through the gaps in the trees. The autumn sun doesn't burn Yates' skin, so they stay out in the open, the breeze ruffling their hair.

Connor flops onto his back, throwing his arms out. "I can't listen anymore. My senses are so tired they could curl up and drown."

Yates chuckles. The boy isn't tired. Yates has seen him exhausted, when his eyelids droop and his gaze loses focus, and he's merely uncomfortable right now. "Your excuses don't work on me, you know."

Connor scowls. "You're strict."

Strict? This is easy compared to Quagmuth's teachings. "I know you can do better," Yates says. He knows it in his heart, wants to see what Connor can do when he really concentrates. "Tell me how the sea is feeling right now."

"You've got to be shitting me," Connor says. Yates raises his brows, but Connor's looking over his shoulder, through the fir trees clustered around them. "The sea? That's half a mile away!"

"I know you can do it." Because Yates could, at his age. That was why Quagmuth agreed to teach him.

"That's bullshit. I can tell you how that tree's feeling. Not the sea."

"Tell me about the tree, then."

The boy closes his eyes, pushing his palms into the ground. After a while, he says, "It's bored. It's waiting for a good storm."

Yates touches the dry soil with a finger, listening. *Where are the gusting winds?* the tree whispers. *When will it rain and soak my roots?*

"What do you hear when you listen?" he asks.

Connor pushes a stone through the soil. "I see pictures in my head. I hear the leaves rustle, but that's it."

"Try again," Yates says. Connor's magic flickers warmly next to his. "What about the tree four yards down?"

And as Connor's forehead wrinkles, Yates reaches over, rubbing his frown away with a thumb. "Don't strain your senses. Nature is a fickle thing, Connor. Follow the sweep of energy to the tree."

Connor presses his mouth in a thin line.

"You're doing it again," Yates says. "Relax."

It takes Connor twenty minutes before he senses the trees at the edge of the forest. "They're singing along to the wind," he says, eyes flying open. "They're fucking singing!"

Yates chuckles. "Language, Connor."

The boy rolls his eyes.

"Think you can listen further out?" Yates asks. The cemetery is Connor's limit so far, and he wants Connor to realize how far he can stretch his abilities. "The dunes past the cemetery?"

"Still damned far," Connor mutters, but he closes his eyes, fingers splayed on rich soil. His breathing slows. His shoulders loosen. Yates watches him, waiting. Nature speaks when you're in harmony with it, when you listen carefully to what it wants to say. Connor sits, still and silent. His lashes flutter. He sucks in a sharp breath. When his eyes snap open, he gapes, disbelief stark on his face. "I heard the sea!"

Pride swells through Yates' chest like a tide. "I knew you could do it."

"It was just a feeling," Connor says, jumping to his feet. "But I knew it was splashing on the shore like... like a lazy cat. I can't believe I heard the sea! I heard the fucking sea!"

Yates springs to his feet right alongside the boy, grabbing his hands. He twirls them around in a little dance, his cheeks aching from his smile. He had expected Connor to hear the dunes, or maybe the sand on the shore. Not the sea, not with what he can do right now. It's amazing. "That's marvelous," he cries. "You're the best student I've ever had!"

"I'm the only student you've ever had," Connor says, but he's skipping along with Yates over the rows of cabbages and dill.

"I can actually teach," Yates breathes. He flops down onto soft ground with Connor. It's exhilarating, seeing the boy's abilities blossom. Connor makes him feel like all his efforts have made a positive impact. Like he has some worth in this world. Like he isn't quite so much a failure as he was before. "Oh, suck my dick."

"Why do you even say that?" Connor asks, squirming around. "No one else I know even swears that way. Did your teacher say 'suck my dick'?"

The thought of Quagmuth uttering those words makes him wince. If his mentor had said that, it would have been to humiliate Yates in front of his fellow students. "No," Yates says. "Especially not him."

"Then why?"

"I... said it out of spite, actually." He chuckles dryly, the memory unfurling in his mind. Quagmuth's ornate sitting room, with its vaulted ceilings and brass candelabras. "A century ago, when my mentor was on his deathbed. He... found out about some things I'd done. I knew I'd fouled up, but I argued with him anyway. I was so very tired of the way he treated me."

Connor cocks his head. "How did he treat you?"

"Not well. He favored his other students." Yates thinks about his mentor, eyes sunken in, his magic fading after eight centuries. Quagmuth never understood him, even as he drew his last breath. "We exchanged some heated words. I'd had enough of his disapproval, so I said, 'Suck my dick' and left. It was the first time I stood up to him."

"You said that to your teacher," Connor whispers.

"I did." Yates grins wearily. Walking out of his mentor's homestead, he had felt like the most powerful wizard. Like he was finally stepping away from his mentor's shadow. If only it were as easy to rid Quagmuth's voice from his head. "I've been saying it ever since. It's not some heroic story, though. I'm sorry."

"I want to say that to the teachers at school," Connor says, his eyes bright.

Yates covers his face. He shouldn't have told him any of that. "Please don't. Your teachers will be furious. They'll want to talk to your father, I'm sure."

Connor droops then, and Yates winces. The boy's father doesn't do much for him. It makes him shake his fist on Connor's behalf, even if he understands why Connor's dad loses himself in alcohol. All Yates can do is teach the boy to cook and do his laundry, so he and his father aren't living in a sty.

"Come on, let's head in for some cookies," Yates says as a distraction. "I baked some chocolate chip ones this morning."

Connor scrambles to his feet, grinning. Yates follows him back into the cargo hold, his heart lighter than before. He'd expected the mentorship to be a burden, but the boy is precocious, a delight to teach, and maybe Yates is a little less lonely, with company like Connor's.

8
Fifteen

ON HIS fifteenth birthday, he finds the wizard on the clifftops. The storm clouds creep in over the horizon, dark and angry, and Connor abandons his ideas of baking a cake. He has no wish to bring his mentor soggy food again. Instead, he takes with him another package of salted fish, wrapped in wax paper, and deposits it in the empty ship.

He finds nothing in the garden and the forest. When he returns to the shore, kicking at sand, he glances at the distant waves smashing into cliffs. And right at the top of the cliffs, a tiny figure stands, arms spread out, the very faintest hint of fire-red atop his head.

Connor runs. He can't explain the need to talk to Yates, to win his praise, but it's an ache in his bones. And so he dashes over damp sand to the cliffs, grabs the prickly, wrist-thick rope hanging down craggy stone. He climbs to the clifftop. Then, he sprints.

The wind at the clifftops rushes through his hair like desperate fingers, drowning out his footfalls, his panting, so Yates doesn't notice when Connor clears the remaining yards and leaps at him from behind, throwing his arms around his shoulders.

Yates staggers, landing hard on the grass with an undignified squawk. Only then does Connor remember that his mentor is two-hundred and thirty years *older* than him, and that his bones might be fragile. He clambers off in horror. "Did I crush you?"

"Suck my dick!" Yates gasps, his cheek plastered against soft grass. His eyes dart incredulously to Connor's, his fingers curling into the ground, knuckles white. He catches his breath. "I nearly died of shock, Connor. What in the murky depths of hell?"

"Language, Yates."

Yates sniffs. "You almost killed me."

"I didn't." The wizard doesn't seem to be in grievous pain—no paling skin, no blood, only a wince as he pries himself off the ground. Connor pulls him to his feet. "What're you doing out here?"

"Enjoying the breeze." Yates smooths down his rumpled clothes. "I haven't been up on the cliffs in a while. The sea always seems so calm from this high."

Overhead, the clouds loom, flashes of lightning staining their depths. The waves crash onto the shore below. The wizard stretches out his arms with a sigh, and not for the first time, Connor notices his pointed nose, his sharp chin. The way he tips his head back, chilly breeze riffling through his hair.

"You know, lying out in the open isn't so bad," Yates says. "I'd forgotten how nice it is." He crouches and plants himself on a grassy spot, lying back with a sigh. "Come on, listen to the wind."

Connor sits, then lies back on lumpy ground next to him, grass tickling his ears. "I've been practicing."

"You'll get even better with more practice." The wizard cups an ear. "Listen."

Rather than listening, Connor watches him. He sees all these things about Yates that he didn't when he was ten, or thirteen: his pale, smooth face, the smile tugging on his lips. His hair is soft-edged, like fire. Connor wonders how it would feel against his fingers. His heart pounds.

He's heard about liking people in school, seen people holding hands. Many more boys with girls than boys with boys. His classmates make out behind the town hall, in alleyways. Warmth suffuses his chest the more he looks at Yates, imagining them pressed close in those places, doing those things.

The people in his classes hook up like magnets snapping together, and Connor doesn't feel a thing beyond friendship for them. With Yates, it's different. All his thoughts at night center around the wizard: Yates showing too much skin, Yates beneath him, Yates kissing him damply, further and further south. Even if Yates says he's two centuries old. It doesn't make sense. Yates is his teacher, his best friend, but also more. Age doesn't matter, does it?

Yates turns to him. "Well?"

"What's it like to be so old?" Connor asks. "And I—everyone else is so young."

Yates sighs, tipping his face up to the sky. "It's

boring."

"Boring?" Everyone wants to be immortal. People try to extend their lives with pills, herbs, and serums. And here's someone repairing their things, who has survived the world wars, the previous century, the decades before TV and pop music, and he acts nothing like a wizened old gnome. "How can it be boring? There are so many things to do."

"Until you've done them all." Yates plucks a daffodil from the ground, knotting its stem with his thin fingers. "People, too. They start to seem the same."

Connor stops breathing. "Am I boring?" he asks, trying not to sound desperate. "I mean, people in Fort Bragg."

Yates laughs. "Well, ever since I met you, things have gotten more interesting."

Connor's heart thumps so loud that surely the wizard hears it. "Really?"

Honesty shines bright on Yates' face. "It's been a joy to watch you learn these past two years. It's like watching a daffodil grow, except you talk back at me all the time."

"You like when I talk back at you." Connor grins, shuffling over to elbow Yates, and Yates musses his hair. Fat raindrops patter down on them, one on Connor's cheek, another on his arm. If they don't leave soon, the sky will open up over them.

Yates doesn't move. Connor almost says, *I like you,* but he doesn't. Yates is his teacher. He doesn't seem interested in a relationship, when all he talks about is magic and stones and the best recipes for shepherd's pie. So Connor contents himself with looking at Yates' mouth, wondering what he'd do if Connor leaned over and kissed him. Whether Yates would kiss back, whether he would think of Connor as someone more than a student.

"How much of the sea can you hear?" Yates asks suddenly, perking up. "You say you've been practicing."

Connor looks to the edge of the cliffs, at the tufts of grass silhouetted against gray clouds. "Maybe a mile out. I don't know. Never really measured."

"What about the high seas?"

He shakes his head. Even on his father's boat, he's never reached where the seabed falls away. It's beyond his abilities. "What's it like out there?"

"I could show you." The wizard's eyes twinkle.

Connor squints. Are they sailing out to sea to do that? "Really?"

Yates sits up, reaching out. "Here, give me your hands. I'll lend you some of my magic."

"How does it work?" Yates has never talked about magic transfer. When was he going to teach him that?

"Like so." Yates sets their hands on the ground, his palms pressing Connor's firmly against the grass. For a long second, Connor only feels the heat of his skin, sees the rise and fall of his chest.

Then he senses it, a tickling brush of heat against his hand. It nudges at his own magic, trailing over his knuckles, and it feels comforting, familiar.

"It takes years to build a connection like this," Yates murmurs. The sea breeze sighs through their hair. "Your magic has to be accustomed to mine, altering slightly so their magical frequencies harmonize. It's a lot easier if we enjoy being around each other, though. Now, I'll lend you just a touch of energy. Don't resist it."

The gentle warmth fits against his own magic like puzzle pieces falling into place. Yates' magic burns powerful and slow, a dancing flicker that soaks into Connor's hands, skimming up his arms. In that moment, it feels as though Yates is living inside him somehow, his magic filling Connor's skin, and he forgets to breathe.

"Try listening now," Yates whispers, glancing over the cliff.

Connor closes his eyes, magic thrumming in his veins. He relaxes. Listens first to the shore beneath them. *It's angry,* the sand whispers. *The waves are high.*

The sand *talks.* Connor holds back his yelp of surprise, reaching further out to where the waves roll along the shore, then past the foamy crests into the sea. *Calm out here,* the waves sigh. *Rain pattering makes us want to play.* Then, he reaches further yet, to where he and his father fish in the deeper waters, perch and snapper darting in shoals around the rocks.

"Further," Yates says. "Past that."

He's never gone beyond those parts. Connor latches onto the softest voices, following them into deeper and darker waters, where the seabed dips down into the bottomless ocean and the boulders stretch into craggy undersea canyons. Gigantic trenches stretch deep beneath the ocean, their shadows black as ink. *Peaceful here,* the canyons bellow. *The ocean sings around us.*

Connor's jaw drops, his eyes snapping open. Yates' hands are still on his. Thunder rumbles, and rain pours around them. "I heard the canyons talk," he says, leaning in. Their clothes are drenched and heavy on their skin. "They said actual words!"

Yates' eyes light up, summer-sky bright, and Connor thinks about leaning in and kissing him. He doesn't, though. Instead, he relishes the way Yates' magic thrums in his veins, the way it caresses his own like a lover's touch. "That's what you'll hear," Yates says, "if you practice hard enough."

"I'll hear it twenty years from now, probably," Connor says. He knows now how much he still has to learn, how much he can do when he gets as old as Yates is. "Wow."

"It's amazing, isn't it?" Yates pulls his hands away. The thin thread of his magic snaps, leaving Connor with the lingering heat of his energy. Yates lies back into the soaked grass, tipping his face up into the rain.

Connor breathes. Raindrops slide down his cheeks, pattering on his head, and all he can think about is the warmth of Yates' magic in his hands, the way it felt so *right*. Like Yates is right for him. The second it flits through his mind, Connor knows it's one of the unshakeable truths in his life, like how he will always love his parents, and how a part of him will always live in Fort Bragg.

"We should probably head back," Yates says, but he closes his eyes against the downpour instead. Connor shrugs out of his coat and throws it over him. Drenched or not, it's still some cover. The wizard snuffles, pushing thick canvas off his face. "Oh, suck it—what was that for?"

"You need a raincoat," Connor says. "Else you'll catch a cold."

Yates throws the coat back, breaking into a wide, gleeful smile. "You need it more than I do, Connor. You're adorable."

After all that's happened today, Connor can't help the heat that surges up his cheeks. He doesn't want to tell Yates what he feels yet, and he doesn't know how Yates will receive that news. So he pulls his coat over his head, hiding his face under it.

There's no way he's blushing like a fool in front of his mentor.

THE HOUSE is quiet when Connor gets home. His father goes out sometimes, and occasionally, he smells like musty clothes instead of alcohol. He doesn't talk much anymore. Connor misses him. He wishes his dad would watch with pride when he sketches a spiral, and light glows from whatever he draws it on. Mom would.

Yates does. Yates leans in when Connor tells him the composition of rocks, and whether a pebble was happy while it rolled about in the ocean.

Connor scrubs at the soup-crusted dishes in the sink, his mouth twitching. The kitchen tiles are grimy, the outer edges of the fridge dusty, but he figures that the house is still clean enough to live in, as long as the trashcan doesn't overflow.

When he's done, he brings his parcel of cookies to his bedroom. They're just as chocolatey as the ones his mom used to make.

BECAUSE THE boy gets surprisingly flustered, Yates finds every chance to tease him. "What nice eyes you have," he'll say. "What a strong man you are, carrying all my vegetables onto the ship."

Connor glares whenever he does that, but Yates never misses the lightness of his footsteps later on.

While rain patters upstairs one afternoon, Yates says, "Your girlfriends must fight to get their hands on you. You know, when you do wander off to school."

Connor looks up from the blossom in his hands, gaping. "Huh?"

"Girlfriends," Yates says, wriggling his eyebrows. A raindrop leaks through the lab ceiling and drips into his hair. "Or boyfriends. Sometimes you stare off into the distance and blush, like just now."

"I don't blush!" But Connor does anyway, a hint of crimson crawling up his neck. His shoulders are beautiful: the broad, downward slopes of his muscles, the sharp lines of his clavicles. Then there's the intensity of his eyes, the chestnut-brown of his hair, the bulk of his chest and arms. Yates doesn't know when Connor started filling out, but he's certain that appreciative gazes follow him around in school.

Yates waves a morning glory at him, its petals fluttering. "If it's enough to distract you from flower bombs, it must be important."

Connor glares. He spoons dried rat droppings into a flower, spilling some onto the dull cherrywood of the lab counter. Which is odd, because he hasn't spilled anything in months. "Not important."

Yates raises his brows. "How many girlfriends *do* you have?"

"You're damned nosy, you know that?" Connor packs the droppings further down with his spatula, then sprinkles in a pinch of powdered potpourri.

"You said we're best friends." Yates shuffles closer, curiosity a sharp itch in his mind. "What were you blushing about, if not girlfriends?"

Connor folds the thin petals in. He sets the flower carefully down on the counter, drawing a chalk circle around it before adding four arrows to direct energy at the flower. "I don't have girlfriends."

"Boyfriends?"

Connor pulls his chalk away from the counter, curling his fingers around it.

Yates feels a twinge of *something*. Maybe delight, maybe unease. "You have a boyfriend?"

"*No,*" Connor mutters. His lips curve down, his gaze lowered as he traces the runes for *heat* and *burst* inside the circle.

The tension in Yates' chest eases. *It's probably because he won't have to suffer through heartbreak.* "You must like someone," he decides. That would explain Connor's shiftiness. "Does that someone not like you back?"

"Shut up," Connor says.

For the first time, Yates can't read his

expression, and he doesn't know what to think. "If you keep at it, he'll probably like you back one day," he says. "Otherwise, he's not worth your time."

"Yeah, well. Maybe one day." Connor sighs, handsome and adorable, pressing a fingertip to the counter. The runes glow briefly red. Energy scatters into the circle, gathers behind the four arrows, then sizzles toward the flower bomb.

The flower lights up momentarily from within, soft white glowing through vibrant blue petals. "What do you think?" Yates asks. These explosives have more energy than the ones he first taught Connor. The runes they're using now are complex, humming with old magic. "Ready to test it out?"

"Hell yeah," Connor says, picking the flower off the counter. His shoulders tense with excitement.

Some things don't change, Yates thinks as he follows Connor to the testing space in the middle of the ship. He's glad for that.

9
Sixteen

ON HIS sixteenth birthday, Connor descends into the shadowy cargo hold and finds the wizard in his kitchen, apron tied around his waist. "Material Girl" plays softly on the beat-up radio, and Yates wriggles, turning in a circle. Their eyes meet. "Oh, suck it," Yates says.

"Do you say that to your customers in town?" Connor asks, heat prickling across his cheeks. Even if Yates only meant it as a curse, it still drops his mind right into the gutter. "Pretty sure those old women would be scandalized."

Yates sniffs and turns away. "No. I'm a professional repairman."

"Didn't think repairmen *could* be professional. It's not like I go around telling people I'm a professional fisherman." While he waits for his blush to subside, Connor tucks his borrowed books back onto their shelves.

Yates laughs, peeks into his oven, then turns and leans against it. Connor imagines the heat seeping into the wizard's back. It's chilly out, and the warmth in the cargo hold clings to his skin.

He wanders over and opens Yates' pantry for

the tub of fish, before stashing the newest slices at the bottom. The memory of Yates swearing nags at him, though. Connor pauses midway. "You were halfway through something, weren't you?"

"No." Yates tugs on the knot of his apron, his grin forced.

"You're lying," Connor says, narrowing his eyes as Yates hangs the apron on the wall. The stove is empty, but he scents the tart, sweet tang of orange muffins. "It's in the oven."

"Why would you say that?" The wizard inches back toward the oven.

Connor knows in his bones that Yates is covering something up. He's been visiting the wizard every day for the past three years, now, and *bullshit* if Yates thinks he's good at lying. "Fine, go ahead and hide it," he says. "It's my birthday. You made a cake for me last year."

Yates throws a halfhearted glare at him. "It was supposed to be a surprise!"

"You always do something for me on my birthday. Why would I be surprised anymore?" When he thinks about it, Connor realizes that he's spent so many birthdays with the wizard. Seven, in fact. And he has only appreciated them the past couple years. It's a pity, but he's quietly looking forward to more.

Yates huffs, peeking into the oven. Inside, Connor glimpses two circular spring-form pans, for two layers of cake. Not muffins. "Fine. No more birthday surprises for you."

"That's not fair," Connor says, his stomach dropping. "You can't just stop like that."

And the wizard turns, a sly twinkle in his eyes.

"You like when I bake cakes for you."

"Just on my birthday," Connor says, his damned face heating up again. He hates blushing, and he hates how Yates' smile widens with glee.

The soft glow of the kitchen lamps lights Yates' face, caressing the curves of his cheekbones and his lips. The ache in Connor's chest throbs to life. He wants to hug Yates, wants to kiss him like every other schoolkid gets to kiss their date. He's thought about it for a year, now. Maybe more.

"Tell me a secret," he blurts, heart thudding.

The wizard blinks. "A secret?"

"Yeah. You know, something you don't tell anyone else." Connor rolls his eyes, hoping it'll hide his nerves. He fiddles with the wax paper left from the fish, tearing little lines into its edges.

Yates clicks his tongue. "You already know some of mine."

He glances up. "I do?"

Yates' laugh is light and infectious, lifting his spirits into a soaring whirl. "Yes, I've shared them with you, silly. Remember the beach behind the cliffs? I've never told anyone else about it. Or the whale crashing into the harbor. Or... well, the bodies. The cemetery."

"Really?" Connor has known about the bodies for ages. The wizard has always treated burying bodies as a daily task, like cooking or cleaning; they're just another part of life. "Why's the cemetery a secret?"

Yates shrugs. "The town knows about the shipwrecks, but the ships are from foreign countries. So long as it doesn't affect their harvest, the townsfolk don't care."

"They care about you," Connor says, unease swimming in his chest. "Right?"

"I'm just a traveling repairman to them." Yates sighs wistfully, turning to check on the cake again. "And that's enough. I don't want anyone getting attached to me. Or me to them. I don't... want to see more loved ones die."

It only strikes him then that Yates has seen more than one death, that what Connor has lived through with his mother, Yates has endured many times over. For someone to have lived two centuries... Yates must have cared for a lot of people who later died. He needs a comforting hug, but Connor doesn't know if he should give him one. For all that the wizard ruffles his hair, Connor has never really been affectionate with him, for fear of Yates finding out his secret. "What about me?" he asks. "What about if I die?"

Yates' lips thin. "I'd rather not think about that."

But the haunted, uncertain look stays in his eyes. Connor has never seen his mentor look so lost, closing himself off, and it reminds him too much of his father. He pulls Yates into his arms. "I won't mention it again."

This close, Yates is a head shorter than him. Connor hasn't really thought about it, when his bones grow and stretch, and he visits the wizard all the time. He remembers himself from two years ago, four years ago, when Yates was taller than him, a knowledgeable, distant figure, someone he could only admire. Now, the wizard's arms wrap around his back, and he leans into Connor's chest, a smile in his voice. "Thank you."

"Are those all your secrets?" Connor asks. He wants to hug Yates for longer, smell the butter and fresh sweat in his hair. Feel the solid warmth of him against his chest. "Or do you have things you aren't telling me?"

Yates leans away, a smile playing on his mouth. "I have to have some secrets."

Connor looks accusingly at him. Haven't they known each other for years? How can he not know everything about Yates, when they're best friends? "That's not fair."

"Tell me your secrets, then," Yates says. Connor's pulse thunders in his ears. Even if he likes the way some boys dress, and even if he looks at the men on the streets sometimes, nothing compares to Yates' warm eyes, the way Connor's ears prick up at his voice. "Are we back on the secret boyfriend thing?"

"You really want to know?" he asks, his voice strangled. Yates can't possibly mean it. It's the only secret he's ever kept from him.

"If you're willing to share," Yates says, smiling expectantly at him, and Connor has wanted this too much to hesitate now.

He leans forward, tilts his face like he's seen people do. Yates' eyes widen. Connor presses a slow, clumsy kiss to his mouth. Yates' lips are softer than they seem, softer than Connor's own, and his breath smells like peppermint. Connor slides their mouths together, Yates' skin catching on his. Yates freezes against him. Was that... unwelcome? *He doesn't like it.* Connor pulls away, his stomach twisting.

Yates gapes. His magic hums in him, a

flickering warmth that radiates through the space between them. "Oh," he whispers. "Oh."

Heat surges back into Connor's face. Yates stares, mouth curving down, and Connor's heart cracks. The wizard didn't want this at all. He's not interested. "Sorry," Connor says, turning, needing to get away. He's messed everything up now, complicated their relationship, and Yates won't want to teach him anymore. How could he think that Yates sees him as anything but a student? How could he have thought Yates wanted his kiss? *I'm an idiot.* "I'll go."

"No, Connor. Don't. Just." Yates swallows loudly. "It's just a—a surprise, that's all." And just as Connor's chest expands with a glimmer of hope, Yates says, "I'm afraid I can't return your feelings. And I'm sorry I didn't notice sooner."

"Why not?" he asks, even though he knows. Maybe Yates doesn't like men, or maybe...

"You're too young," Yates says, his eyes dark with regret. "And you're my... my student. I could never do that to you."

"But you're my best friend," Connor says. It doesn't sound any better. He can't expect Yates to like him with just a kiss.

"That's another reason." Yates steps away from him, rubbing his arms. "I don't want to destroy all this. I'll be your teacher and your friend, but that's where the line is."

His chest squeezes tight. Connor quells the disappointment welling in his ribs, turning away. He can't breathe. "I gotta go."

To the side, he sees Yates glancing at the oven, at the cake that's still not done baking. "Will you return tomorrow?" Yates asks carefully.

Connor sucks in a shaky breath. "Yeah. Yeah, I'll be back."

And he flees, hurrying out of the too-small cargo hold.

THROUGH THE circular kitchen window, Yates watches the boy retreat into the forest, hugging himself. He's never had someone so young fall in love with him, and it makes his insides clench.

All Connor knows is the tiny bubble of his world. Yates doesn't want to break him, doesn't think he deserves anything like romantic love himself, especially not from a child he's taught for years. Connor is so *young*. There are so many people out there, younger men who have energy like Connor does, men who haven't influenced Connor like he has.

You have no use for inane fancies, Quagmuth would have said. *A true wizard has focus.*

Yates doesn't want to put his student through that. It's not right. And even though he has no answers, he remembers the slide of Connor's lips on his, Connor's hesitance, his damp skin. It had felt better than he'd expected it to. It shouldn't have felt so good, in fact, when they shouldn't consider romance at all.

Yates raises his hand, hesitates, before he swipes Connor's kiss off his mouth. He doesn't let himself regret it.

With time, he's certain that the boy will get over him.

AT HOME, Connor pokes at the half-cooked fish on the stove, heart-sore. Dad sits on the couch, nursing another beer, and Connor doesn't feel like talking at all.

WHEN HE gets home from fishing the next day, Connor still hasn't made a decision. Thoughts of Yates have haunted him all night. He doesn't know if Yates thinks less of him now, or if Yates will still teach him. He contemplates the satchel by the door, thinking about going to school for once. Maybe the teachers have forgotten him. Maybe he should have gone to school more often. Maybe he shouldn't have kissed Yates.

Connor reaches for the school bag, thinking about the faceless high school crowd. Then he thinks about blue eyes, and his breath catches and twists. He can't avoid Yates forever. Avoiding Yates is equivalent to Yates sending him away, and he needs to talk to him. See him smile. Maybe Yates will hug him for no reason.

He's out of the door before he knows it, striding toward the forest. His skin itches for touch — a hug, or even just a nudge.

Connor slows as he approaches the clearing, jamming his hands in his pockets. The ship still stands upright on its struts, the garden sprawled out around it, butterflies flitting. Everything feels alien to him. He takes a deep breath, steps forward.

Yates' head pokes up from the flowerpot garden on the deck. Uncertainty freezes Connor's limbs. He half-expects Yates to tell him to leave.

Then the wizard turns, his eyes flickering with concern. "You'll grow roots if you keep standing there," Yates says. "The cake's still waiting, you know."

Relief crashes through him like a wave. Connor sucks in a breath of crisp air, his heart pumping again. "Yeah," he says, his voice uneven. "Coming up."

He doesn't want to lose the rest of this. A best friend and teacher is more than what he has back home.

DAYS LATER, when it's far too late to address the topic, Yates says, "About the other day."

He glances at Connor to gauge his reaction. On the tiled floor in the middle of the ship, Connor stiffens. "The other day."

Yates tries not to cringe. Should he even be bringing this up? Is this what teachers do? But they're friends, too, aren't they? "Yes. Your... affection."

A red tint sweeps up Connor's neck. Then he's glaring, looking away uncomfortably. "You make it sound like I'm sick."

Yates stops himself from hiding his face. He's *two-hundred* years old. He should be more dignified than this. He thinks about Quagmuth's scowl, the underlying disappointment in his eyes, always directed at Yates. So he hardens his expression. "I'm your teacher," he says. "If I call it affection, then affection it is."

Connor glares, folding his arms. "You don't

know anything about it."

Yates knows plenty. Even if he hasn't had students, he's known enough adolescents who have allowed emotion to sway their choices. Julie, the girl in the next town over. Peter, from fifty years ago, before the second world war. Yates should stop this before Connor mires himself in infatuation. "Wizards should never give in to emotion. That's something you have to learn, Connor."

"We're all humans," Connor says. "I can't stop feeling... things."

What things? Yates wants to tease. For the sake of being a good teacher, he says, "Sometimes, in desperate situations, you need your sharpest intellect at your disposal. A moment's hesitation can lead to an ocean of difference. Life and death. Right and wrong. Throwing a shield up before lightning strikes. You can't let emotion cloud that judgment."

Connor settles back, digesting his words with a smaller frown. "I understand."

When Connor doesn't try to refute his words, Yates relaxes. Maybe he's getting through to the boy. Maybe he's doing right as a teacher. Maybe he hasn't ruined things between them, after all.

10
Seventeen

ON HIS seventeenth birthday, Connor wades into the waist-deep brine and hauls bodies from the ocean.

This late in autumn, the surf leaches heat from their skin, and it's only because of the sprawling crosses drawn into sand that they're still braving the tide, hooking arms around stiff bodies and dragging them to shore. Three yards away, Yates reaches into the rolling waves. For all that he grins and musses Connor's hair, he never is playful when they search for bodies. *The dead deserve respect,* Yates says, but the shadows in his eyes hint at more than that.

Who did you lose to the sea? Connor wants to say. But Yates never asks about his mother, and so Connor won't pry, either. He's wary of being chased away, of hearing about a past lover, of having Yates close him off, so he watches what he says. He knows better to guard his secrets, now.

The sea brushes past his legs, sand tickling his toes. *Warm,* the sea murmurs around him. When his foot nudges something solid, he clenches his jaw, sucks in air, and plunges into the water.

Beneath the surface, the ocean rumbles. His breath gurgles in his ears, and his fingers snag on drifting fabric. The body comes up through the waves with him. Connor blinks saltwater from his eyes and wades back to shore.

The corpse is a blonde woman, eyes frozen shut. His heart clenches. He tears his gaze away, focusing on the shifting sand beneath his feet. Then he strides into the cemetery and lowers the woman at the end of a bedraggled row. Footsteps thump behind him.

"Get warmed up," Yates says, dragging another corpse up alongside the blond woman. It leaves a trail in the dirt, wet and dark, and Connor looks at the sea of headstones around them.

It's been two months since the wizard allowed him to join his search for bodies, on a day when the waves roared and crashed, and heavy rain poured on them. There had been too many corpses, people from a sunken cruise ship further out to sea. Yates had had Connor dig the graves, but it seemed as though there was always another body to be buried. At the end of it, the wizard had collapsed against him, shaking and drenched, all the spells along the shore bled dry.

Connor follows the familiar tracks back down to the sea. He rinses his hands in the shallow waves, then wanders over to a drawing in the sand. It's a Celtic cross, for perseverance. There, he dips his toes into the blue glow of its outline.

At once, warmth washes into his body, from his feet to his legs to his torso to his arms, banishing the cold. He breathes in slow, his skin tingling, and it doesn't feel like the seasons are changing, doesn't feel like he's just been in the thankless sea. Instead, Connor feels alive, full of energy, like someone's pulled a warm blanket over him.

He tips his head back, the breeze tickling his face.

"Okay?" Yates asks quietly by his side.

Connor nods. "Yeah."

"You don't have to help if you don't want to," Yates continues, and Connor can almost hear him picking at his shirt hem. "Go back to the ship and get some rest."

He scoffs then, cracking an eye open. "Me? Aren't you the one who's two centuries old?"

The wizard smiles wryly, turning to face the sea. His hair plasters dark against his head, and he doesn't seem old, not to Connor. Connor inches over, nudging him lightly. This, Yates still allows, perhaps because Connor hasn't talked about the slow lick of flames in his chest. But he hasn't forgotten that kiss from a year ago, and that fire still burns.

Connor hopes, and keeps his dreams in the secret pockets of his heart.

"I'm not a boy anymore," he says into the breeze. "I haven't been for a while."

Yates glances sidelong at him. Connor meets his gaze, holds it for as long as he can. In the end, it's the wizard who breaks the stare, taking in a deep breath. Connor wants to know what Yates thinks of him now, but he doesn't dare ask, not with something so important. Yates is the brightest spark in his life. "I'll draw more spells," Yates says. "I don't want you catching a cold."

Connor tries not to let his disappointment

show. He turns away, wriggling his foot into the sand. "You owe me a birthday cake."

The wizard's eyes twinkle. "I haven't forgotten," he says. "If we finish this early, I'll even make you some sardine sandwiches."

And Connor cheers right up, because sardine sandwiches are still his favorite food. Yates makes the best ones. Yates knows that, knows he'll do anything for more of them, the bastard. "Fine," Connor says, but he's grinning now. "Cake and sandwiches."

"It's a promise." Yates sets his hands on Connor's shoulders, walking him back into the ocean. "Now get to work."

YATES LOOKS after Connor on the beach, tracing his path as he strides across the tide-darkened sand, waves catching his feet. He's no longer the excitable boy that Yates knew seven years ago. Now, he's almost a man, and Yates doesn't know what to think.

Connor gives him lingering stares sometimes, that Yates pretends not to notice. He can't respond to them, can't acknowledge the boy's interest. Connor is so young. An innocent, almost, and Yates can't fight the nagging doubt that he's influenced the boy somehow, imprinted on him without meaning to.

But Connor brings a spark of life to his otherwise mundane existence. After years alone on this foggy shore, Connor makes him laugh. Yates doesn't know what his best option is. He's blundered: lost friendships, disappointed his mentor. He doesn't want Connor to be just another mistake. Doesn't want to lose him. Connor has worked himself into long hours of his day, every day of the week. Yates is too selfish to send him away.

So he tucks his hands in his pockets and heads for the forest, knowing that Connor will be back tomorrow. That, in itself, is a relief.

BACK AT home, Connor sits on the couch next to his father, looking at the stubble on his jaw, the dullness of his eyes. His clothes are frayed, and he stares uninterestedly at the music videos on TV. In the years since his mom passed away, his father's chestnut hair has grayed, and the wrinkles on his skin have deepened. New scabs cross his arms — accidents from when he's brought beer out on the fishing trips.

"Does it really help?" Connor asks. "Drinking this much?"

"What's it gotta do with you?" Dad mutters, flipping past women in bikinis and basketball matches on TV. "Run off with your girlfriend."

Connor sighs. "Yates isn't my girlfriend." He takes the bottle dangling from his dad's fingers, setting it on the coffee table. "You need to stop doing this. Mom wouldn't want to see you become this... ghost."

Dad's clenches his jaw, his arms tensing. "What d'you know about what she'd want?"

Connor winces. He hasn't tried talking his

father off alcohol in a while, and he remembers why he stopped. "This isn't good for you. We can't keep getting into accidents. Any worse than cuts, and I don't think we can afford treatment."

"I'm fine," Dad snaps. He takes the bottle back, gulping from it. "Shove off. I don't need a damned nanny."

Deep down, Connor wonders what his old, cheery dad would think of himself now. He remembers his father hanging paintings on the walls with his mom, remembers late nights when he sneaked out of his bedroom and found his parents dancing in the kitchen. *Your dad carried me through the doorway when we married,* Mom had told him once. *We were eighteen. The only time he was happier was when I told him I had you in my belly.*

Connor misses his mom again. His chest aches. "I miss her too," he says. "She wouldn't want to see you hurt."

"Fuck off." His dad scowls, chucking the beer bottle at him. Connor catches it in one hand, ignoring the slosh of liquid onto his knuckles. Better a mess than glass shards on the floor.

"Just try to cut back, okay?" he says, setting the bottle back on the table. He doesn't know what else he can do, other than say what Yates told him to. "Stop drinking for my sake. Can you do that?"

Dad purses his lips, looking away. "I'll try."

Yates says that some wounds don't heal that quickly, and Connor knows his father still hurts. He wishes he knew how to mend wounds like that.

There's nothing else he can do for his dad now, so he grabs his parcel of cookies from the kitchen, and retreats to his room

11
Eighteen (Part I)

LIGHTNING STRIKES on his eighteenth birthday.

They're on the clifftops again, Yates waving a short stick, storm clouds crackling above. Connor thinks he's insane, but the heavens seem to favor the wizard: lightning carves a jagged white line further out at sea, thunder roars, and wind whips around them, bending the grass at their feet.

"This is nuts. We'll get struck down," Connor yells. Yates waves him off. The only thing taller than them is an old spruce further along the cliff. "You're gonna kill us!"

"The most powerful magic," Yates shouts back, "can be wielded when you combine the different elements together. For instance, this." He draws runes down the side of the stick—*heat, electricity, storage*—and raises it up to the heavens again. "*Lignum vitae.* Wood of Life, Connor. Watch."

Lightning strikes before either of them can move. It rips a blinding line down to Yates, searing the air around them. A heartbeat later, thunder explodes above, bellowing like a furious beast, and Connor can't hear anything past the shooting pain in his ears.

All he sees is white. His ears ring, the scent of ozone sharp in his nose. He tries to reach his senses out, but he can't feel the heat of Yates' magic. *He's gone? He can't... That idiot!* Fear claws up his throat. He can't lose this man. Can't think about a world without Yates.

Before the colors in his vision fade, he's stumbling forward, almost whimpering, trying to find his mentor. Yates waves from feet away. His hair sticks out, smoke rising from its ends, and relief wells up in Connor's throat. "I thought you were gonna die," he says, hating that his voice breaks. "Damn you!"

But Yates just smiles at him, warmth shining in his eyes. "I'm still alive, aren't I?" He shakes the stick at Connor. "This wood—"

Connor tugs him against his chest. Yates' voice muffles against his shirt, and Connor wraps his arms around him, his heart pounding. "Don't do that again," he hisses.

He knows now that Yates isn't fragile, that he can take some knocks and bumps, and so Connor squeezes him tight, trying to tell him all the words he doesn't want to hear. *I love you. You don't know how important you are to me.*

The wizard coughs and struggles. "Can't breathe. Let go, Connor!"

Connor releases him. Yates sags against his chest, panting. When he looks up, his eyes are unguarded and blue as the summer sky, and Connor leans in, needing to feel Yates' lips on his own.

He's halfway to Yates when he realizes he's

about to kiss him. His stomach twists. He wants that kiss, wants Yates sinking against him. But Yates hasn't said anything about Connor's feelings, and Connor knows a kiss will drive him away. So he quells the whirl of panic and relief in his chest, staring down at the wizard, aching.

"I thought you were going to die," Connor says. It feels like a cop-out.

"I wasn't. I know my risks." Yates lingers against his chest for a few more seconds, before frowning at himself and pulling away. He taps the stick in his palm. It's not even singed. "You should have learned two things: first, the nigh indestructible quality of *lignum vitae*. Second, the conversion of energy into life magic. Now, watch."

In the midst of rumbling thunder, Yates crouches before a patch of soil, brushing away leaves and flowers. Slowly, he traces lines into the sand, the tip of the stick glowing a brilliant bluish-white. Where it touches, sand melts into red-hot glass: first a curve, then a spiral. Rain begins to patter down, fat drops landing in their hair.

Lightning flashes again, blinding white. The sky fades to a belligerent gray, and a flicker of orange flares through the forest. Yates cries out. "Oh, *suck* my dick!"

In the distance, flames lick around a fir tree. It's unnervingly close to where the ship is, a thirty-minute sprint from the cliffs. Connor clenches his jaw. The ship can't be burnt to cinders, not when it's become a second home to him. "Damn it!"

"Hurry, the rope," Yates says, pushing him along.

Rain falls, stinging droplets flying into his eyes.

His feet pound over grass, and he slips twice on smooth stone. Two boulders sit by the lone spruce, the rope down the cliffs anchored around them. He grabs it, scrawls an adhesive rune on one hand, and descends so fast the rope burns his palms.

"Oh, Connor," Yates sighs above the rain, exasperated. "You know spells to protect your hands."

"No time for that," he snaps back. The moment he hits the rocks at the bottom, he's sprinting across the shore, winding into the forest where he'll get better traction.

Yates falls behind. "Your legs are too long. I can't keep up!"

He grumbles and turns, slowing as he passes through the straight, dark trunks of the trees. When the wizard catches up, Connor grabs his arm and pulls him along. The watchful firs skim past them in a blur.

The blaze devours the trees, crackling and leaping, its glow flickering through the leaves even before they've reached the ship. Yates groans, but he pumps his legs faster to keep up with Connor's strides. When they break into the clearing, flames lick around half the ship, more than the rain can quench. Heat ripples from it in waves. Yates snatches a twig off the ground. "Connor—the arrows!"

As the wizard begins drawing a large circle around the ship, Connor follows, sketching the first arrow. Then the next and the next, all pointing inward. Yates completes the circle and turns to face his home, carving symbols for *air* and *fast* and *cold* into the soil.

He jabs the stick of *lignum vitae* into the ground. The magic in the wood sweeps out beneath them, spreading through the circle. Then it swoops within the barrier and rushes at the ship as an icy wind.

The flames wink out with a string of pops. They leave the ship standing in the middle of the clearing, wood smoking, holes burned through the starboard side. Yates' shoulders sag. Connor grimaces. The rain continues to pour, soaking his shoes.

Slowly, they circle the ship to inspect the damage, feet splashing in puddles. A layer of char covers the surface of the hull. The stern has held steady, and along the sides, parts of the ship have disintegrated into ashes, exposing the interior. From the ground, Connor sees the remnants of the kitchen and the bookshelves, their backs burnt off. "I'm surprised the fire didn't spread more."

The wizard winces, stopping by the largest gap of all—ten yards of the side, with some support beams gone. Connor can't help staring at his hair, the way it gleams darkly against his head, a deep red that he wants to touch. Yates wipes the rain from his face. "I had to replace some of the wood in the ship. The newer parts burned."

"There'll be leaks until we can fix it," Connor says.

"It's not so bad—I've had worse."

"I'll help." Connor stops by his side. His own clothes are soaked, and he doesn't care. Yates is here, alive and warm.

Yates leans into him. "Thanks," he says quietly. He twists his fingers together. "I appreciate it."

Connor shrugs. Truthfully, he just wants an excuse to see the wizard all the time.

LATER, AS his dad reaches for an unopened bottle by the couch, Connor says, "I want to live on a ship."

Dad pulls his hand back. "You don't mean our boat. That's barely big enough to sleep in."

Connor shakes his head, heat prickling on his cheeks. "Yates has one."

His father stares at him for a while, and it feels like everyone can read his secrets. Connor hates that. But Dad just looks away, hooking a bottle opener against the lid. He's still going through two twelve-packs a day. "If you want, I guess. Best if you help me with the fishing, though. I'm getting old."

Connor bites down his disappointment. Dad doesn't care, not like Mom. Mom would have wanted to hear about Yates' ship. "Of course I'll help," he says. He wouldn't desert his father. His parents have taught him that people are stronger with others around to buoy them. "That was always the plan."

THE DAY after the lightning strike, Connor scales the makeshift ladder up the side of the ship. In the hours since the storm, Yates has pinned lengths of tie-dyed cloth to the open walls, blue-and-white fabric that flutters in the breeze.

"It feels like the bathroom is so open otherwise," the wizard says when Connor ducks under cloth to enter the cargo hold. The place reeks of smoke. "Like the entire forest is peeking in."

Connor snorts. "The bathroom never had walls."

"Of course it does: the ship's walls." Yates laughs, reaching into his cookie tin. He freezes, then peers inside. "Oh, suck it. I'm out of cookies. These were the chocolate chip ones, too."

Connor glances around the kitchen. The fire didn't reach the food stores—the pantry and cabinets are all unmarred—but a hole gapes at the back of the stove, and some of the runes along its edges have burned away. "That's all you've been eating? Cookies?"

Yates grins sheepishly. "Yes?"

He sighs, rubbing his face. "You're *two-hundred* years old."

"All the more reason to be eating cookies." The wizard sets the empty tin on the island counter, wandering over to the pantry. "Are you going to help with the repairs, or are we studying something new today?"

"We're going to fix this place," Connor says. Yates needs actual food and something better than cloth walls. "At least some tarps to keep the rain out."

"I'm afraid I don't have that," the wizard says, cringing. "Strange, isn't it? I repair things for people, but neglect my own home."

Which is why Connor's here, isn't it? To help Yates take better care of himself. He decides for them. "We're making a list today. Get the things for the ship, then start work."

Yates grins brightly at him, and his stomach flips.

AS THINGS go, the list of materials Yates needs far exceeds what he can afford. They carry bundles of tarps beneath their arms, and Connor holds bags of nails in one hand, their footfalls muffled against sand. "At least you live in a forest," Connor says. "We can't afford all that wood otherwise."

"You will help cut the trees down, won't you?"

"'Course I will. I want you to teach me more magic." *Or just smile. That'll work, too.* Connor steps closer to him, just to feel the heat of his arm.

The wizard's eyes light up. "I'm sure we'll be able to continue soon."

"Maybe if we have all the materials," Connor says. "Dad and I don't make a lot of money. I can't help pay for this."

Yates wrinkles his forehead. "I don't expect you to contribute to the expenses, Connor. You're my student."

And it's the same argument again: no help, no intimacy—because he's too young. Connor glares. "I spend all my time at your place. It's my home too."

"Well. I'm your teacher, so it's my responsibility."

"I want to help."

"And you are. I couldn't possibly carry all these back to the ship myself." Yates nods at the bundles between them. "Thank you."

But he still thinks of Connor as a student, as someone below him, and it's not enough. Connor wants to be his equal, wants Yates to regard him as someone desirable. He wants Yates to kiss him.

"Fine," he says, his thoughts churning. Maybe he isn't ready yet, but someday, he'll convince Yates to change his mind.

12
Eighteen (Part II)

IT TAKES them days to saw logs and shape the planks. As they wait for the wood to season, they cut more timber, filling the cargo hold until there's barely space to walk. When that happens, Yates teaches Connor to combine the different forms of magic: pushing life energy into barriers, using shape magic to grow plants, and storing energy from nature in wood.

Connor runs late one day, when the fishing boat sails into the harbor on the heels of a storm. While waiting for the rain to pass, they'd reeled in more fish, which Connor had gutted, filling first the salting buckets, then the iceboxes. By the time he reaches the forest, it's well past noon, and he stinks of fish.

He doesn't find Yates in the cargo hold, or on the deck. The crops around the ship are newly-weeded, but there's no wizard to be seen.

Caked with dried sweat and scales, he decides to take a bath.

Connor has never seen Yates bathe, but he's seen the pails of rainwater on the other side of the kitchen. He fills the tub with them, squeezes two lemons into it, and strips. He cleans under his nails, scrubs the fish scales off his arms, washes his face. By the time he's done, Yates still hasn't shown up.

He stands, looking around. *Of course* he's forgotten to grab a towel, and *of course* they have to be in Yates' closet in the corner of the cargo hold.

He lifts one dripping leg out of the tub when the makeshift doorway flips open, and Yates pokes his head in. Connor freezes. Yates stares. Yates' eyes sweep down his body, then back up, and his throat works. He moves, but whether he's trying to climb up or down, Connor doesn't know, because he yelps and disappears from view. Something thumps outside.

Connor crosses the cargo hold before he thinks, stepping over the timber on the floor. He sweeps the tarp open, and his stomach clenches at the sight of Yates lying flat on the ground.

He descends the ladder. Below, Yates squawks, his hands clawing into dirt. Connor pauses. Yates blinks and blinks and *blinks,* blue eyes darting between him and the forest. He steps closer. Yates scrambles backward. When Connor crouches by him, Yates' eyes drift down his chest, then away. And back to his chest.

"No," Yates groans, covering his face with a dirt-speckled forearm. "Get... get dressed."

"What, you've never seen a guy before?" Connor asks. Yates can't stop staring at him. He isn't making a face or being flippant. Instead, he's just lying there, trying to drag his attention somewhere else. And so Connor opens his legs.

Yates' gaze drops to his groin, and the noise coming from his throat sounds like a dying animal.

He struggles onto his front, burying his face in the dirt, and drops clumps of soil onto his head. "No," he says, muffled. "Go away. Get dressed. Please."

"I... didn't bring fresh clothes," Connor realizes. After the fresh fish was sold, he'd hurried all the way from the harbor to the forest, leaving his father to cart the salted fish back to the house. And none of Yates' clothes fit him: his shoulders are broad, muscled from hard work on the ocean. "Just the ones from the morning."

Yates scoops dirt up around his face. With a growl, Connor grabs him by the shoulder, flipping him over. "Don't do that."

The wizard's hands fly right to his groin, but it's too late. Connor glimpses the straining fabric before he can hide it, and it sends an answering heat through his gut.

"You like how I look," he says. How did he not know that? That Yates likes men, that maybe Yates likes him?

"You're my *student*," Yates splutters. He struggles back onto his front, pushing his face into the ground. "Go home. Come back tomorrow."

"You're attracted to me," Connor says, trying the words out on his tongue.

Yates' breath rushes out. "Nothing's going to happen," he says, voice strained. "You're my student. That's where the line is."

Why does it always come down to him being a student? Connor glares at the dirt-strewn locks of Yates' hair. His father has been calling him a man in front of all the other fishermen. He's not a child, not someone Yates can evade. "I'm eighteen, Yates. I'm old enough to make my own decisions."

"And this is my decision." Yates drops more earth onto himself, then turns his face away. "I'm bound as your mentor. I will not betray this bond."

Heat wells up in Connor's chest. Yates never said he wasn't interested, and it sounds like he's just hiding behind excuses. They aren't in a school. No one cares if they do anything. No one knows about them. Yates says this like he doesn't know Connor's been in love with him for fuck knows how long. "What if I want this?" he snaps. "What if we have sex?"

Yates freezes. His fingers curl into the earth, and he bows his head. "Then I'm no longer fit to be your teacher."

"No one says we can't, except you," Connor says. They could be lovers and partners and friends. Not just a teacher and his student.

Yates shakes his head. "This is final, Connor. Get dressed and go home."

The wizard has to be joking. Connor nudges him with a foot. "Hey."

Yates doesn't answer.

"Yates."

Silence.

"Yates!"

"Go before I sever this bond," Yates says, and Connor's stomach shrivels. He can't risk that. Can't risk being shut out of Yates' life.

"Fine." And so he returns to the ship, pulling on his clothes. When he leaves the clearing, Yates is still lying on the ground, clumps of soil in his red hair.

HOURS LATER, when the sky has darkened, and when the crickets sing in the forest, Yates sits in the bathtub, panting.

He didn't expect this. Not for Connor to put obscene thoughts into his head, nor for him to find a deep well of hunger in himself. Alone in the forest, he'd settled into not seeing another soul for days, and at his age, sex has become an afterthought.

Being a teacher means patience and giving and selflessness. Not staring at an expanse of bronzed skin, thinking about his mouth on places it shouldn't be. Not remembering that he hasn't been touched in decades, knowing exactly who he wants between his legs. He's watched Connor *grow up*. It shouldn't have taken one look for all his thoughts to sink into the gutter. His body had responded with ferocious, visceral need. Before today, Connor has been someone he admired a little too much, perhaps. Now...

The pearly streaks lie stark against the tub. They glisten up at him, recriminating, and Yates covers his face with his hands. Disgust crawls up his throat. He hasn't been able to get those images out of his head: Connor on the ladder, Connor leaning over him. Connor and his legs—

Yates groans, pressing his forehead against cool steel. This cannot happen again.

THEY DON'T talk about it.

BEFORE THEY can build momentum, the ship repairs hit a hurdle. Connor's dad meets with a boating accident one day—beer on board again—and he fractures his hand slipping on a stray fish.

Jaded, Connor steers the boat back into the harbor. He accompanies his father to the smaller hospital, the one that has subsidies for the public. They spend the entire morning there. By the time Dad's hand is bandaged and he's discharged, dusk has fallen. It's too late to make a trip to the forest. Connor stays in, cooking with the faded recipes on the wall. He's memorized them by heart, but he likes reading the familiar looping script, and his father never says anything about removing those cards. They're not a reminder of Connor's mom, after all.

When he sets buttery squash cubes on the table that night, Connor says, "I like someone."

Life sparks in his dad's eyes. It's a sight better than the slump of his shoulders and the dimness of his gaze. Connor knows the feeling. He's seen Dad covering his face, seen him sitting hunched on the side of his too-large bed, and he knows that Mom's ghost hangs over them both. Dad tries not to drink. Sometimes he drinks half a bottle and puts it back into the fridge. Sometimes he thumbs the bottle cap, glances at Connor, and turns away from it entirely. Sometimes the bottles surround him like a wall.

Connor hopes the bandaged hand will turn his dad away from the alcohol. And so he tries to help, giving his dad something else to think about. Even if it's a secret. "His name is Yates."

His father snorts. "You talk about him all the

time. Guy with a ship."

So maybe this isn't really helping. Connor sighs, setting fried fish on their plates. "Yeah, well."

Dad studies him. "He treat you okay?"

Connor nods. Yates treats him too well, maybe. He gives him free access to the charred library, corrects his drawings, and never treats him like an idiot. "He just—he says I'm too young."

"Yeah? How old is he?" Dad holds his fork awkwardly in his other hand, jabbing it into a squash cube.

Two centuries, Connor almost says, but he remembers that most people don't get that old. That only magic folk can have lives like that, and how the hell is he magic, if his parents aren't? "Uh, forty-eight."

It still sounds terrible when he says it.

"Couple years younger than me." Dad raises his eyebrow. "You've been talking about him since... since you were, what, fourteen? He's not some child molester, is he?"

Heat sweeps through Connor's face. "What?" he splutters. "No!"

His dad leans forward, staring hard at him. "I should meet him sometime, this Yates. See if he's trustworthy."

"He is," Connor says. "I trust him with my life."

Dad raises an eyebrow again.

Connor flushes, jabbing at his fish just so he has something to do. "I just... I-I want him to like me. That's all."

And that's the most difficult thing he's had to

admit aloud. Connor knows what he wants, but hearing it, and knowing that Yates doesn't like him that way... It hurts.

"So you're asking me for help."

"I guess. I don't know what to do."

His father sets his fork down on his plate, leaning back. "Back when—Back when I met your mom," he says, his words halting. "In school. We were seventeen."

"You were still in school?" Connor asks, dropping his fork. His dad has never talked about this, not to him. "I thought you were fishing!"

Dad grimaces. "My father didn't fish. He sent me to school. The rest of my brothers were home-schooled."

"Why?"

"Because they were *magic*," Dad mutters, sullen. He stabs at his fish. "And I had no spark. They kept me out of their games and meetings and shit. When I married Mags and moved to Fort Bragg, they were glad to be rid of me."

Connor's appetite vanishes. "Oh."

And it all makes sense. Dad refusing magic back when Mom died. Dad rejecting all mention of it, snarling when Connor even breathes the word. Dad never talking about his family, never visiting Connor's grandparents, or his aunts and uncles.

His dad inhales, holds his breath, then releases it. He pops a squash cube into his mouth. "Anyway. This Yates."

He's magic. And so am I. Connor watches him, uncertain. He doesn't want to talk about magic right now, doesn't want to mention Yates teaching him, because he knows how some secrets should be hidden away. So he says instead, "Tell me more about you and Mom. I want to hear about how you met. How you asked her out."

Dad cracks a tiny smile. It sheds the years from his face. "We were good, Mags and I."

The brightness in his eyes gives Connor hope that his dad will be fine, someday. His father is still in his husk somewhere, emerging when he isn't drunk. And as his dad talks, Connor wonders if he'll ever look sappy like that, reminiscing about Yates. Some days, it seems like a frivolous wish.

13
Eighteen (Part III)

DAD SEEMS better after their talk: calmer, the tension in his shoulders eased. He sails out with Connor in the morning, cranking the fishing nets one-handed, and points out the cormorants soaring on the drafts high above. Connor hands him soda—Dad hesitates before accepting it—and they settle back in their chairs, Connor gutting all the fish now that his father can't. Dad apologizes for the accident.

Later that afternoon, he finds Yates wandering on the shore. The wizard hurries up when he glimpses Connor, his forehead furrowed. "Is everything okay?"

"Yeah." Connor glances back at the tiny, pastel-colored houses miles away. "My dad broke his wrist on the boat yesterday." He almost doesn't want to say it, because it means he has even less money to help with the ship's repairs. It makes his skin itch with guilt.

Yates sets a hand on his arm. "I'm sorry to hear that. You're fine, though?"

He feels like smiling, then. It's nice. Nice that Yates cares so much about him. "Yeah. But I've got more things to do when we fish. Loading the boat and all that. How are the repairs going?"

Yates grins dryly. "Slow. I never did like repairing things."

Connor sighs and steers them back into the forest. "We haven't even got most of your ship patched up yet."

"I know."

"And you're just wandering around!"

"I was waiting for you." Yates' eyes slide over to him, and Connor's heart quickens. He still doesn't know how to deal with this. He's interested. Yates is, too. The wizard's gaze flickers down Connor's body when he thinks he isn't looking, and Connor doesn't miss the way he wets his lips. But Yates will also end his mentorship if anything intimate happens between them, if he oversteps his boundaries.

Connor follows the lines of Yates' limbs instead, the fine bones of his hands, the points of his elbows, the slope of his shoulders. He shoves his hands into his pockets, thinking about the support beams they have to rebuild, the starboard side that has to be sealed before it gets too cold, so Yates can be warm for the winter.

That's something they can both work toward.

YATES' FINANCES encounter a hiccup as winter eases into spring. They've patched most of the largest holes, hard Douglas fir bent to fit the sides of the ship. The new planks stand out from the surrounding wood — pale yellow against charred blue paint, and Yates insists that any new coat should match the old.

None of the hardware stores in Fort Bragg carry that particular shade of blue. They don't have the right colors to mix it up with, either. Connor asks the cashier, Sheila, at Mack's, who calls three other suppliers for updated paint catalogs. "They'll arrive in two weeks," Sheila tells him.

Which works out anyway, when a tidal wave washes out the Pacific Coast Highway further south, and food imports grind to a halt.

They've got plenty of fish. Other foods, like vegetables and flour and chicken, take longer to arrive. The prices in the grocery stores swell like the tide, and Connor pauses at the produce aisle, thinking that potatoes count as vegetables, too. In his head, Mom says, *You must eat colorful foods to stay healthy.*

Deep in the forest, Yates pokes at the slow-growing vegetables in his garden, a frown on his face. "I'd much rather have cookies," he says, "except flour is the most expensive right now."

They don't paint the ship for months, and most repairs are forgotten in favor of keeping their pantries stocked.

BETWEEN HIS father's hospital bills and the food shortage, repairing Yates' ship becomes something of a joke between them.

"Did you bring the resin?" Yates will say. Or, "When do you think this ship will be ready to sail?"

Connor scoffs every time. "You'll sail it to the bottom of the ocean," he'll say. "Resin is for wimps."

And Yates will laugh, the melody of it settling into Connor's chest.

Between his lessons and cutting wood, Connor pushes magic into the ground so new leaves unfurl in the garden. He can't practice at home or his dad will notice, but at Yates', he germinates daisy seeds and makes flowers bloom.

It has to be just the right amount of magic, Yates said. *Too much magic, and you'll only get leaves. Too little, and it won't grow at all.* The pots on his deck are full of spinach and basil—leaves that will wilt to a coin-sized lump on the stove. Connor brings handfuls home sometimes, and the rest of their money goes into mending the fishing nets.

Oftentimes, Connor will glance up from the garden soil to find Yates staring at him, his own hands stuck in dirt. Yates will smile and glance away, but it doesn't stop his heart from skipping. *What do you think about when you watch me?* he wants to ask. The words have been waiting in his mouth for months, now, but he's lost his courage to try.

He doesn't want to lose both a mentor and a best friend, so he bows his head, scrawling protective runes into the soil.

DESPITE YATES' hopes, drought creeps up in late spring, leaving the farming communities of California parched and brown. Fish doesn't get any more expensive, but other meats do, and prices on everything have gone up to offset the increased water costs.

Connor has named the ship. "The Old Boat," he says. "It's fragile and elderly like you are."

Yates tells him he's not old, and Connor raises a pointed brow. He's a fraction of Yates' age. He has his father's sharp eyes, the corded muscles of his shoulders, the bulk of his body. Sometimes, Yates thinks he might even be able to lift the ship.

Connor grins, and Yates finds his breath catching. Sometimes, Connor bumps into him so he loses his balance, then grabs him by the arm, steadying him.

Deep down, Yates craves more of that contact, needs that heat on his skin. He hasn't forgotten the bathtub incident. It's shameful, what he does with that memory, but as Connor stares at him with those dark eyes, Yates *knows* he wouldn't mind. It makes him hate himself.

He's shaped Connor into a person he respects and is fond of, taught him his own morals; that's a teacher's job. Not something a lover should do.

So when Connor walks up to him and nudges his shoulder, smelling like fresh sweat, Yates stops breathing. He's torn between pushing him away and burying his nose in his chest. His hunger itches at the back of his throat. He turns instead, clapping dirt off his hands.

"We'll see if there are more inexpensive repairs we can do," he says.

The disappointment in Connor's eyes sends guilt winding through his stomach, but Yates forces himself to look away.

Drawing these boundaries between them is the only thing he can do, at this point.

A MONTH from his nineteenth birthday, Connor carries two drums of paint to the ship. He treads carefully into the clearing, sets the drums down, and climbs the rope ladder to the deck. "Hey."

Yates pulls a weed from his daisy pot, his eyes bright. "You're late."

"Yeah, well." Connor shrugs, heat prickling at the back of his neck. "I got you something."

Yates' face *glows*. "You did?" He dusts his hands off, hurrying forward, eyes darting over Connor's hands and pockets. "What is it?"

Connor nods beyond the railings. "Down below. I'm not carrying them up here."

"You didn't..." The wizard leans over the deck wall, and his eyes grow wide. Before Connor can answer, he's scrambling down the ladder, skipping the last few rungs to land before the drums. There, he crouches, blue eyes skimming over the labels.

Connor fights down a smile. "You're grinning like I brought you a ton of salted fish."

"It's better than that." The wizard hugs a drum of paint to himself. "You shouldn't have. These were expensive."

They're also five months of Connor's savings, tucked away under his bed when he first found a vendor selling that exact shade of velvet blue. The rest of the paint drums are still at the shop. Yates pries the lid open with a trowel, and his jaw slackens. The paint inside is rich and deep, like the purple-blue sky on a stormy night. It'll dry to match the rest of the ship.

Yates sets the lid carefully back, hammers it down to secure it, and leaps to his feet, right up into Connor's chest. "Thank you," he breathes, his lean arms wrapping around Connor's waist. His magic flickers and dances like a crackling fire. "This is the best gift I've ever received."

"It's just paint," Connor says, but they've been working on the ship for almost a year: reconstructing beams, sanding down planks, spreading resin over freshly-seasoned wood.

"It's not, and you know it." Yates' voice muffles against his shirt. His shoulders lift, then settle, and Connor realizes that Yates is breathing him in, that Yates is entirely plastered against him, holding him tight, and he wants more, wants things to stay as they are forever.

So he slides his arms carefully around Yates' shoulders, pulling him close just to feel the weight of him, smell the musk and earth in his hair. Yates leans in closer. Like he wants him.

"What do you want for your birthday?" he asks sometime later, his face still in Connor's shirt.

You. Connor sniffs at him, over and over. He can't have enough. "Nothing. Maybe a sardine sandwich."

Yates chuckles, his shoulders shaking. He's a bundle of heat and laughter in Connor's arms, precious and beautiful. "Okay. I can do that."

When Yates pulls away and looks up, his face is barely inches from Connor's. His eyes are sparkling, his mouth damp, and Connor aches to kiss him.

"Are we painting now?" Yates asks. He tiptoes forward, his lips whispering against Connor's cheek, a warm, light touch that lingers on his skin.

"Yeah," he says, turning to hide his blush. *Yates kissed me.* "But we'll have to sand the resin down first. Can't just wait for the trees to do it."

Yates laughs, hugging him tight before slipping away. "Okay. Let's do that."

AT HOME, Connor can't help smiling. He's sneaked another recipe card from Yates—paprika and buttered fish with garlic toast—and he whistles as he makes dinner.

"Found a golden fish?" his dad asks, gulping from a fresh bottle. "Never seen you so happy."

"It's nothing," Connor says, but he's still grinning. Even his dad's drinking can't dampen his mood.

"Yates, huh?"

He minces the garlic. "I got him some paint for his ship. He hugged me."

"Good for you." Dad sets the half-full bottle on the table, rocking his chair backward. "Bring him back for dinner sometime."

"Yeah, I will," Connor says. He knows why he hasn't: Yates looks thirty instead of forty-eight. Or two-hundred and forty-eight.

He doesn't know how to explain that, so he whistles along to "Just Another Day" on the radio. It feels like Yates is right there in the kitchen with him.

YATES LEANS back in his bathtub again, head tipped back, one hand between his legs. His fingers work over slick skin, squeezing slow and tight, and his breathing stutters. He thinks about musk and fresh sweat and a hot mouth on his neck, then further down, licking to his tip, and he's coming so hard he can't breathe, can't think, his body tense, toes curled.

By the time his heart slows, and by the time the stopped cogs of his mind grind into motion again, he's shaky and weak, guilt clinging to his skin like sweat.

He can't think about Connor this way. He can't. But Connor is sweet and kind and just a little bit sarcastic, and he's no longer the boy he was at thirteen. Yates wants to press up close against him. Wants to sink his teeth into Connor's skin. Wants Connor to drive into him and make him forget about everything else.

He rubs his hand over his face. How much had he influenced Connor's infatuation? He's betrayed his student, hasn't he, doing something lewd like this? His stomach twists. He needs to tell Connor never to return. He needs to stop keeping secrets like this.

Yates pulls a towel over his head, sick with himself. Someday, he'll find the guts to stop this madness.

14
Nineteen (Part I)

ON CONNOR'S nineteenth birthday, they layer the ship with its final coat of paint. Connor had arrived late from fishing to find Yates out painting by himself, his face alight with anticipation. Now, hours later, the wizard sweeps his final brushstrokes across the hull, then leans back to survey the ship, running a paint-smudged hand through his hair.

"It's over, Connor," he breathes, his voice growing higher. "It's done. We're done!"

Yates' grin is almost too bright to look at. But the same triumph surges through Connor's chest when Yates drops his brush into the paint bucket and turns, pulling him into a tight hug. His blood roars in his ears. It's been an entire fucking year since the ship caught fire, and they're finally done. "You think?"

"Yes. I'm so glad we did it," Yates says, his words coming fast, his fingers stroking down Connor's back, their chests pressed tight together. Heat flickers low in Connor's gut, a visceral response to the victory pounding in his veins, and he wants to push Yates against the drying paint, wants to kiss him senseless and grind into him. Instead, he drops his brush and swallows, threading his fingers through Yates' hair. It's soft, slipping against his hand, feathery and light like silk. Yates leans into his touch.

It's taken months to complete the repairs — reforming the hull, scrubbing the surfaces down, applying coat after coat of velvet-blue paint. Earlier, Yates had worried about the two inches of paint left in the drum, wondering if there would be enough to cover the rest of the starboard side.

"I'm glad too," Connor says. "Been through a lot of shit to get this done."

Yates' laugh rumbles throaty and low against his chest. "Language, Connor."

Connor snorts. "I'm nineteen. My dad's a fisherman. He swears more than I do."

Yates turns, his gaze lingering on the smooth, painted surfaces of the ship, the clean windows, the squat cabin perched on the deck. It would have been ready for the water if the engine mechanisms worked, but Yates wants the ship anchored here, so Connor has never tried to repair its transmission.

He buries his nose in the soft down of Yates' hair, smelling the tang of his sweat. "No more wood-cutting," he says. "Glad that's done with."

Yates hasn't pulled away. He strokes a hand up along Connor's back, then down, and Connor knows he's got his eyes closed, face tucked down so he can't see who he's touching. "I feel the same," Yates says, his breath warm on Connor's collarbones. It makes him shiver. "Many times, I thought we'd never see it done. We've had so many hurdles: the money, the drought, your dad's bills. I've been boiling salted fish for months. I guess I'm a little tired of that."

A nagging worry unfurls in Connor's stomach. "You don't want me to bring more fish?"

"No, no. That's not what I meant." Yates leans closer, his nose nudging Connor's throat, and Connor's heart kicks to life, pounds against his ribs so hard that surely Yates must feel it. "I should find other ways of cooking fish. That's all."

And Yates brushes his lips against Connor's neck. Connor's mouth goes dry. Yates hasn't done this before. He's never even hugged him for this long, only studied him with those pensive eyes, and surely Yates knows what he's doing to him.

Connor slides a thumb down his spine, drawing a groan from his lips. The sound slips into Connor's ears, down his nerves, between his legs. Connor knows the telling heat in his groin. He pulls his hips away so he isn't pushing against Yates, except he wants Yates to feel him, feel how much he wants him. He wants Yates rocking back. Wants him squirming, hungry.

"What're you thinking about?" Connor asks, following the lines of Yates' back, the hem of his T-shirt tucked into his pants. His pulse beats in his cock, and he isn't thinking clearly anymore. "The ship?"

"Mm-hmm. It's magnificent." Yates leans back to survey his home again. "Do you think it should have a name?"

"I named it," Connor says. "The Old Ship."

Yates slaps his arm lightly, grinning. "That doesn't count."

"Yeah, well, I should go clean up. Change my

shirt." *See to this hard-on before you notice.*

"Mm. I may as well do the same." Yates pulls away, studying his own clothes, and Connor tries to quell the mix of horror and excitement coursing through his veins. With the ship complete, it feels as though Yates will notice his arousal anytime now. He doesn't want Yates telling him to go home.

Connor walks stiffly to the other side of the boat, scales the rope ladder, and Yates climbs up after him. It feels as though the wizard can see through his pants. Once his feet land on the deck, before Yates' face shows above the railings, Connor rubs himself, sighing at the pressure. He waits for Yates to get onto the deck, lets him open the cabin door and descend into the cargo hold first.

When Yates' hair disappears through the trapdoor, Connor turns, thinking about climbing off the boat and slipping away into the forest to jerk off. Yates pokes his head back up. "Aren't you coming?"

He bristles.

The wizard takes another step up, concerned. "What happened?"

"Nothing." His voice comes out as a growl, and Yates' gaze sweeps over his body, assessing him for damage. Connor tries to turn. Yates sucks in a sharp breath, and Connor *knows* what he's found, can't meet his eyes.

Yates falls off the ladder with a *thump*.

"What the hell is wrong with you?" Connor snaps, at the same time his brain says, *Yates is hurt, make sure he's fine, you need to go to him.*

He finds the wizard at the bottom of the ladder,

sitting up and rubbing his elbow. "Ow," Yates says, his body swathed in the dim shadows of the cargo hold. "That hurt."

"Is it bad?" Connor asks, hurrying down the ladder. He crouches down next to Yates to probe his scalp for bumps. "Hit your head?"

"No." Yates licks his lips, looking at him, then away, before his eyes dart down to Connor's groin. His throat works.

"If you want it, say something," Connor mutters, heat creeping up his cheeks. He can't believe he's even saying this. "Don't just fall off the damned ladder."

"I—I can't." Yates' tongue flicks across his lower lip, and Connor wants to kiss him all over again. "You know that."

Connor ignores the disappointment seeping into his chest, getting to his feet. If he can't hide his arousal, then the least he can do is wash his face, and maybe some of the sweat off his arms. He pulls his shirt off. Behind him, Yates makes a low, strangled noise. Connor turns. "What?"

Blue eyes tear away from his chest, down his straining pants, and to the side. Yates' chest heaves. "Suck it," he whispers, eyes dark with self-recrimination.

Connor throbs. He glances down at the hard line in Yates' pants, and feels himself grow damp. "Suck what?" he asks, the words rumbling from his throat. He wants Yates' mouth further down, dragging along his cock.

"Nothing." Yates rolls onto his feet, stepping toward the kitchen.

Anger spikes through Connor's veins. "If you

want me, just say it, damn you," he hisses, crossing the three feet between them. He's been waiting for years, now. Yates knows that. He doesn't miss the way Yates' gaze drags down his thighs. He snares the wizard's arm, turns him around. Yates' eyes widen like a caught animal. He's never looked like that before. "Touch me," Connor whispers, his hand slipping down to Yates', catching his palm. "Please."

"You know I—"

Carefully, Connor pulls his hand closer, pressing it lightly to his groin. The heat of Yates' fingers soaks through his pants, light and firm, and Yates' breath rushes out. Connor's pulse pounds in his ears. Yates is going to pull away, and Connor is in too deep to let go.

Yates' fingers twitch against his cock. He glances to the side, teeth sinking into his lower lip, and strokes down to his base. Then up, to his head, and Connor doesn't dare breathe, when anything could break this. But he wants this more, right now. He rolls his hips against Yates' fingers, a thrill shooting down his nerves when Yates flattens his entire hand against his cock, moaning. The sound goes straight between Connor's legs.

He releases Yates' hand.

"I—" Yates hasn't pulled away. "I shouldn't."

"You want to." His voice catches in his throat, and he looks down at the telling strain of Yates' trousers. Yates can't act on his desires, is too scared to try.

So Connor touches a knuckle to his neck just to feel his heat, the way he's tense, needing. Beneath his skin, Yates' magic flutters, warm and bright, and Connor follows the line of his throat down to his collarbones, skimming over his chest. Yates' nipple hardens against his fingernail, a tempting point behind his shirt.

And Yates' palm rubs lightly against his cock, hot through his pants. Connor steps closer. Yates *wants* him. It feels like progress, like bliss and acceptance. And maybe if Yates can't see him as clearly... "I'll—" He clears his throat, his heart pounding. "I'll turn off the lights."

Yates' gaze skitters away, but he nods. Connor backs him up against the kitchen island, his cock nudging into Yates' palm. There's a dark spot on Yates' pants now, even if he can't meet Connor's eyes. Connor picks up a forgotten piece of chalk on the counter, sketches his arrows, along with the runes for *extinguish* and *light.*

One by one, the lamps around them go off, until only a single sconce glows from the far end of the cargo hold, casting them in shadow.

Pressed between Connor and the island counter, Yates holds himself still, tiny worry lines on his forehead contradicting his hard cock, the way his fingers twitch against Connor's pants.

Slowly, Connor cups his cheek, tips his face up. Yates' eyes slip shut; an invitation.

When Connor kisses him, he sighs, parting his lips. Yates tastes like tea, and Connor learns him slowly, the silkiness of his mouth, the wet flick of his tongue. Then Yates pulls his hand away from Connor's cock, his hips rolling forward, and Connor's throat goes dry.

He holds Yates to the counter by his hips, pushing their cocks together, their bodies separated by mere layers of fabric. Yates shudders, gasps softly into his mouth, and Connor wants him closer, wants to never let him go.

The next kiss is deeper, full of lips and teeth. Yates pushes into his mouth, sliding against his tongue, tasting him, and Connor groans, surprised. He can't believe they're pressed so close, that Yates wants him. There's so much of Yates he wants—he wants to smell him all over, taste his skin, suck his cock until he arches and cries out—but he doesn't know how much time he has. The old Yates could come back and say *no,* and all this will be over.

So he kisses Yates carefully, rucking up his shirt, distracting him from his thoughts by grinding their bodies together, slow and heavy. Yates squirms. He bucks his hips, cock slipping off Connor's bulge, nudging into his thigh, and Connor shivers. Yates is this aroused, all because of *him.*

He reaches down, touches Yates through his pants, feels the weight of his desire, the way he pushes into Connor's hand, willing and hungry. He tugs Yates' belt loose, pulls his zipper open, its rasp loud in the cargo hold. Then, Connor pushes Yates' briefs down.

Yates' cock slips out of its confines, jutting up, more demanding than Yates himself has been, and Connor gulps. He circles his fingers around it, hears the hiss of Yates' breath through his teeth. Connor traces down the ridge of his underside, learns the way he curves just slightly, the way his skin slides away from his head. For years, he'd been wondering about this. About what they could be.

When he touches his finger to his tip, Yates gasps. His hips snap up, smearing slick over Connor's fingers, and it makes him throb, makes his pants tight. Connor wants to be everywhere at once—Yates' chest, his groin, his calves. He kisses Yates again, deeply, circles his damp head just to hear his sharp cry, then drags his mouth down the length of his throat. Yates' pulse beats against his lips.

Connor sucks lightly on his skin, and Yates gasps, his fingers scrabbling along the counter. He curls them into Connor's side, his breath rushing hot into Connor's hair, and Connor kisses down to his nipples, biting lightly on them through his shirt. Yates arches toward him, reaching up to yank him close, his breathing ragged, his nipple hard against Connor's tongue. He likes this. Likes what Connor's doing to him.

It sends an electric sizzle up his spine. Connor rubs his palm firmly over Yates' cock, and it leaves a wet trail over his skin. Then he smears Yates' slick all over his tip, kisses down his chest, and as he nears Yates' hips, his stomach quivers.

"Please," he hisses, his fingers winding through Connor's hair, pushing him down. "Please."

Please what? Connor wants to ask. Instead, he follows the fine trail of hair down Yates' abdomen, drags his nose down the musky, damp length of Yates' cock. He smells it from base to tip, and back down, into his hair, nudging his balls with his nose. Yates whines. He thrusts up, grinds his cock against Connor's cheek, leaving a smear of wetness on his skin.

Connor licks slowly over his velvety base, up

along the fine veins to his head, and drags his skin down to expose his flushed tip. There, he circles Yates with his tongue, lapping up salty slick, blowing lightly on his skin. Yates swears, leaning back on the counter. His hands push down on Connor's head, and Connor takes him in.

"S-suck it," Yates hisses, a low edge of desperation in his voice. It's the only thing Connor hears in the shadows of the ship.

Yates fills his mouth, a smooth, silky weight. When Connor wraps his lips around him and sucks, a groan rips from Yates' throat, raw and animal. Connor has never heard anything like it. He wants to hear it over and over, wants to hear Yates' hunger, so he takes him in further, then slides him out, licking his tip, the same spot beneath his head where Connor likes touching himself. Yates jerks up into his mouth, nudging his lips with his cock, his breathing a broken string of sobs.

Connor pulls away then, until he only has Yates' tip in his mouth, and laps over him, toying with his slit, licking at the slippery drop that oozes out. Yates' fingers tighten painfully in his hair. "Don't stop," he says, his voice wavering between a growl and a whimper. "Please."

And so Connor lets Yates' skin slide back over his head. He licks at its opening, pushes his tongue between his skin and his tip, circling his head, and Yates gives a low, harsh groan, his thighs shaking. So he closes his mouth around Yates, pushes his skin down with his lips, and laps slowly around his head. Yates swears, holding him down, his hips rocking up so his cock pushes deeper into Connor's mouth.

But Connor needs him, too. He stands, pulling his pants open, and the pressure in his cock eases. Yates' eyes glint in the shadows. He leans against the island counter, swallowing when Connor steps close. Connor anchors his hand on Yates' hips, pinning him against the counter, his bare cock sliding slow and firm against Yates', pleasure whispering into his body. He groans, pulls Yates close, wrapping his arms around this man—his mentor, his best friend, his secret love.

It's almost too much. The weight of Yates' cock, the heave of his chest, his shuddering gasps when Connor pushes against him. Yates trembles in his arms. Connor presses a kiss to his forehead, reaching down to wrap his hand around them, smearing slick all over their skin until he doesn't know if the wetness on him is his or Yates'. He thrusts up, hissing at the heavy slide, and Yates swears, rocking up, fucking into his hand.

Connor loses track of how long they do this, when Yates' cock grinds against his own, and they're both trapped in his fist, his precum leaking onto Yates. He bucks his hips harder, squeezes tighter around them, and Yates leans into his chest, his breath puffing warm through Connor's shirt.

Tension swells in his body, in part because of them touching, in part because Yates is here, pressed up against him. Connor comes hard, pleasure crashing over him like a stormy wave, and he isn't aware of anything but Yates, Yates, Yates.

When he can think again, he finds Yates squeezing his waist, rolling his own hips. "Come on," he says, his voice unsteady. "Need—need more."

Connor dips his head to breathe him in, his sweaty hair, his damp skin. Splashes of pearly slick smear on his pale chest. Connor gulps. A hint of white trickles down the dusky outline of Yates' erection—dregs from Connor's climax—and it sends a hum of satisfaction through his chest.

Connor scoops up the rest of his cum from Yates' chest, slicking it over Yates' cock. The wizard trembles, his breath stuttering, cock jumping in Connor's grip. "Suck—Oh, damn it, Connor," he growls, thrusting up into Connor's hand. "Damn you."

You know who you're doing this with. Connor's pulse thunders. Yates is acknowledging *them*.

Suddenly reckless, Connor leans in, kissing him slow on the lips. "Suck this?" he whispers, swirling his grip around Yates' cock, covering the entirety of it in his own cum. Yates hisses like the air was punched from his chest, and Connor smirks, pushes a cum-slick finger under his skin, circling his tip. "Tell me."

Yates groans, thrusting up at him. He slips a hand behind Connor's neck, pulls him closer to kiss him hard, pushing into his mouth, and the slide of his tongue is demanding, desperate. "Suck me," he gasps, pushing down on Connor's shoulder. "Now."

Connor's heart pounds. His knees bang against the island counter as he crouches. He trails kisses down Yates' chest, down his abdomen to his straining cock, and laps a slow, wet line up its length, tasting the bitter tang of himself on Yates' skin. Yates makes a low, keening sound in his throat, rocking up. Connor lets him wait a long moment, licking around his head, sliding his skin down, then up, until Yates swears again, bucking his hips. His magic flares beneath his skin like a roaring flame.

Further up, on the counter, Yates' fingertips glow a soft orange, five points of light on the countertop. His arms tremble. Smoke drifts up from the smooth wooden surface, and his fingertips whiten. He's charring the counter, teetering on the edge of his control, and it sends a thrill across Connor's skin.

The wizard's thighs quiver against him. His gasps ring loud in the shadows, and Connor licks along his cock. Where he tastes the bitter tang of his cum on Yates' skin, Yates' tip is salty with slick, and Connor sucks hungrily on it, eager to taste his pleasure.

He takes Yates as deep as he can. Yates fucks up into his mouth, panting, a thin sheen of sweat on his groin, and as Connor sucks long and slow on him, Yates pulls him closer, spine arching, his cock growing thicker. His moan cracks just as Connor hollows his cheeks, and then he's spilling, hot and heavy and bitter on his tongue.

Connor swallows all of it. He pulls away slowly, listening to Yates' ragged breathing, releasing the wizard so he slumps back against the island counter.

For a long moment, neither of them speak. Connor wipes his mouth, straightening to his full height. This hasn't happened before. Now that he knows what Yates feels like against him, he wants more, wants Yates closer, wants to bury his face in his neck. He wants to wake up next to the wizard, make him laugh, snuggle up to him in bed.

"Oh, gods," Yates mutters, turning over to hide his face against the counter.

A whisper of unease skitters down Connor's spine. Yates presses his forehead to smooth wood, and Connor remembers him falling off the ladder a year ago and sending him away. He tries to distract them both. "Plans for the ship?"

"Connor. Why—You shouldn't have... Oh, blazes." Yates' voice climbs, tinted with growing horror. "Why?"

"Why what?" Connor clenches his fists just so he has something to hold on to. His skin crawls. Yates sounds desperate, different—like he had when he saw Connor naked from his bath. "Why I sucked you off?"

Yates flinches. "We shouldn't have done that. I shouldn't... shouldn't have touched you."

Connor closes his eyes briefly, quelling his fraying nerves. He doesn't want Yates to send him away, doesn't want to go for months without seeing the wizard. "We want each other. Isn't that enough?"

Yates pushes himself away from the counter, straightening. He sketches a quick rune on the table, sends it away to light a lamp. Then another and another, until all the lamps in the cargo hold burn bright, and Yates still can't turn to face him. "I'm your godsforsaken teacher, Connor. I'm supposed to shape you into an upstanding person, not take advantage of you!"

"You didn't take advantage of me," Connor says, anger flickering in his gut. He grabs Yates' shoulder, spins him around. Yates flails, grabbing the counter. His knuckles whiten. Connor releases him. "I chose this myself."

Yates' eyes flash. "And how do you know that I didn't somehow forge your attraction to me?" Connor blinks. That isn't possible, but before he can speak, Yates continues. "I've influenced you too much to be your lover, Connor. You need to leave."

"No!" Connor steps forward, hesitating. Yates' eyes are wide and haunted, and he knows this man better than he knows anyone else. Yates is almost a part of him. "No. I'm your student. You can't throw me out, Yates." Because if he leaves now, Connor knows he won't be allowed to return.

"You can't be my student anymore. Don't you see?" Yates covers his face with his hands, his shoulders slumping. "This wasn't supposed to happen. I—I should have stopped this."

"You wanted me," Connor says. "Still want me." He steps closer. "Yates, please."

He pulls Yates into a hug, feels the heat of his smaller frame, the press of Yates' arms against his chest. Yates sags into him for a heartbeat, then jerks away, as though his skin burns. Bright heat thrums at his fingertips. "No, Connor. We can't do this. It isn't right."

"Who the fuck cares about it being right?" Connor snaps, his breath catching. How else can he change Yates' mind? What doesn't Yates already know? They'd be good together. They've gotten along so well through the years. "I love you, damn it!"

"No," Yates gasps, shaking his head, even as

his eyes glimmer with *want*. "No. Get out of this place, right now."

"You can't make me," Connor says, regretting it the moment it leaves his mouth. Yates is his mentor. He's shown Connor how to bury bodies, how to listen to rocks a hundred miles away, how to make flower bombs that explode with purple sparks. "You're my best friend. You can't send me away."

"You forget who you're talking to," Yates says, his voice strained. He reaches for the chalk on the counter, scribbling the runes for *mind* and *erase*, and Connor's heart stops beating. He isn't fast enough with his own spells, can't draw up a strong enough defense. Yates has had centuries of practice. "Go now, before I make you forget."

His blood chills. Yates is everything to him, and Connor can't lose this, can't lose so much of him at once. So he backs away, aching to pull the wizard close. He shouldn't have done this. Shouldn't have ignored the consequences. "This is just between us, damn you."

"It's not just between us." Yates' eyes flicker over Connor, raking over his face and his chest, down to his feet, and Connor realizes that Yates is memorizing him, burning him into his mind. "I betrayed this bond, Connor. I'm not fit to be your teacher."

"Then don't," Connor snaps. "I don't care if you aren't!"

Yates' fingertip whitens next to the runes, ragged shapes next to five charred lines, and Connor tenses. Yates will run magic through the spell. How the fuck can he do that, as though

Connor's memories of him aren't important?

"No. No, don't," he chokes, stepping back. "I'll leave."

Yates hardens his expression. "Don't turn back when you go."

Connor swallows. He looks again at Yates — his rumpled red hair, the brilliant blue of his eyes, the gleam of his lips. His shirt is still rumpled, his pants undone. Connor remembers the dusky notes of his sweat, the heave of his chest, the way his voice broke.

He sets his foot on the ladder, one rung at a time, his heart heavy. Before he crosses the trapdoor, he pauses, meeting Yates' eyes.

"I love you," he says again. Yates glances away, the corners of his mouth pulling down.

Connor leaves.

It takes everything he has not to glance over his shoulder. He crosses the garden into the forest, trudging through the trees. As he stops to pull his clothes on right, magic prickles in the air, a brush of warmth over his shoulders. He turns sharply, looking behind.

The ship is gone. The trees stand around him, no velvet-blue between their trunks, and his stomach turns. He traces the path back to Yates' home, back to the clearing.

Except there's nothing there but more trees, and an invisible barrier he smacks his head against. He runs his palm over the cool, thrumming surface, anger scraping in his heart, swelling and acidic. *How can you do this to me?*

The barrier stands when he slams his fist down on it. Is this all he means to Yates? Someone he doesn't want to see anymore? *How can you shut me out when I need you?* Connor bares his teeth, kicking at it, raining fists down until his hands throb, and all the energy flees his body.

He wants to believe that the barrier is temporary, that Yates will take it down in a week, or a month. But he knows Yates better than he knows himself, knows that they've broken their boundaries today, and the loss of it hasn't struck him yet.

Connor clenches his jaw, stepping away. He'll return tomorrow.

YATES SLUMPS against the kitchen counter, face in his hands. None of this is right. Connor is gone. The barrier hums around him, and the cargo hold echoes with silence.

He doesn't dare think back on earlier. If he does, he'll soften and forget why the separation is necessary. Why the barrier is crucial. Why he can never meet Connor again. Why... *Connor.*

The name rolls across his tongue like a lover's whisper. Yates cannot forget the slide of Connor's skin, the heat of his mouth, the touch of his breath. Connor had felt like surging fire and ravenous hunger, even if he caressed Yates like he was someone precious. They had been intimate in the shadows, Connor unraveling him, pressing their bodies together, stealing the words from his lips. On the counter, five lines char through wood, matching the points of his fingers.

He'd made a promise to a boy years ago. At the

merest suggestion, he had forgotten himself and slept with Connor, betraying that promise, betraying the memory of his own mentor.

Disgust wells up in his throat. Yates turns, sweeping things off the counter—the pot lids, the spatulas, the stack of recipe cards that has shrunken over the years. He's in Fort Bragg to repent, not to find a handsome young man to bed. Magic shouldn't be used for frivolity. Some things should stay buried, and he should remember that. The recipe cards scatter across the kitchen, sliding across the floorboards. Yates glares at them. He needs to forget Connor. Needs to think about something other than mahogany eyes and a strong chest.

He's striding toward the lab when he glimpses an old wooden calendar on a side table. *November 7,* the faded lettering reads. Next to it, a note he'd taped on just this morning. *Connor's birthday. Don't forget cake.*

All the breath rushes from his lungs. Yates stares at the note, horror and disbelief flooding his mind. None of this should have happened, not at all.

15
Nineteen (Part II)

IN THE first days, Connor waits. He figures he has time. The afternoons yawn before him, hours he'd otherwise have spent practicing spells with Yates. He doesn't know how else to spend his days, so he sits under a fir just outside the barrier, waiting for Yates to emerge.

Yates doesn't appear.

A week in, Connor's patience begins to wear. He sketches tiny spells in the dirt, ones that Yates taught him, ones he learned from Yates' library. They shoot at the invisible wall, sparks of red light bouncing off. Connor watches the way they dissipate, unimpressed. Yates knows the power of his strongest spells. The wall will repel them.

He tries the stronger spells anyway, ones that mimic lightning and fire, even ones he vaguely remembers. He cuts himself once, blood dripping from his hand when a spell goes wrong, and he swears, suddenly angry that Yates has caused all this, that Yates is the reason he hurts.

But he also remembers he's the reason Yates banished him, because he forced Yates' decision, so he sits, now furious at himself.

He tries again and again, targeting specific points on the barrier. Connor exhausts his knowledge and energy trying to break the spell, but it stands, mocking when he bashes it with an angry fist.

He digs his fingers into the dirt next. The barrier extends underground, and Connor should have known that Yates is a bastard, when he digs seven feet down, and his fingers meet yet more obstruction. By the time he climbs out of the hole, it's dusk, and his stomach rumbles. He remembers the warm golden lights glowing from the portholes of the ship, but the shadowy forest ignores him, aloof and uninviting.

Connor grits his teeth then. Yates knows he's waiting. Yates hasn't once stepped out of the shield, and he doesn't know why the wizard has to be such an *idiot*. What has Yates been eating? He doesn't have supplies to last a week.

The next day, Connor brings with him salted fish, and leaves it hanging on a branch.

HIS STOMACH jolts when he returns to the same spot two days later, and the fish dangles from the branches, untouched. In his stubbornness, he hasn't stopped to consider that Yates might be injured, that he might have begun tinkering in the lab and forgotten to feed himself.

"Yates," Connor yells, banging on the shield. "Eat your damned food!"

Yates doesn't answer. Connor can't hear anything from behind the barrier, and it makes his scalp prickle. The shield is the only evidence that Yates is alive. He'd have to maintain it every day for it to still stand, and Connor is quietly glad for that knowledge. But fury still roils in his chest.

"This isn't a joke," he says. "Damn you!"

He stalks to the cemetery. The graves are all weeks-old, and the dirt hasn't been moved. On the shore, he finds no fresh bodies.

Connor glares at the grave markers, then heads for home.

SOME DAYS, Yates watches him through the windows. Connor curls up beneath a fir, dragging a twig through loamy earth, and Yates' throat goes dry at the thought of him.

It can't be healthy to want someone this much, even three months after he's sent him away. Regardless, he presses his face to glass, hugging himself tight as his eyes trace Connor's chestnut hair, his strong arms, the way he looks right at him, as though he can see Yates through the barrier. It makes his stomach squeeze, makes him crave Connor's heat. If he thinks hard enough, he can imagine Connor's arms wrapped around him, strong and safe.

Yates wishes everything were different. That he met Connor at a different point in his life, that he'd never taken Connor in as a student, that he'd never met the boy at all.

I love you, Connor had said. The words still echo in his ears. Yates hasn't had love in a while. Hasn't deserved it. But Connor's affection is like a blanket, a safe place he can hide in. Sheer need crawls up his throat. He tries his best to swallow it back down.

You are a wizard, Quagmuth said an eternity ago. *Human burdens will thwart your judgment.*

But that always happens, doesn't it? All he's done is flit from one clouded judgment to another, and he's hurting now, all over again.

CONNOR BRINGS fresh salted fish sometimes, leaves them hanging along the pathways to the shore. He leaves blankets wrapped in waxed paper, too, but all his gifts lie untouched, and Connor ends up wrapping the blankets around himself when it rains.

There are new graves in the cemetery. Ten new ones in two days, and not a flash of red hair anywhere. Yates had to have dug them in the night and early morning to finish them before he arrived. He winces at the thought of Yates in the surf, chilly wind blowing around him, the wizard's teeth chattering. So he leaves blankets by the trees, ventures into the waves himself, and pulls bodies out so Yates doesn't have to.

The next day, the shovel disappears. The message is clear: *Go away.*

Connor brings his own shovel. The day after, the cemetery vanishes behind a barrier, along with the shovel he left. He storms all the way to the forest and pounds on the invisible wall, furious. It's been five months.

"Get out here and face me, damn you," Connor

snarls. "I know you're in there!"

The birds in the forest chirp, and the trees ignore him. Connor turns away, the whispers in his heart bitter and swirling.

SOME NIGHTS, after it rains, Yates creeps out of the barrier. Every bit of his mind says *no* when he pulls open waxed paper, shaking off clear droplets of rain.

He pulls the blanket over himself, over his head, shutting out the world beyond. Inside the blanket, it smells like salt and ocean, like soap and fish, like *Connor,* and Yates curls up in it, tugging it close. It feels like an embrace.

When dawn draws close, he emerges from his cocoon, no more a butterfly than before. Yates folds the blanket up exactly as it was, wraps it in paper, and leaves.

Connor never finds out.

CONNOR STAYS home after the cemetery disappears. He goes out for groceries and returns to find his father surrounded by bottles. He sighs, drags a chair out just as Dad tips beer into his mouth.

"What happened this time?" Connor asks, tired. He doesn't have the energy to care anymore. Yates has abandoned him, ignored all his salted fish and blankets. He's brought them home, tucked the fish into plastic tubs and the blankets in his bedroom.

"I saw your old sailboat. From your birthday," Dad says, setting his bottle down. "Mags and I picked it out at the market. She said you'd love it. And she was right, wasn't she? You want to live on a ship."

His throat squeezes so tight he can't speak. He swallows. "The ship is gone," he says. "I can't go back."

And it sounds like defeat, like loss. If Yates cared, he would have said something. He would have kept a blanket, accepted a fish. Or even left a drawing somewhere that says he's alive. He hasn't. He doesn't fucking care, and Connor hates him so much. Hates him for all the hurt, hates him for the hole in his chest he can't patch. He can't look at other men without thinking about Yates.

He's spent *years* telling his dad about the wizard, and Yates is gone now.

"Yates?" his dad asks, rubbing a weary hand across his face.

He can't help the sting in his eyes, the way his vision blurs. Connor swipes his tears away, reaching for an unopened bottle on the table.

HIS HEAD swims. He tries to talk to his dad, but his words slur and don't come out right. He tries to remember Yates, the crystal-blue of his eyes, the way his mouth curves into a smile, but the memories are fuzzy, full of gaps, and Connor is suddenly afraid — so afraid — that Yates cast his spell and he has nothing left of the wizard.

Connor is drunk, and he *hates* it.

HE STAGGERS to the forest the next morning, nursing a hangover. There's a patch of flat, grassy ground where the cemetery used to be: an illusion and a barrier rolled into one. Connor can't walk through the place anymore, has to resort to walking behind the empty land, skirting around it to where the ship is.

Along the way, his head pounds, and the sun glares in his eyes. He stumbles over the roots on the forest floor, winding between firs until he's lost.

He walks straight into the barrier, pain bursting through his head. Why is all this happening to him? Does Yates hate him now? A tendril of fear tightens his throat. He snarls and bashes his fist into the shield, screaming words he doesn't mean. *Fucking twisted asshole. You're a goddamned waste of my time and my life. I wish I never met you.* When he's done and all the anger is gone, Connor turns, stalking back home.

He's spent eight months waiting. He's not coming back.

YATES STARES at the empty path on the outskirts of his barrier, half-expecting Connor to show up. He knows he shouldn't. He heard every word of Connor's outburst, and he knows he deserves all the names Connor flung at him. He's failed as a mentor and as a friend, and he doesn't know how he can repair any of it.

Slowly, he climbs out of the ship, taking one slow step after another, careful to glance around in case Connor appears. He shouldn't be afraid of him, but he is. He's wasted Connor's time, formed a wreck of a relationship with him, left him heartbroken and miserable.

Yates picks his way through the forest, peering at the empty branches, at the old footprints fading into the forest floor. He thinks he'll see something familiar—a salted fish fillet, a blanket, anything—but there are only trees and birds and moss, and the emptiness of the place sinks into his bones.

He had hoped for Connor to leave long before this. Now that Connor has sworn never to return, Yates wishes he had stayed instead.

16
Twenty

ON HIS twentieth birthday, Connor stays home. Dad is drinking at the kitchen table again, and Connor understands why he never stopped. Memories are dangerous, cutting him when he tries to remember the better times.

He tips his head back against the living room couch, muted sitcoms playing in the background, frayed fishing net in his hands. If he closes his eyes, he can still remember this day a year ago: the soft caress of shadows, the ragged hiss of breath, the smooth, damp skin, that hungry mouth on his.

The memory is sharp and blurry all at once — he no longer knows if he's messed up the sequence of events, but he's played it over and over in his mind, until he knows every touch on his skin, until he knows Yates' breath on his neck, the weight of his body and the arch of his back. Sometimes he alters it: his nose on Yates' spine, Yates splayed beneath him, heavy-lidded and inviting.

It washes over him like familiar music, soothing and playful and kindling, and the ghost of Yates' lips brushes over his cheek.

Glass shatters in the kitchen.

Connor's on his feet in moments, eyes snapping open. He finds his father with his face in his hand, broken brown glass at the base of the wall, shards strewn across the floor. "What happened?"

Dad shakes his head, jaw clenched. "Nothing. Everything's fine."

Connor nudges the pieces of glass with his shoe, his skin prickling. This doesn't happen often at all. His dad doesn't smash bottles even when he's drunk. "You're as fine as a rotten fish."

Dad curls his hands into fists, his shoulders tensing. "What do you fucking know," Dad snaps, pain etched into the lines of his face. Connor's ribs tighten. He doesn't know how he can help his dad. He's tried and tried, and nothing works. "Go back to that Yates."

"I can't," he growls. Dad says it like it's a fucking option. Yates hasn't been a haven in a year. "And unlike you, I'm not drinking! Even if it fucking hurts!"

"Don't give me that shit." Dad stands, the chair rattling behind him. His knuckles whiten against the table. "None of my business if you don't drink, but if you're gonna be a bastard, stay in your damned room."

Growing up, his dad had been someone he admired, someone he wanted to grow up to be. Connor went to school talking about his father as a fisherman, about the catches they made at sea. He still has memories of sitting on Dad's shoulders, the world sprawled at his feet. Except the man in front of him isn't that person.

Anger flares in his veins. He should leave his father alone, let him cool down. They've always managed to ease out of these confrontations. But drinking makes a person forget, and how can Dad try to forget Mom? Doesn't he value those memories? Even if they hurt?

"I still miss her, damn you," Connor says, contempt loosening his tongue. "I lost my best friend. He's a damned coward." It hurts all over again, thinking about Yates, but it's a dull ache now. He can't purge those memories, a ghost of Yates that still lives in him. "So shut up when I say stop drinking. I'm doing fine without booze. Why can't you?"

Dad punches him in the face.

Pain explodes in his head. Connor staggers back, slips on a shard and swears, falling backward. His skull slams into the drywall.

When he blinks, he's sitting against the wall, blood smeared on his fingers. "You hit me," he says. Dad has never hit him before, and a tiny frisson of fear shoots down his spine. How the fuck can he do that to him?

Dad steps closer, and Connor tenses.

"Fuck," Dad says, dropping to his knees. His eyes are wide, his face pale. Glass grinds beneath his shoes. "The hell, Connor. Don't die. Don't fucking die on me."

"I'm not gonna die," Connor snaps. His head throbs. "The fuck were you thinking?"

Dad can't look away from his bloodied hands. He reaches out, then hesitates, holding back. "You're sure you aren't gonna die?"

When his dad's shoulders sag further, his gaze uncertain, Connor relaxes, leaning back against the wall. What would Yates say if he told—No, he isn't going to hear about this. *Damn you, Yates.* "I'm not gonna die because of some fucking hand wound. But you just hit me, damn you."

"I—" Dad gulps a deep breath, running a hand through his hair. "I-I shouldn't have done that. I wasn't thinking right."

"You weren't thinking at all," Connor mutters. His head still hurts, and his fingers are starting to throb. But the fury has seeped out of his dad, leaving him slumped and small. "You were drinking. That's what caused it."

"I..." Dad falls silent, all gray hair and bloodshot eyes. Connor feels a pang. He knows the pain his father has been through. He knows what hurt and disappointment feel like. He's no longer a kid—hasn't really been a kid since his mother died. Surely Yates knows that. "I'm sorry," Dad says, rubbing a hand across his face. "I've been a goddamned bastard."

At least Dad cares, Connor thinks. *Unlike you.* He shakes away the blue eyes in his mind. "'S long as you remember that," he says. Blood wells up along his cuts. "I need stitches."

Because magic can't solve this, either. He can use it to feel better, or to shelter himself from the rain. But unless he has an excess of energy, he can't heal wounds. Can't revive anyone. He hasn't got the resources to resurrect his mother anymore, and it feels like another of his dreams has withered.

He hasn't used his magic since the day he turned his back on the ship. The runes and spells still linger at the back of his mind, and Connor misses them, suddenly.

As Dad stands and groans, Connor gets to his

feet, washing his hands at the sink. He'll get stitches at the clinic. Then he'll start practicing his circles again. Losing Yates isn't the end of everything.

His blood swirls with water down the drain, and for the first time in ages, Connor feels as though he has a purpose again.

WHEN HE returns from the clinic, the sun setting behind him, he finds the floor cleared of glass. In the corner of the kitchen, his dad pushes a new plastic bag into the trashcan.

"I'm throwing out the booze," Dad says, eyes downcast. "It's... not worth hurting you over. I'm sorry."

Connor watches him. In the past, his father had joked frequently, sharp-witted and carefree, always looking to his mother for her reaction. The man in the kitchen now has a belly from drinking, and he moves sluggishly, bogged down with age. They haven't known each other in years.

It unnerves him, how time does this to people. His dad grabs the full bag of bottles, glass clinking, and steps outside. The dumpster shuts with a bang. When his dad walks into the house again, he glances at Connor's bandaged hand. "Stitches went okay?"

"Yeah," Connor says. The clinic was full of people he didn't recognize.

His dad walks over to him, gaze lowered. "I know you haven't forgiven me yet," he says, "and I don't think I can forgive myself. But... you want a hug?"

Despite his misgivings, Connor nods. It's a step forward. "Yeah. Okay."

Dad wraps his arms around him, sturdy and solid, patting his back. Connor's throat tightens. It feels like he's found a lost piece of his past.

WHILE HIS dad cleans the rest of the house, Connor practices chalk drawings in his room with his bandaged hand. The first circle comes out crooked. He scowls.

Why don't I draw a circle, and you follow the lines?

He shoves the voice out of his head, penciling circles on newspaper, frowning when the newsprint makes it difficult to judge them. He tries the floor next, digging chalk out of his bedside drawer — *Here, these are for you to practice at home* — and almost throws it across the room. But his mom would have wanted to see him succeed, so he grits his teeth and traces circle after circle on the floor, scrubbing them away when his dad knocks on the door.

"I'm thinking we should go out for lunch," Dad says when he pokes his head in. He's clean-shaven today, his eyes a little clearer. He sneezes. "Holy hell, it's dusty in here. Have you been pulling up the floorboards?"

"Nah. Just cleaning out under the bed," Connor says, wiping his chalky hands on the back of his shirt. "Lunch?"

"Just you and me. We haven't done that in a while."

Connor doesn't miss his father looking at the bruise on his cheek, but he says nothing about it. If his dad needs a reminder, he's happy to provide one. "Sure," he says. "Lunch sounds good."

Dad's smile makes him look like a different person, and Connor hopes they're headed in a better direction now.

THEY HEAD down to a new burger joint next to Mack's. "I've been eyeing this place for a while," Dad says. "Every time I make a run down here, it always smells like someone's backyard grill. Sheila—cashier at Mack's—she says it's good."

From a block away, Connor catches the savory tang of grilled meat: charred and smoky and flavorful, something he hasn't learned to cook. The recipe cards he has are mostly for fish and vegetables; they've rarely had money for beef. But he knows where to find more recipes. There's a stack of them on a rune-carved counter in a ship.

"You've never stopped here?" Connor asks, breathing out. The ache in his chest seeps away.

His father rubs his head sheepishly. "I wasn't spending money too well. Never really had enough. I'll try harder."

"You'd better," Connor says, immediately wishing the words didn't sound so casual. He hasn't really talked to his dad in a while, and he shouldn't act like they're still familiar with each other.

His dad grins, embarrassed. His gaze wanders up along the crowded sidewalk. "I know I haven't been the best. But I owe it to you to do better, and I will. Okay?"

Connor chuckles. It's a hopeful beginning. "Okay."

They get a table by the picture windows. As they walk through the bustling restaurant, Dad waves at a woman a few tables down — bubbly and chatty. The cashier at Mack's. Connor nods at her.

The things on the leather-bound menu aren't very expensive, but as he holds the weighty brochure in his hands, Connor knows he can buy groceries for three meals with the price of the cheapest tomato-and-beef sandwich. The waitress comes by. Connor asks for water. After a moment's thought, his dad asks for water, too.

Dad talks about the sea, the fish migrations, and stricter regulations coming down on the fishing community. When their orders arrive, the smallest burger is tiny, dwarfed by its slice of cheese, and Connor sighs.

"Want some of mine?" Dad says, waving at his own steak sandwich with a knife. The seared meat glistens, and it makes Connor's stomach twist. It has to cost at least twice as much as his own. It also looks delicious. "Here," his dad says, slicing off half the slab and transferring it onto Connor's plate. "I can't finish it all, anyway."

He's sure his dad is lying, but it makes his eyes sting. Connor nods, blinking rapidly as he stares out the window.

A shock of red hair flashes by across the street, vibrant like fire. His stomach drops.

"Saw something?" Dad asks.

Connor's voice flees his throat. The person

disappears behind a corner, and dull sedans roll by between them. From the little he saw, he can't tell if it was a man, whether the person had crystal-blue eyes, whether... He shakes his head. "It's nothing."

Dad cuts into his steak, studying him. "You stopped talking about Yates."

He doesn't know how the name still makes his heart stumble, even now. Connor jabs his fork into his burger. The beef is just the right mix of spicy and juicy and char, and he suddenly understands why people would come to this place, why the tables are all packed. He wants to cook like this. Would Yates like it? *Why am I still thinking about that bastard?* Connor sighs.

"Want me to go over and punch him?" Dad asks.

Connor's considered doing that himself, but the feeling never stays. He doesn't want to hurt Yates. "Nah."

"What happened?" His dad winces immediately after, as though he thinks he doesn't have the right to ask. And maybe he doesn't, but ignoring his question won't solve anything.

Connor starts on his burger. "He didn't want to see me anymore."

"Didn't want to commit?"

He shakes his head. It's embarrassing, thinking about that lewd afternoon in front of his dad. He wishes his face would stop heating up. "He had second thoughts, I guess." But it isn't that. And he can't tell his dad who Yates is, because for all his dad is repentant, he still holds his prejudices against magic folk. "He doesn't want to see me again. I'm... I'm getting over him."

But is he really, if the mere sight of red hair makes him want to bolt across the road?

"I'm surprised you didn't start drinking."

His dad grimaces, but Connor shrugs. "I didn't want to forget."

Dad reaches across the table to clap him on the shoulder. "You're a braver man than I ever was."

Connor looks back down at the food on his plate, his appetite waning. If bravery is all it takes, then he'd be back in the ship by now, wouldn't he?

BACK HOME, Connor pulls the recipe cards off the kitchen walls. He tucks them under the sailboat, face-down, and closes the closet door on them both.

IT'S BEEN almost two years, and the ship is driving Yates insane. Next to his two centuries, eight years with a person shouldn't have carved this many memories in him. He sees a young boy sitting cross-legged on an empty floor, throwing flower bombs up into the air. He sees an adolescent curled up in his armchair, reading *Life and Magic,* though it's far too advanced for his level. He sees a young man with his hands full of earth, transplanting a lavender bush that has overgrown its pot.

He sees a man, broad-shouldered and cast in shadow, standing over him in the darkness, winding him up with need. That memory haunts him through the nights.

Sometimes, he peeks out the windows, expecting Connor to be waiting on the path for him. Sometimes he expects impatient fists on the cabin door, followed by excited shouts of *Let me in!*

The five charred marks still linger on the island counter. Occasionally, Yates peels off the embroidered table mat to look at them, just to remind himself that it hadn't been a dream. That Connor had touched him and claimed him. Made his toes curl and his back arch for the first time in decades.

The chalk runes are gone. When Connor still visited, waiting for Yates to lower the barrier, he'd considered erasing Connor's memories. It would have been easy, too. Connor stayed for hours, not moving from his spot.

Today, Yates steps out into the cabin, where the runes for the boundary lie. Connor isn't coming back. He knows this in his bones when he brushes his fingertips over chalk, smudging away lines of power. In the same heartbeat, the barrier falls away around the boat, dripping like a sheet of water.

In the depths of his heart, Yates wishes that Connor would return.

He needs to forget him. He can't.

17
Twenty-One

ON HIS twenty-first birthday, Connor goes to the library. It's anticlimactic. In movies, people celebrate their twenty-firsts with parties and alcohol. At twenty-one, Connor has dated a few other guys, learned to kiss and fuck, and a tiny part of him cringes at what he'd considered a kiss two years ago.

In the library, books fill the history section: *The Great Wall, Medieval Tales, Egyptian Pharaohs.* Nothing about wizards or magic, not even a whisper of Merlin. Sometimes, in the children's section, he finds books about circles and crosses, but those are the basics of magic. He asks the librarian for more books by the same author. The librarian clicks her tongue and says there aren't any more titles written by B. Wandolf.

He visits the children's section to search again anyhow. He's been through the used bookstores in Fort Bragg; there's nothing here that will help him move beyond Yates' lessons. Instead, he finds tomes on mythical beasts, krakens that live in the sea. Disappointment wells up in his throat. He knows where the advanced books are — behind a barrier with a wizard who doesn't want to see him.

Sometimes, Connor wonders if his mom would have been disappointed that he ruined his chances at learning magic. He wishes she were alive so his dad would be happy, instead of staring listlessly into space at the dinner table. Despite forgoing the beer, his father never smiles. He dusts the wedding portraits on the wall, trailing his fingers over their smooth black frames.

Connor wishes he had someone to talk to about the quiet yearning in his ribs. He wishes he had a best friend again.

He steps out of the library, hands in his pockets, the afternoon sun glaring down. A couple of girls rush out after him, whispering. "I *know* you want more books, but this really can't wait," one of them says, her footsteps jaunty. "The repairman's here! He only stops by twice a month, you know. He'll fix your glasses."

"No one repairs broken glass," the other girl says, squinting, her face lacking spectacles. "It's impossible!"

"Well, my mom says he can. You know how picky she is."

Curious, Connor trails behind them. He's seen repairmen come and go in Fort Bragg. Some who ruined more than they repaired, some who fixed things decently. One who returned crushed antique mirrors to their original forms, and who did it flawlessly. He knows; he tagged along with him once.

They reach a side street near the roundabout, where the businesses are slow, and the trees on the sidewalk push needle-like branches into the sky. A gaggle of people crowd around a bench—mostly older ladies, a handful of men in casual wear, and some schoolgirls. They're talking amongst themselves, too loud for Connor to pick out voices.

The girls from the library join in. Connor settles on the next bench, waiting for the crowd to disperse. Waiting doesn't bother him—it's most of what he does before the first haul of the day. It takes a lull in the demands to hear the repairman's voice—strained high with stress. "I'll have your handkerchief fixed by tomorrow, ma'am!"

Connor's heart trips. He knows that voice, has heard it thousands of times: high with laughter, low when teasing. He's heard it lilting and sharp and needy and... It's Yates, goddamned Yates who has hidden himself away for two fucking years.

He doesn't know how to deal with the emotions welling in his chest. There are too many things he wants to say, too many accusations. *How could you shut me out? How could you make me hurt so much?*

He can't decide what he wants to say first. So he waits until the crowd dissipates, until there are five people left surrounding the bench, and Yates can't take off or threaten him with magic. He stands, walks behind Yates' customers to approach him from the back. Yates' hair is fire-red, combed down, his shoulders thin, and Connor wants to lean in, wants to press his nose into his hair. He wants to know if Yates still smells like loamy earth. He's supposed to be angry.

"I'll—I'll get to you in a moment," Yates says in a rush. He pauses, and Connor remembers that Yates can feel his magic. Because he can feel the dancing heat of Yates' as well, standing this close, the way it blazes like fire at a hearth. The familiarity of it makes his throat tighten.

Yates turns, his skin pale, his eyes startlingly blue. He looks up at Connor's shirt, over the round plastic buttons, to his neck, then his face, and his eyes widen with despair.

"I have a heart," Connor says. "Can you fix it?"

"No. No, I can't," Yates says, his chest heaving, his eyes skittering back to the scrawled names on his notebook, that same looping script. "I can't mend hearts. Please go to a doctor. Now, Mrs.—"

"You broke mine," Connor says.

Yates freezes. The people around them begin to stare, eyes flickering over them both, and Connor feels a glimmer of triumph when Yates flushes. "Mrs. Norfolk," Yates splutters, turning to a short old lady with wavy white hair. "Your kettle—"

She sets a hand on Yates' arm, frowning, and glances toward Connor. "You should fix his heart, dear," she whispers. "He seems upset."

Yates pales. He turns partway, stops himself, and Connor's heart beats in his ears. Yates is so close. He can't decide if he wants to kiss him or cuff him or both. He should walk away. Yates doesn't care, hasn't cared for two years, and Connor deserves better than this. "I'm leaving," he says, turning. "Goodbye."

Yates whips his head around, mouth falling open. Connor pauses. The wizard's eyes burn with a desperate yearning, raking over him, from his face to his chest and back up, and damn it if Connor can't still read all his expressions. Yates swallows. Connor feels a twinge of triumph, a whisper of relief that he hasn't been alone in his longing, that Yates still wants him as much as he does.

"Damn you," Connor says, turning back. He wants so much from this man. Still needs him, because nothing else can fill the hole in his chest. "Do you—" He swallows. "D'you still have space for a student?"

Yates' eyes cloud over. "No," he says, his voice strangled.

Connor swears. It can't work out between them, not like this. He wants to learn magic. He wants Yates, but Yates won't have him, and he should forget that this ever happened. That Yates hasn't tired of him, that Yates doesn't want him enough to take him back.

He shoves his hands back into his pockets, striding down the sidewalk, his heart splintering all over again.

To his left, Yates watches him leave, surrounded by broken things and waiting people.

IT FEELS as though the world should be crumbling.

On his bench, all Yates can see is the broad span of Connor's shoulders, his thin T-shirt stretched over bronzed skin. He can't help noting the littlest things: the way Connor bows his head, the heavy tread of his feet, his steps full of purpose. He's choosing to leave, and Yates cannot breathe.

Is this what Connor felt when Yates sent him away two years ago? Like something had pierced him through the chest?

Connor was a student then. Growing, reckless, cheerful. He's no longer any of those things. When he felt the familiar, warm flicker of Connor's magic, Yates had been prepared to see the same boy at nineteen, somehow, even though people age faster than he remembers. At twenty-one, Connor's shoulders have broadened. His shirt clings to the smooth expanse of his pectorals. His eyes have aged, dark and weary, and his mouth... Yates shouldn't be thinking about his mouth.

And so Yates can never be his mentor again. Maybe a friend, but not a person who holds power over him. And Connor had asked for him to be his *teacher*. What was he to say but no?

Now, he's given Connor a choice. And Connor has chosen to leave.

Yates looks back down at the ragged shoes, cracked boxes, and dented pans crowded on the bench, all in various states of disrepair. His remaining customers turn their knowing gazes on him. He feels raw, exposed, and there's nothing to hide him right now, no ship for him to retreat into.

Yates lifts his chin, trying to smile at Mrs. Norfolk. Connor may be gone, but he still has a living to make, a life to lead. He has no one to depend on but himself.

A WEEK later, while they're waiting to reel the nets in on the boat, Dad says, "I'm going out on a date tonight. Don't cook for me."

Connor pauses in the middle of gutting fish,

stunned. "Date?"

His dad raises an eyebrow. "You know I've been seeing the girl at Mack's. Sheila."

He's been vaguely aware of his dad talking about the cashier, but he hadn't thought Dad had actually been interested in her. Hadn't thought his dad would want to see anyone else. With dread growing slowly in the pit of his stomach, Connor asks, "What about Mom?"

Dad's lips thin. He digs his knife carefully into the belly of a fish. "She's not coming back. I need to move on, Connor."

"But you can't—can't abandon Mom." Connor sets his knife down, staring at his father, at the firm set of his shoulders. It feels like betrayal. "What will she say?"

His father sighs. "Mags will understand. I'll always love her. That won't change. I just... want a companion." Dad meets his eyes, looking right into him. "You understand that."

Neither of them mentions Yates. Yates, who was there for Connor when his mom died. Who stepped in as his friend and confidant and mentor. Who helped Connor through his grief. He aches to hear the wizard's voice, suddenly. Chest tight, Connor lowers his head. Dad needs someone who won't leave him. Mom can't do that. "Yeah. I understand."

Dad nods, gutting another fish. "What about you? You're still young. There's plenty of time to make your own decisions."

Connor knows that. Knows there are guys out there who are interested in him. But he can't forget the way Yates stared at him, two years after they parted ways, his gaze so damn starved. There's no one who wants him as much as Yates does, and Connor regrets walking away, now. "Don't know."

"No worries." Dad reaches over to cuff his shoulder lightly. "Just gotta be patient."

"I will," Connor says.

When he gets home later, he practices drawing his shapes again, remembering the mellow voice that had taught him his magical theories.

18
Twenty-Two

ON HIS twenty-second birthday, Connor walks the five miles to the sea-glass beach. It's been years since he visited the place — Yates had brought him here twice when he was fourteen, to see light from the sunset glinting off pebbled glass. In the years since, there had been no time: too many spells to learn, too much time spent at home or on the fishing boat.

Right now, Connor doesn't want to spend another moment with Sheila in his parents' house.

He can't hate her. Sheila is short and dark-haired, full of honest smiles. She laughs along with his dad, eyes crinkling, and listens when Dad speaks, leaning her head on his shoulder. She cooks sometimes, sharing recipes with Connor, and she even convinces his dad to eat the bell peppers he hates. Connor doesn't know what to think of this relationship, except to decide that he doesn't like it. He should move out. He has no space for a stepmother in his life.

So, he heads to the beach, walking until gritty sand melds into stone pebbles into green and brown bits of sea-glass, and he stops, breathing in the salty breeze.

Something snuffles. Connor turns, but all he sees is a flash of white darting behind a boulder. A bird? By the time he steps closer, there's nothing behind stone but footprints. Human-sized footprints. And a flare of bright, warm magic. His heart quickens.

"It's you, isn't it?" he asks, swearing to himself. How does Yates show up on his birthdays, even when Connor doesn't want to see him? What spells did he use to turn himself invisible? Why doesn't he have the guts to show himself?

With hope and longing and bitterness roaring in his chest, Connor whirls around. He's had enough of Yates, had enough of all the shit in his life. He trips over his feet. He throws a hand out to catch himself, stone jabbing into his palm, and he curses. When he regains his footing, he stalks away, lifting his hand to examine its angry red mark. Pain throbs in his skin like a second heartbeat.

Glass beads crunch. The well of magic presses closer. It raises the hairs on his arms, and Connor glances to his right, where the magic pulses strongest. Something touches his palm. It's dry and light, like a finger, and warmth spreads through his skin. It feels like home and safety. Like healing and bright points in his childhood. Like Yates.

Connor swallows hard against the tightness of his throat. "Why do you keep doing this to me?" he says between clenched teeth, surprised that he can still feel hurt. "Go find someone else to screw with."

The magic dims, as though Yates flinched. Connor stalks off down the beach. He doesn't need a damned wizard to soothe his hurts, when he hasn't recovered from the separation three years ago.

Yates doesn't follow.

Connor slows when sea-glass mixes with gray pebbles on the beach, his heart thudding. This feels wrong; he shouldn't be leaving. He's missed the damned wizard. He hasn't seen Yates in years, and he doesn't know if he ever will again. There's still a hole in his chest waiting to be filled.

So he turns back, hating himself for giving in, and sits down in front of the boulder. His spine thumps against stone. Yates' footprints and magic creep closer; just a whisper of heat at first, then brighter, like a tiny flame. It settles next to him, pushing a shallow, round indent into tiny pebbles, and Connor can imagine Yates curled into a ball, arms wrapped around his legs.

"Stop being a coward and show yourself, damn it."

Yates stays invisible. Silent. Connor glares at the waves rolling in, digging his fingers into translucent glass beads.

"Once upon a time, there was a monster who lived under the sea. It hated boats that sailed too close, so it grabbed them and flung them deep into the ocean."

"Bullshit."

"How else do you think my ship ended up in the forest? The others aren't so lucky. They're smashed to pieces, and the people in them wash ashore."

"Is that why you pull the bodies out?"

"Perhaps. But that's how this beach was formed. The glassware from the ships pour out, and they grind down into pebbles in the ocean. Aren't they beautiful?"

Connor scoops up a handful of sea-glass, pouring it out of his palm. The pieces tinkle down like beads. "I still hate you," he says.

A sharp breath comes from his side.

"I can't forget you, damn it." Anger clamors in his chest, and he smashes the beads against the boulder, baring his teeth. The sea-glass rains back down onto the beach. But Yates sits with him, listening, and Connor thumps his head against rock. It's easier like that, talking to empty air. He can't see what Yates is thinking, whether Yates really cares. "I haven't been happy. My dad's got a girlfriend. I... I tried with some guys. None of it worked out."

Yates doesn't answer. The waves crash on the shore, yards away from Connor's folded legs. The wizard is close enough to touch. It would be so easy to reach for him. But Connor has his pride; he's not going to start anything between them, not anymore.

"I just—I want to know how to get out of this," he says. "'Cause I can't move on. My dad's moving on. You are too, aren't you? I can't. Wish I could."

Further from the wizard, where Yates can't see, he sketches in the pebbles by his thigh: a circle for a boundary, a cross for perseverance, a rose for love. His skin prickles under the weight of Yates' gaze. It feels intimate, like a touch, except Yates doesn't move closer, doesn't admit to his presence. How long will he stay like that? Until one of them leaves? Connor pounds his fist into the glass beads, forcing his anger out. He should let this go. He doesn't want to hurt anymore. With a sigh, he leans his head back against the boulder.

For a time, they sit by the sea. Yates stays silent, his magic burning warmly by his arm. Connor closes his eyes. When he opens them again, the sun is further down in the sky, and Yates' magic is still there, next to him. Yates sat with him for hours. He wipes his face with the back of his hand, his heart thudding slowly. This is hopeless; he knows that.

"I'm leaving," Connor says. "Take care."

He can't read Yates' eyes, not when he can't see the damned wizard at all. And that's fine. That's good. It helps him turn his back on the beach, stepping away. Someday soon, he'll be free of the pain that comes with loving Yates.

That thought hurts more than it should.

YATES CRUMPLES against the boulder, panting. Pain sluices like fire along his tendons, stinging ant-bites marching across his skin. He squeezes his eyes shut. Concentrates on breathing. He knew the penalty for invisibility. He knew it would hurt, and yet... it had been worth the agony to stay by Connor's side.

He presses his forehead to warm stone, focusing on the crash of waves, the stillness of the boulder, air flowing into his lungs. Magic shouldn't be used this way. He shouldn't have camouflaged himself into the environment, pushing all his magic toward his skin, but it had been the only way to hide. So Connor wouldn't take one look at him and leave.

Of course Connor had to show up on the sea-glass beach. Of course they couldn't miss each other by half a mile. Just when he'd thought he'd skip Connor's birthday this year.

Yates digs his fingers into the pebbles, biting into his lip so he tastes the coppery tang of blood. It hurt, seeing Connor again. Seeing him walk away. Thinking about him with other people. He forces down the scrape of envy in his throat, the thought of Connor in someone else's arms. All he'd allowed himself was Connor's presence—Yates doesn't even deserve that much, after banishing him.

And yet Connor had stayed. Trusted him enough to doze off by his side. Yates wants to wake up next to him, see his dark eyelashes flutter in the morning sun.

He shakes his regrets away, rocking forward onto his feet when the agony subsides to a throb. "Are you out there?" he asks, staring out at the glittering sea. "You haven't been wrecking ships lately."

The sea doesn't respond. It's been calm the last few weeks, and Yates should be burying bodies. Should be giving all the lost souls a decent farewell, unlike how he fouled up his brother's death. He needs the reminder.

He looks between the waves and the distant speck of the town, then back at the boulder where Connor had sat. His stomach drops. Three shapes trace through the pebbles: a circle, a Celtic cross, and a rose. A prayer for unyielding love.

"You shouldn't," Yates whispers, heart squeezing tight. "You should forget me."

Connor isn't there to answer him, and the ocean breeze sighs in his ears.

SIX MONTHS later, over a fried fish dinner, Dad says, "I proposed to Sheila."

Connor freezes, horror coiling in his stomach. "What?"

"She said yes." Dad grins, cutting into his fillet with his fork. "Hey, at least be happy for me, won't you?"

"But..." He wants to protest. Say that he wants his mom back. But Connor knows he can't do this to his dad, when Sheila has been visiting every other week, bringing them cookies.

"She'll be moving in," Dad says. He glances out of the kitchen, at the photos on the walls. The old, yellowed photos of Mom and Dad are all in Connor's room now, and the new, framed photographs are of his dad and Sheila posing from various places around town—the beach, the restaurants, the park. Connor remembers building sandcastles while his mom lounged on the beach, remembers her strolling with his dad in the park. He can't glimpse these pictures without his stomach twisting.

"We'll move the rest of Mags' things into your room. That okay?"

"I guess," Connor mutters. He shovels mashed potatoes into his mouth, tasting little. It feels as though his father is cramming all the memories of his mom into an unseen corner. How do you pack your first love into a box? He wishes he could. Put all his thoughts of Yates into a crate and sink it into the ocean. Maybe he *should* have let Yates erase his memories.

"The urn, too." Regret flashes through Dad's eyes. "I think you'll keep her safe."

"Yeah." A lump rises in his throat. He remembers his mom in the kitchen, dancing quietly with his dad. Remembers them hugging when Connor reeled in his first fish. He still misses her. Wishes she were around to tell him how she feels about Dad marrying someone else. What she thinks about Yates, and how Connor still can't forget him. What would she have done in his stead? "I will."

"Thanks." Dad reaches over to squeeze his shoulder.

Connor thinks about shrugging his hand off. Everything's changing too quickly: Dad moving on. Proposing to his girlfriend. Carrying on with his life. Connor has done nothing: he fishes with his dad in the mornings, tends to the boat and practices his shapes in the afternoons. *Some days,* Yates once said, *I feel as though I'm lodged in time. Everyone else is moving on without me.*

Connor hadn't known what he meant, but now he understands. Was that why Yates turned him down? Because he was too naive?

His mother's ashes watch them from the mantle, and Connor ducks his head, his fork scraping against the plate. *I wish you were here,* he thinks. *I miss you.*

"I'M SORRY," Dad says one balmy afternoon, his eyes shadowed. The leaves rustle outside the house, and the neighbors' wind-chime tinkles. "There weren't any other wedding slots available. I've talked to the pastor about it."

Connor sucks in a shaky breath, his chest

burning. "It's on my birthday," he growls. "You can't do this to me."

"We'll go out for dinner the day after." Dad sets a hand on his shoulder, meeting his eyes. "Just you and me, okay? Like old times."

"Old times had Mom in them," Connor says. Not Sheila. Not just him and his father sharing a restaurant table by the window. But this is his life now: Yates and his mother gone, his dad with someone else. Connor doesn't have anyone to spend his birthday with. It's pathetic. He turns away, heading for the door. "But yeah, whatever."

Behind him, his father sighs. Connor doesn't respond, instead stepping out into the chilly October sun.

19
Twenty-Three (Part I)

ON HIS twenty-third birthday, his father marries Sheila. They recite their vows at the nearby church, five blocks from home, and Connor sits through the ceremony in a new button-up shirt and pants, trying not to tug the uncomfortable clothes loose.

Dad and Sheila kiss when the pastor declares them man and wife. Around, the fishermen cheer, and Sheila's coworkers clap and whistle. Connor cringes, not looking at them at all. While everyone heads to the reception area for a lunch of grilled perch and sugar cookies, he slips out through a side door, pulling his necktie loose. Cookies remind him of baking in a shadowy cargo hold, and he doesn't want that right now.

He heads down the sidewalk to the house. After today, Sheila will be living there with them, and he'll have to think of her as his stepmom. It feels wrong. He's certain that his mom doesn't want Sheila in the house, either.

In the living room, Connor stares at the framed pictures of his father and Sheila. They're always smiling in the pictures — eyes crinkled, faces bright. On his bedside table, the pastel-blue urn sits, dusted and out of place. "Hey," he says. The urn waits expectantly for him. "We're leaving."

He takes the urn down. Walks out the house with it.

Connor only stops to think when he's halfway down the beach, the waves lapping feet away. "Where do you want to go?" he asks.

His mother keeps silent.

With a sigh, he trudges on, one hand tucked in his pocket. The urn sits skin-warm and heavy in his other palm, quiet. To his side, the waves crash, foam sweeping up the beach. His shoes leave sharp-lined imprints in the sand.

Connor doesn't think about the distance he walks. He thinks about the sand beneath his feet, the roar of waves, until the water seems to pull further and further back into the ocean. He doesn't notice it until there's yards of wet sand — three yards, then five, then ten to the edge of the waves. There's never been this much of the shore exposed, even during low tide. Unease prickles at the back of his mind.

He tucks the urn under his arm, looking around. No one along the beach, no one to tell him if he's missed something. He clenches his jaw, wracking his memory for a voice.

Everything in nature is made of energy. Wood has the strongest voice, but with practice, you'll hear the voices of the stones, and the voices of the sand. Can you hear the sea?

Connor drops to a crouch, sinking a hand into the sloping shore. He hears the earth first, the quiet of the grains at his feet. *Shhh,* says the sand, stretching for miles along the coast. *The water is leaving.*

It doesn't make sense. So he listens to the brine between the grains, the water pulling away from the shore. In his mind, he sees it sweeping out like a retreating tide, crabs scuttling over the beach, tiny fish dragged along with the waves. The ocean draws away, like a beast with a hurt paw, and Connor reaches out further.

Far out to sea, the waves lengthen, as though pulled by a force much further away. And further yet, in the distance, Connor imagines the hiss of water and energy traveling fast, piercing through the ocean. *Angry,* it murmurs. *We move with fury.*

The wave will return, faster and higher than before, to swallow the forest and the town. *The people at the church!* He recoils from the thought. Dad doesn't know. Connor has no way to return to Fort Bragg before the wave hits. He'll be swept out to sea before he can get there, but he needs to make sure his dad makes it through. He needs to anchor himself to a tree. Or sail out. He needs a boat. A ship.

There's a ship in the forest.

Heart slamming against his ribs, he sprints down the shore, his shoes kicking up sand. There isn't time. He has to get to Yates. Barrier or not, Yates' ship is two minutes away, and this is someone he can save. He'll tell Yates to save the rest of the town.

Connor's strides lengthen. A path opens in the dunes—the way through the cemetery. Did Yates drop the barrier? It doesn't matter that they haven't spoken in years. Yates' life is more important than that. His feet pound down the worn dirt. The wind whips through his hair as he plunges into the forest, firs towering over him. Everything is still, calm.

"Yates!" Connor crashes through the low shrubs, urn clamped tight against his chest. "Yates, get on the ship!"

Connor tears down the familiar trail to the garden. Behind, the first wave crashes down on the shore, furious. He glances over his shoulder, stomach jolting at the frothing crests further out to sea. The second wave surges in, breaking over the cemetery, water gushing across the tombs to the forest. Twigs snap beneath his feet.

"Yates!" When he bursts into the clearing, he finds the wizard crouched in his garden, mouth hanging open. Blue eyes dart over Connor—face, chest, legs. Connor vaguely remembers that he's still in the suit from the wedding. "There's a wave coming in," he yells. "Get on the ship!"

Yates glances to the sea and pales. A wave swells up past the trees, blocking out the sky. "Climb on," he snaps. His fingers dig swift runes into the dirt. "I'll draw a shield."

"No!" Connor darts forward. Sweat slicks the urn in his hand. "Fort Bragg. Save the people there!"

"Fort—Oh, blazes. It's too far!" Yates winces, but his fingers scrawl new runes. The wave towers up above the firs, a churning wall of mud, and Connor's heart stops beating. There's maybe ten seconds before it crashes. He falls to his knees next to Yates. The wizard sucks a sharp breath, fingers flying over dirt. "Fifty arrows. I—Suck it, there's no time!"

165

Connor claws arrows into the soft earth, his fingers too slow. Beside him, Yates tears through two columns of spells: *wall, wall, wall.*

The wave shatters at the tree line with a deafening roar. Water rushes through the forest, a dark swell. Connor swears. They have twenty-eight arrows. He's still scratching them into the soil when Yates plunges his fingers into the earth. At once, a blast of magic sears through the runes. Connor yanks his hand away from its stinging burn. The ruts in the ground flare a radiant blue, and sizzling energy sweeps away from them, in the direction of Fort Bragg.

Next to him, Yates sags, weary.

Brine surges between the trees, a murky brown wall that roars through the garden.

"Conn—"

The churning water crashes into them. It slams Connor into the side of the ship, knocking the breath from his lungs. He swallows a mouthful of seawater. For a full minute, the wave pins him to the ship, water rushing past him, splitting around the hull like a river around a boulder. Behind, the ship groans, its submerged struts snapping. It lurches backward. Where is Yates?

Connor tries listening to the water for him, but he can't relax enough to hear. The waves splash around him, and there's no mess of red hair in sight. Just as he's about to dive down, Yates breaks the surface of the water with a wet gasp, paddling frantically. "Get on the ship!" Yates shouts.

The wizard doesn't wince—he's not injured. Beyond the trees, another wave sweeps forward, smaller this time. Connor struggles to draw a rune on his hand while he treads water, his mother's ashes clamped awkwardly in his arm. The urn slips. It splashes into the water and sinks like heavy stone, down into the shadows. His stomach lurches. He can't lose his mom's ashes.

A hand wraps around his forearm. "I'll get it," Yates says in a rush.

All Connor sees is a flash of blue eyes before the wizard dives down, his hair dulled by the water. It's too much to digest—Yates, swimming down after his mother's ashes. Just *seeing* him again, after two years. The wizard's pale hands wrap around the urn, ripples smudging the outlines of his arms, and Connor doesn't know what to think.

Yates breaks the surface, water streaming down his face. "Hands out."

Connor reaches out for the urn, but Yates presses a finger against his palm, scrawling an adhesive rune onto his skin. His fingers trail light and cold, and he's setting the urn in Connor's hands, pushing him toward the rope ladder. Magic tingles in Connor's skin.

"Climb!" Yates shoves at him. Connor climbs, and the wizard follows.

The next wave crashes. The boat lurches further sideways, and Connor scrambles up. Past the railing, soil and clay shards have scattered across the deck. The ship cants into the trees, branches sweeping out over them. Pottery remnants scrape down the floorboards. Connor lowers himself gingerly onto the deck, making space for Yates. "Get us out of here!"

"What?" Two feet away, Yates climbs over the

railing, his feet skidding against the floor. His eyes flicker over the broken pots, and dismay flashes across his face. "I'm not leaving."

"We need to get back to town, see if my dad's okay." Connor glares. "The spell wasn't complete."

Yates winces. "It wasn't, no."

"So get us out of here." The wizard hasn't changed. He still is fond of the townsfolk. He can still feel guilt. He isn't as heartless as Connor thought he was.

Yates turns away, avoiding his eyes. "I'll try."

It feels like a rejection. Yates doesn't want to look at him, even now. To hide his hurt, Connor looks over the rails.

With a groan, the ship slides free of the branches. He relaxes his hold on the railings as it tilts upright, glad for support beneath his feet. Yates sinks to his knees. But the ship doesn't slow—it drifts quietly through the clearing, pushing against the trees on the other side, until another wave breaks against the ship, angling it so it fits into a gap between the firs. The ship floats through the forest, trunks and branches scraping along its hull.

"We're heading out," Connor says, thrilled and wary at the same time. He'll get to town a lot faster by sailing. He'll get to see if his dad is fine. He'll have something to think about other than Yates being so close.

"Oh, suck it," Yates says. "It doesn't sail."

Unwillingly, Connor glances at him. Yates' face is upturned, light caressing his skin. Connor's heart kicks. Even amidst the churning waves and tipping ship, Yates is beautiful—cheekbones high, lips pink, eyes clear and intelligent. Red stubble dusts his cheeks, and his shirt clings to the flat expanse of his chest, the thinness of his arms.

Connor aches, looking at him. He hasn't seen Yates in two years. The last time he saw the wizard, Yates had been surrounded by his customers in town. They sat at the sea-glass beach together a year ago, but he hadn't thought he'd needed to see him again this much. Hadn't expected the hole in his ribs to yawn open.

"You can sail it with magic," Connor says.

"The ship is heavy, you know." Yates meets his eyes. In that heartbeat, Connor reads his apprehension, the way his shoulders hunch. He fills Connor with all kinds of questions. *Did you miss me? Did you regret being my teacher? Did you love me at all?*

It hurts to think about, so Connor stalks to the front of the ship, avoiding the plants where he can. There's still time to rescue them—he's broken pots before, and Yates has taught him to mend simple things. Yates has taught him how to mend everything but his heart, and here they are again, on the same ship, close enough to touch.

He swallows, tightening his arm on the urn. Mom would have known what to do. He wishes he had her advice, wishes he'd asked her all these things before she died. What would she have done in his place? Would she tell him to forget Yates? Connor wipes the brine off his face, stepping aside to let a tree branch sweep by.

The ship pushes through slanting rays of light, out into where the cemetery lay. Except it's now a sea. For miles around, all Connor sees is the forest and the ocean. No sand, no pastel houses. His heart squeezes. "We should get to Fort Bragg."

"I'll sail the ship," Yates says, clearing a segment of the floor. With some chalk from the cabin, he traces runes onto the deck, pushing his palms down to power them. Warm magic sweeps through the ship. It floods the floorboards, then the rudder and the steam engine, and the propellers hum to life. Yates clenches his jaw, his bangs falling into his face. Connor wants to step closer.

Instead, he stands and stares. Yates' eyes are barely open, and as the ship gains momentum, his chest heaves. Connor doesn't have magic like this. All he can do is watch Yates, helpless, and he wants this man all over again. Yates has hurt him. Thrown him out, ignored him, kept him away. But Yates has also wanted him, sat with him for hours on the beach, spent years teaching him the intricacies of magic. Right now, Yates is pushing the rest of his magic into the ship just because Connor asked.

Yates has given Connor part of himself, and Connor can admit that he still loves this man, even now. So he steps forward, kneeling down next to him. The wizard's heat seeps into his skin. Connor reaches up, brushes wet strands of hair away from his face, his fingertips skimming Yates' forehead.

Yates startles. His eyes land on Connor, and as he scrambles away, his gaze drags down to Connor's mouth, to the crouched mass of his body. "What—What are you doing?"

Connor shrugs. "Just realized something." *I still love you,* he wants to say. *I want to stay with you for a long time.*

But Yates will throw him off the ship if he breathes those words, so he swallows them, feeling their bitter scrape down his throat.

Yates gulps, his gaze skittering off. "I'm sailing the ship to Fort Bragg. When we get there, you'll go home."

"Fine," Connor says. It's a lie.

Yates ducks his head, pressing his hands back onto the deck. Connor feels the calm of his magic sweeping out into the ship once more, a familiar, gentle touch. He leans against the cabin door just to have Yates' magic brush his skin. It feels like heat and home, like the cornerstones of his past and the insane fantasies of his future. It feels *right*. Even if he's spent so long trying to remove Yates from his life.

The ship lurches, throwing them forward. Yates tumbles. Connor flings his arms out to catch himself, palms landing hard on the floorboards. Water drips onto his head. "What the fuck?"

"Oh, *suck* it," Yates mutters, rubbing his wrists. "Why do you have to do this now?"

"I didn't do anything," Connor says.

"I'm not talking to you."

Wood creaks behind him, low and ominous. Bewildered, Connor glances around. Thick maroon pillars curl around the ship, wide as tree trunks. They slide over the cabin and railings, bulging, squeezing around the ship so it creaks. Brine sluices off round purple suckers. *They're tentacles,* Connor realizes as one limb pushes up above the ship, water raining from its tapered end. Horror coils in his stomach. "What the hell is that?"

"The kraken," Yates says flatly. "It woke up."

20
Twenty-Three (Part II)

IF THERE'S a hell on Earth, Yates is convinced that this is it.

Glistening tentacles coil around the ship like giant snakes, scattering water into his eyes. The tidal wave has washed his ship out to sea. The kraken lurks beneath them, Yates' home snared in its grasp, and Connor is three feet from him, his face raw with shock.

"Does the world have a grudge against me?" Yates asks.

Connor rolls his eyes, but his shoulders tighten. "Get us out of here."

"I can't." Because even though he banters with whales and trees and stones, the kraken has no desire to make friends. Beasts make the worst companions, especially one that has stewed in its misery for centuries, throwing ships out of the ocean. "It'll hurl us into the sea!"

The next tentacle slithers over the stern, squeezing so tight the wood creaks. Yates' stomach roils. He can't risk the ship, but he doesn't want to hurt the creature, either. A heat spell would loosen its grip. He hurries to the nearest limb, reaching out.

Connor snags his arm, jerking him back. "The hell are you doing?"

"Stopping it before it destroys my ship!"

Yates tugs his arm free, gathering magic at his fingertip. Between saving Fort Bragg and sailing the ship, he has enough magic left for only a few spells. The ship groans around them, its beams trembling under the force of the kraken's grasp. Yates crouches, scrawling a rune for *shield*. He has enough magic left for one barrier, maybe.

But the ship lists to the side, broken flowerpots scraping across the floorboards. He stumbles, shoulder slamming against the door, and pain hisses through his body. "Oh, suck it!"

Next to him, Connor breaks his stumble with both arms outstretched, grimacing when he hits the cabin. The tip of a sinewy tentacle crashes between them, splintering the cabin door. Yates leaps away, his heart thumping. *Connor?*

Another tentacle slams onto the deck, squeezing between the cabin and the railing. The wood around it creaks, straining, and Yates' stomach clenches. He throws his arm out, scrawls a rune for heat onto drenched, leathery skin. Magic flares out through his finger, but the tentacle merely squirms. He jabs more energy into the rune, a sudden spike, and the limb snaps into the air, its end lashing across his chest like a sack of bricks. Yates stumbles backward, gasping.

"Yates!"

More limbs shoot up from the ocean, swaying above the ship like a towering purple forest. A tentacle whips into the cabin window. Glass shatters. Yates needs to do something. He can't just watch the kraken tear his ship apart, not when he's spent so long repairing it.

Something wraps around his chest. He jerks away, heart leaping to his throat, only to have the same warm limb drag him backward, against a sturdy wall of muscle. It's *Connor,* he realizes, when his spine fits against the defined contours of Connor's chest, and hot breath feathers over his ear. "You okay?"

He stops thinking. He should be focusing on the kraken. He should be saving his home, but *Connor* is touching him, and all he wants is for Connor to hold him like this.

Connor's fingers press into his chest. He pulls Yates tighter against himself, and Yates gasps, staring blindly at the strangling clutches of the kraken. "Answer me. Yates!"

"Yes," he gasps, sagging against Connor just to feel him again. "Yes, please."

"How do you make it fuck off?" Connor growls. The ship jolts, throwing them across the deck, and Connor slams him into the side of a tentacle. Yates' breath rushes out of his lungs. Connor swears. "Where's your biggest knife?"

A knife? Against a creature twice the size of the ship? "We should talk to it," Yates says. Attacking the kraken will only rile it further. "Be polite."

"Fuck talking." Connor turns, scrawling the rune for *electricity* into a sucker.

Ice slicks through Yates' veins. He snatches at Connor's hand, but the spell pushes into leathery skin before he can stop it, a jab of hot energy. The kraken's limb lashes out, flinging them both back into a railing. Connor grunts. Yates lands heavily on his chest and groans, throwing a hand out to stop him when he straightens. "Let me try."

With thick tentacles sweeping broken pots and mud over the floorboards, Yates scrawls the runes for *talk, listen* and *beast* on his throat, turning to face the sea. "Please stop," he shouts, cupping his hands around his mouth. "Lord Kraken, please listen to me!"

The tentacles around the ship still. They ease off, and relief slides through Yates' limbs. Waves break against the ship. Then, in a low, thunderous rumble, the kraken roars, *"Someone speaks to me."*

"It's me, Lord Kraken," Yates yells, scrawling an additional rune, for *loud*. "The wizard by the sea. Yates."

The same rumble comes again, reverberating through the ship. *"You disrupt my sleep."*

"The fuck is happening?" Connor backs away, scanning the deck.

"Shh." Yates curls his fingers into the railings. The kraken is a sprawling, murky shadow beneath them, and there's no way to extract them without using all his magic, or the ship's. "There was a disturbance, Lord Kraken. I deeply apologize for your awakening."

The tentacles tighten around the ship, lashing through the air. Droplets of brine patter across his face. *"Filthy humans and your filthy lies. You are not sorry."*

Yates winces. He doesn't want to deal with another kraken. "Please, Lord Kraken. Let us pass. We mean no harm."

"No harm. No harm, the human says!" The

tentacles tighten around the ship, squeezing so hard that the wood beneath them groans, splintering at the rails. Yates glances at the broken timber in dismay. *"Taint the sea with your magic, steal the fish from these waters, and say you do no harm!"*

"What's it saying?" Connor turns to the tentacles, uncertainty flashing through his eyes. He clenches his fists anyway, magic sparking at his fingertips.

He can't let Connor lash out at the kraken. But the beast isn't relenting, and they need to calm it down. Quietly, Yates says, "It's not working. It'll take a while."

"Fuck the kraken." Connor turns to a tentacle squirming feet away, scrawling a rune for *heat* on it. Before Yates can move, he slaps his palms against leathery skin, sending a pulse of magic through it. "Take that, you bastard!"

Panic curls through Yates' chest. "No," he chokes. "Not now!"

The kraken roars. Connor leaps back from its writhing tentacles, stepping in front of Yates. The maroon limbs tighten around the ship, drag it down sharply. Waves splash up around its sides. The shadow in the sea darkens to a burnt umber. Then, it erupts through the water's surface: first a pair of cruel, twisted horns, then beady black eyes, dark as ink, and a bearded, gaping mouth crusted with gray-black barnacles. Brine flows in rivulets off the beast, down its maw, to the scales of its broad sternum. It's twice as wide as the ship, looming taller than even its tentacles.

Yates stops breathing. He doesn't want to fight

this monster. Too much is at stake, and he's no match for even one beast. The one time he tried making peace with a kraken, it had ended in devastation. "Lord Kraken," Yates shouts, nails digging into wood. They can't possibly survive being hurled into the sea. He won't have his home shattered just like that. "We beg your forgiveness!"

The kraken stretches its mouth wide and *roars*. The air around them shudders. Yates crumples to his knees, pain pounding through his ears. The beast's tentacles ram Connor against the cabin, and Connor slumps to the floor, stunned. Yates stops breathing. Before he can move, the kraken raises its limbs, dragging the ship out of the water. Connor sways forward. *Is he hurt?* The thought makes Yates' throat close.

The tentacles constrict around the hull. Yates throws himself at Connor to anchor him down. A second later, the deck tilts. He lurches away from Connor, and his heart clenches. He scrawls an adhesive rune onto the deck, presses Connor's palm down on it. Connor grabs him around the waist. Racks, plants, and pots of soil scrape down the deck, falling past the railings into the sea. Dismayed, Yates watches them go. He spent years cultivating those bonsai.

Then the floorboards ram up against his hands and feet, and the kraken flings them through the air in a tremendous sideways thrust.

The ocean's surface hurtles by ten yards below. They're joined to the ship only by a single spell — Yates' hand on Connor's, Connor's arm around his waist. There's nothing beneath them but ship railings and glittering sea, and the wind shrieks in their ears. Their momentum heaves them forward. Yates' stomach plummets.

"Yates!" Connor snaps, holding him tight, urn tucked between his knees. "Hang on!"

The water's surface draws closer. The impact will smash the repaired segments apart, and Yates cannot allow that to happen, cannot allow Connor to crash into the ocean. He forces magic into his fingertip, scrawling the runes for *shield* and *ship* and *sphere*, and shoves his energy into woodwork, gasping as the magic in the ship reacts to his own, sweeping to every corner, to the bow and stern and sides.

An invisible sphere solidifies around the ship. They slam into the ocean with a violent splash, pushing a deep indent into the water's surface. A wall of brine crests around them, threatening to submerge the ship. A long moment later, the shield floats them to the ocean's surface, and the ship rocks violently to the other side, sending Yates sprawling across the deck. He scrabbles for a handhold and slams his shoulder against the railings. Connor swears, his feet skidding over the floorboards, the urn rolling away from him.

The ship rocks again, and they tumble to the other side of the deck. Yates skins his knuckles on the floorboards. It takes the ship minutes to stabilize. Yates groans, keeping his eyes shut until his nausea fades.

Then, he flattens his ear against the deck and reaches out with his senses. He hears nothing but the quiet calm of the sea, the whisper of the wind. Half a minute later, when he still doesn't sense the kraken, he drops the shield around the ship. It splashes gently into the water, bobbing on the waves.

Footsteps thump toward his head. Connor drops to a crouch beside him, hauling him up by his underarms. His eyes bore into Yates'. "You okay?"

It feels as though he can peer right into Yates' thoughts. Yates tears his gaze away, scanning their surroundings. The sea whispers calmly, and Connor kneels right before him, bruised but otherwise unhurt. Relief fills his lungs. He's never been so glad to see Connor alive, never felt so elated for his return, so he tucks his face into his shoulder, exhaling shakily. "Yes. Oh, heavens, yes. I'm fine."

Connor's arms slide around his back, pulling him close. His shoulder presses warm and solid against Yates' cheek, and his arms are strong, safe. Yates leans in, breathing in the damp brine of his shirt, the sweat on his neck. He never thought they'd be this close again.

"Thought we were gonna die back there," Connor says, his voice rough. "You idiot."

He can't help but laugh. This is ridiculous. The ship. The kraken. Connor on the muddy deck. "This isn't happening," he says. The ship is still floating, and nothing was anchored in the cargo hold. The shelves below-deck are full of plates and glass receptacles. His breath catches. "Oh. Oh, no. Oh, heavens, Connor."

He pulls away, rising shakily to his feet. The splintered cabin door creaks open when he tugs. Inside, the jars that lined the shattered windows are strewn across the floor, in fragments of jade-green and blue. Yates holds his breath when he pulls the trapdoor open.

Below, warm light glints off a thousand ceramic shards. The calendar sits on top of a smashed clay doll, a gift from an old nursemaid friend, and scarlet glass beads gleam between sugar and tiny screws and plastic bottles. His chest tightens.

Yates swallows his whimper, climbing gingerly down the flour-dusted ladder. Further inside the cargo hold, the utensils sprawl over the library floor. The books lie open halfway across the room, and the lab shelves gape emptily, broken glass and dried herbs a mess on the counters. It'll take a month to put everything back together. Yates can barely take one step now, and all he wants to do is burrow into his bed.

Connor steps down from the ladder, setting one hand on his shoulder. His fingers squeeze lightly, sturdy and warm. Yates stiffens. He shouldn't be this close to Connor. His life is a mess. His home floats out at sea, and most of his beloved knickknacks are shattered. "Hey."

He looks up hesitantly. This is the most vulnerable he's been in front of Connor, and Yates has nowhere to hide his weaknesses, not in front of this man. Before he can find the words to push him away, Connor steps forward, arms whispering around his back.

"That kraken was a damn pain," Connor murmurs. He pulls Yates close, his heat soaking into Yates' skin. "Glad you're here with me."

His heart misses a beat. Yates doesn't know what to say, not when so much has happened between them, when so much has happened today.

He hasn't had this touch in a while. Hasn't had it in years, since Connor was last in this ship, pressed against him in the kitchen.

Heat trails down his body, and Yates remembers exactly why he pushed this man away. Connor was his student. He's given Connor a part of himself, shaped him into the man he is now, and it isn't fair to want Connor as a lover. He pulls away. "I'll get you back to Fort Bragg," he says, even as his skin longs for Connor's heat. "I just have to regain my strength first."

Connor reaches out, as though he wants to pull Yates close. He lets his hand fall instead. "Yeah, okay. I'll wait."

As he turns away to clear the mess, Yates feels the weight of Connor's gaze on his skin, the unspoken words hanging in the air between them. He ducks his head and gathers broken shards in his hands, searching for a spot to stash them.

The past is shattered. Not everything can be put together again.

21
Twenty-Three (Part III)

"I NEED a bath," Connor says, his skin itching. The past hour has been a mélange of damage control: scooping debris into piles, rescuing edible food, and dropping the anchor so they'll stay close to the shore. He scratches at his arms, resisting the urge to rip his sleeves off. Even if it's an ugly brown right now, the shirt is new, remnants of soil clinging to fabric. "Seawater itches like a bitch."

Yates pieces together glazed ceramic shards at a low table next to the library shelves. "You're still a fisherman, aren't you? I would think you'd be used to seawater by now."

"Not like this." Connor sighs. Spots of fire trail down his body, from his scalp to his armpits to his groin, and he doesn't want to scratch at himself like a goddamned monkey. *Fuck it,* he decides, unbuttoning the shirt. "I don't swim in the sea. Not a fish."

At Connor's words, the wizard's lips pull into a smile. He draws a chalk circle to keep the magic in place, then scrawls runes next to his work. Connor shrugs the shirt off his shoulders.

"You do go through a lot of—"

Blue eyes snag on his chest. Yates' gaze follows the splay of his shirt down to his abdomen, and his tongue darts over his lip. It sends a whisper of hope through Connor's veins. "I wash my arms after we fish," he says, then drops the shirt on the floor. Yates' eyes rake over his pectorals, down his bare arms. Does he know how hungry he looks? "It's not like I let brine dry on my skin."

"I guess you don't," Yates says. He blinks, looking back down at his ceramic pieces—red lines on white surfaces, one of Yates' treasured oriental plates before it smashed.

Connor grabs a bucket of fresh water from the kitchen. They'd purified a few since drifting out to sea. Yates has promised to sail them back to Fort Bragg tomorrow, and Connor tucks away the worry he has for his father, focusing instead of the wizard. He sets the water bucket in the tub, grabs a steel bowl, and unbuttons his pants.

"You're... really bathing," Yates says, his voice strained. Connor steps out of his pants, his pulse racing when Yates' gaze strokes down his legs, to his feet, then back up his thighs. "I—I should head upstairs."

His breath catches. *No*, Connor wants to snap, but he doesn't know how to say it without sounding desperate. "Just look away. You're gonna get a sunburn if you stay up there for too long."

Yates' eyes drift up Connor's chest, then down, and Connor turns, tugging his boxers off. Behind, Yates makes a soft, strangled sound in his throat. It makes heat rush down to Connor's thighs, makes him think about pulling Yates close. Instead, he steps into the bathtub, sitting down.

Yates clears his throat. "I'll... just go for a few minutes. That will give you enough time for your bath."

"I thought the ship would be crushed for sure," Connor says to distract him. He scoops a bowl of water, emptying it over his head. The attack from an hour ago still seems surreal. He's never seen a beast twice the size of the ship. Worse, an actual kraken. Those rumors back home are real. "The kraken was choking it to death."

Yates fiddles with his ceramic pieces. "Oh, that. Most of the ship is made of *lignum vitae*. It withstands a lot of damage, if you remember."

Lignum vitae. It jolts something in his memory. *Lignum vitae. Wood of life.* Connor frowns, studying the wizard. They could have used the magic in the ship to escape the kraken, instead of letting it fling them further across the sea. There's enough wood on the ship to provide that magic. "We repaired it a few years ago, after the lightning strike. It was mostly the sides that needed patching."

The wizard nods. He fits two pieces of a plate together, sketching chalk runes on the table's surface. "The rest of the ship wasn't burned. When the kraken first hurled it into the forest, some of it was damaged—I filled those holes up with Douglas fir. Those were the parts we had to repair."

Connor splashes water over his arms, watching the rivulets run down to his elbows. "So there's still a hell lot of *lignum vitae* left. Why didn't you use it with the kraken?"

"It's a rare material. Remember the shaft bearings we found in Mack's? Your dad hadn't even seen them before. I didn't want to drain the ship's energy just because of a beast. Saving it for a rainy day, if you will."

Connor remembers lying on a cliff, raindrops in his face. He remembers Yates standing and waving a stick, lightning striking wood. He remembers the horror of thinking he lost Yates. "Yeah."

"I'm relieved that the ship is mostly intact this time," Yates says. His chalk runes glow a faint blue, and the edges of the ceramic pieces knit together. His smile fades. "But there's a lot to repair around here."

"Like us?" The words fall from Connor's mouth before he can help it. He stops breathing.

Yates tenses. But he doesn't leave, instead pushing another two shards together. He seals the crack between them. Then the next pair, and the next. "I'm not sure what you want, Connor," he says. "But I'm not able to provide it."

"You can." Connor scowls. Yates hasn't changed, has he? He still thinks Connor's too young. "I'm a fucking adult now, Yates. I make my own decisions."

"Is that why you walked down the shore with your mother's ashes?" Yates glances up at him, as though afraid to meet his eyes, his hands shaky.

He clicks his tongue. "My dad married his girlfriend today. I didn't think my mom wanted to stay in the house after that."

"Oh." Yates' shoulders sag. He takes the mended pieces out of the circle, placing new shards in them. "That's... It's your birthday, isn't it?" He winces. "That's not very nice of them at all."

Connor shrugs. Right now, not knowing whether they've saved Fort Bragg from the waves, he can't muster any anger toward his dad. "He said the church was all booked up. Told me he was really sorry and all."

"I wish it were different."

"Yeah, well." Connor pours more water over his head, rubbing grime from his face. He lathers his hands with rosemary soap, pushing it through his hair, down his arms. It's a relief to be clean again. The sensation is something to hold onto, when he doesn't know if his dad is okay, and Yates is four yards away, years of hurt standing between them. "But we need to repair this."

Yates brushes off his chalk drawings, sketching a larger circle on the table. "Repair the ship?"

"No. Us."

The wizard's shoulders stiffen. His next words are so quiet that Connor has to strain his ears. "You'll do better without me."

And that reels a boatload of hot anger through his chest. Connor growls. *Fuck* if Yates gets to decide that. *Fuck* if Yates' feelings are all that's important. He's on his feet and moving across the floorboards in a heartbeat, Yates turning to stare in wide-eyed shock. "Don't give me that shit. I know what I want."

"You're too young to know," Yates says, dropping his half-mended plate with a clatter. Connor towers over him, and Yates' eyes flicker down his body, over the bubbles smeared across his chest. "Connor, please."

Connor crouches down in front of him, legs open, one soapy hand slipping behind Yates' neck, holding still against warm skin. The wizard smells like dried sweat and brine. "Look at me," Connor says, heart pounding. How many times has he dreamed of being this close to Yates again? How many times has he thought about that gaze trailing down his body? "Look me in the eye and *mean it* when you say you don't want me."

Yates gulps. His gaze darts to Connor's shoulders, his abdomen, his groin, and Yates' breathing stutters, loud in the inches between them. His eyes scream *want*. An answering hunger roars deep in Connor's abdomen. Yates squirms. "I... Oh, suck—This isn't right."

Slowly, Connor leans in, so his knees scrape against the floorboards, and his lips brush Yates' ear. "You want to taste me. I can read you, Yates."

The wizard sucks in a sharp breath. It's all Connor needs to know. He tilts his head, pressing a soft kiss to Yates' cheek, then the shell of his ear, circling his earlobe with his tongue. Then he takes it into his mouth. Yates moans, a low, guttural sound. His fingers land on Connor's thigh, an electric touch trailing down to his knee, then up the muscles of his leg, learning the grooves of his skin.

An inch from his groin, Yates pauses. His fingers curl, then slip down slowly, between Connor's thighs, and Connor is hard in seconds, a rush that makes him throb and his head spin. Yates' hand is on his cock. He can't believe it. Yates' fingers brush all the way to his tip, cool and gentle, and pleasure feathers through his body. Connor swears. He wants more.

As though he's jolted from a daydream, Yates flinches. His magic flares under his skin. "No," he gasps, scrambling backward, his eyes anchored on the library shelves. "I can't—can't do this."

Connor's roar swells in his chest, held down by a shred of discipline. Yates has been doing this for four goddamned years. He's so tired of the wizard and his stupid games. Instead, he glances down at the telling line in Yates' pants. "You want to fuck me, damn you," he growls. It kindles anger in his gut, knowing that Yates wants him, that Yates is still the same idiot he was before, pushing Connor away when he'd much rather grind up against him. "Look, I'm not going to ask you to teach me again. I don't want to be your student."

Something flickers in Yates' eyes.

"Can we be friends?" That one sentence makes him feel like he's cracking his walls open. He doesn't know what he'll do if the wizard rejects him again. Go home and fish, and be content with that? "Just... just friends. Okay?"

Yates' fingers twitch against the floorboards. "Just friends," he says. "I... can do that. Yes."

Relief surges through his body, and he rocks back onto his heels, breathing out. "You won't hide from me again?"

Yates turns away. "I can't promise that."

He can't help the hurt in his ribs. Yates has agreed to be his friend; it has to be enough. His heart says it isn't. "Okay. Fine."

"Get dressed," Yates says, pushing himself to his feet. "I'll be upstairs."

Connor watches as the wizard scales the ladder, his head bowed. It feels like a step forward, but Yates is still distant, and Connor wants to hold him close. Yates won't allow it.

He trudges back to the tub. There are things to clean up around here, crockery he can mend. If he repairs enough of Yates' things, maybe Yates will let him mend their relationship, too.

22
Twenty-Three (Part IV)

YATES REALIZES he's a coward.

He's spent an hour staring out to sea, mulling over ways to send Connor home, and yet... he still doesn't have a solution. After four years of avoiding him, Connor is here again, on his ship, and Yates doesn't have enough magic to sail them to town. He should harness the energy in the *lignum vitae*. He should exhaust himself to get Connor beyond his reach.

Yet a part of him wants Connor to stay. It revolts him to know he wants to bed a person a tenth of his age. Connor hasn't lived through the panic of the world wars, hasn't been taught by any other wizard. He hasn't had a disapproving mentor mutter in his ear, *If you fail others, then you have failed me.*

Yates doesn't want to feel like a failure anymore. He's tired of the reminders that he isn't good enough, that he wants something so perverse: a child he has shaped into a man. It violates all the rules he knows.

So he leans against the cabin wall, resting his

head on smooth wood. None of this should be happening. His home shouldn't be a mess. He shouldn't be out at sea. Connor shouldn't be here, a temptation and a safe harbor rolled into one. In his arms, Yates doesn't feel like a failure. He doesn't think about the mistakes he's made in the past, the flesh sagging off his brother's bones.

The ghosts from a century ago still haunt him, and Yates is weary of their weight on his shoulders.

He pries himself off the cabin wall. The rough grain of the floorboards brushes under his fingertips, and the waves splash softly against the side of the ship. His stomach growls. He should eat. Cookies, maybe, or cake. Yates freezes. It's Connor's birthday. He's forgotten it again, pushed Connor away on his birthday for the third godsdamned time. In his mind, Quagmuth whispers, *I am disappointed in you.*

He groans, rising to his feet. He's agreed to be friends with Connor, and so he'll bake him a cake, or make him a birthday dinner. Something that will ease the misery of this situation. Yates winces. So much of this is his fault. He shouldn't have taken Connor in, shouldn't have kept Connor as a student when he began to desire more. They shouldn't even be friends again.

When he descends into the cargo hold, he finds Connor in a beanbag chair by the library, thumbing through a book. He's wearing a bath towel around his waist. Just that. Yates can't help but follow the muscular lines of his abs, the curves of his pectorals falling into shadow, the bulge of his arms. Dried seawater itches across his own skin, and he barely remembers that he hasn't rinsed off the brine from the flood.

Connor glances up, his shoulders tensing. "Thought you were gonna stay upstairs longer."

Yates steps closer to read the text, sagging at Connor's defensiveness. "I didn't know you were still interested in those books."

Connor snaps the book shut, setting its spine against his thigh. "Refreshing my memory. Something chased you down?"

The books in the library teeter on the shelves, stashed with no thought for subject or size—tomes hastily tidied after the kraken. Which one was Connor reading? *Was he waiting for me?* His pulse skips. Connor can't possibly want him, so he heads for the kitchen, trying to ignore the sting in his heart. "I realized that I was being rude," Yates says. "I should have baked a cake for your birthday."

Connor snorts. "We're stuck on the ocean. Don't need a cake. I'm not ten anymore."

I used to bake you cakes, Yates wants to say. *You'd grin and hug me.* He buries those words, buries the tendril of hope that sneaks into his stomach. "I'm baking one for me, then."

Connor watches him, gives a half-shrug, and turns to the crockery shards piled by the library table. "Sure."

And so Yates prepares the batter, beating together eggs and flour and milk. For all the glassware that the rocking ship shattered, there is still dried fish tucked into plastic containers and potatoes in wicker baskets. Yates is grateful for that.

Behind, Connor pieces the plates together, his face taut with concentration. He draws his chalk circles confidently, steady lines that speak of practice, and Yates can't help the fierce pride that roars through his chest.

I love you, he wants to say, and the shock of it mutes his tongue. He doesn't know what sort of love it is, whether it's one a mentor feels for his student or something more. The urge to hug Connor and kiss him is inappropriate. He wants to anyway. It makes him remember *failure* and *I will make you proud*, and he turns back to the counter, his heart thudding dully. Maybe they shouldn't even be friends, if he can't straighten out what he's feeling right now.

He grabs a dish towel and wipes the counter down, wishing he could clean his regrets away.

Later, when the scent of vanilla wafts from the oven, Yates cracks the door open, peeking inside. Sponge cake rises in the little spring-form pans. His spirits lift. Carefully, he sets the pans on cooling racks on the island counter. Connor edges over. "You actually made cake."

"I thought you might like it."

"I'm too old for cake." On the other side of the counter, Connor studies the cake pans. Then his eyes wander across the cherry-wood of the island, to the five charred marks closer to him. His eyes widen in recognition.

Yates swears under his breath, heat flooding his cheeks. He'd given up on covering the marks, hadn't even thought about placing a mat over them when Connor stepped into his home. And now the reminder is here, sitting between them: short, dark lines from a years-old memory, brief moments of stolen kisses that Yates still treasures.

"You liked it," Connor says, his eyes flickering up to Yates' face.

Yates looks away. He can't admit to that. Can't admit that he still wants Connor close. "Do you want icing on the cake?"

"Yes." Connor huffs. "Damn you."

Yates tries to laugh. It falls flat between them, so he stops, hugging himself. "You've been practicing your magic."

Connor jerks his shoulders. "Some. Not much."

"You didn't... find another teacher?" Yates chances a glimpse at him. Connor's shoulders are corded with muscle, his biceps defined. It would be nice, he thinks, if he could just forget their history. Maybe he should have erased his own memories.

"No. I searched for books, but I couldn't find any."

"Oh." He snags a piece of chalk from the side of the counter, sketching runes to tease air over the cakes, cooling them. The runes are familiar. Something he can ground himself with. While Connor waits, he beats together butter and sugar into frosting, and cracks open an unbroken jar of blueberry jam. "I'm sorry it's been difficult for you."

"Are you?" Connor glances at him again, his fingers tracing over the burn marks. Yates should really cover them up. "Did you know how pissed I was?"

"Some." He remembers the names Connor yelled at him. Thinks about them often. To avoid his eyes, Yates unlatches the spring-form pans, smears jam over one slab of cake, and carefully transfers the other onto it. "I heard what you said, that day in the forest. You were right to call me a bastard. I'm sorry I was a waste of your time."

It still hurts, saying it like that.

Connor studies him. A long moment later, he shakes his head. "You were a bastard."

Yates flinches.

"But I shouldn't have said those things either," Connor says. He steps around the counter, toward him, and Yates' breath catches in his throat. He wants a hug. He wants far more than that, more than he deserves. Connor stops inches away, his magic a bright, warm spark. "'Cause when I think of you, that's not who you are. It wasn't a waste of time."

Yates chuckles then, mirthless. What has he done with Connor that isn't atrocious? "Really?"

"Yeah. You're kind. You spent years teaching me magic. You were there for me, Yates. I haven't forgotten that." Connor closes the distance between them, wrapping his arms around Yates' back. Heat bleeds through his clothes, and Connor's embrace is sturdy, a cocoon of safety that Yates doesn't have strength to pull away from. Connor smells like rosemary and musk, like fresh sweat and *home.*

"Oh." He trembles, relieved. Connor doesn't hate him. He buries his face in Connor's shoulder, breathes him deep into his lungs. "I... I missed you. While you were gone."

"Yeah?" Connor's voice rumbles through his chest.

"We can be friends," Yates says again, wishing they could have more than that.

"Okay." Connor's fingers sift through his hair, gentle strokes that say too much. Yates pretends not to hear it, pretends not to notice the way Connor brushes his mouth over his nape. It sends a thrill down his spine. "Thanks for the cake," Connor says.

"I made it for me," Yates says. He curls his fingers into Connor's waist, wishing this moment could last forever.

HALF AN hour later, Connor scowls at the yellowed pages on his lap. The text does not explain shape magic, or how to combine runes with life for a stronger casting. When he first read it years back, Connor had assumed that "circles of three" meant three separate circles, instead of concentric rings joined to create a formidable barrier. Yates didn't teach him this.

He leans over the sunlit drawings on the deck, replicating the faded circles in *Advanced Shapes*: first the smallest, then a second, and a third. Next, he draws the straight lines to connect the barriers, and between the rings, the runes that will hold the spell steady.

The binding of life energy to once-dead material involves energy in excess of a thousand-fold, the author had written. *To do so requires circles of three at minimum. Quagmuth the Wise, inventor of the ten-circle spell, once drew a barrier to trap the mother of krakens.*

The ten-circle spell is what he needs to contain the energy for a revival, but Connor knows he's not ready for that yet. Perhaps in a few years, when his magic has grown. He pieces together ceramic shards for a bowl, places them in the middle of the three circles, and sketches the runes to seal the cracks. *Heat, grow, knit,* he scrawls on repeat.

Footsteps thump behind him. Connor turns, chalk in hand, to see Yates stepping out of the cabin, clean shirt clinging damply to his chest. Water drips from his hair. Connor hadn't expected him to be done with his bath this soon, but Yates treads more lightly now, his limbs loose and relaxed.

Blue eyes flick over the chalk barrier, and Yates' lips press into a line. "Not like that," he says, crossing the empty deck to crouch by Connor. He scoops the chalk out of Connor's fingers, smears away his lines and runes with a thumb. "Fewer lines. With three circles, you'll need three lines to hold them in place, not four. Having more lines than the circle count disrupts the shape balance."

The words wash past Connor's ears. He stares as the wizard draws three lines joining his circles, equidistant from each other. Since the day he cut him off, Yates hasn't corrected him, hasn't talked about magic theory. To see this side of him after years, patient and focused... It makes his breath catch.

"For the strongest shield, you'll want to leave little space between the circles. Think of it as walls stacked against each other. This also means you can't draw large runes, since the runes shouldn't touch the boundary lines." Yates' fingers fly through the shapes with deft strokes, quick taps of chalk on wood.

Connor doesn't want him to stop. Something pangs in his chest, sharp and bittersweet; he hadn't thought he'd miss that spark in Yates' eyes again, the way he talks so easily about magic. "The book didn't mention the number of lines."

"The book doesn't explain a lot of things," Yates says. He finishes off the spell with little runes to the side, before clapping chalk dust off his hands. "Which is why I said to ask me if you don't understand—" His eyes grow wide, and blood drains from his face. "Oh, *suck* it. No. Forget I said that."

Disappointment swamps Connor, a heavy, smothering wave. He glares, watches as Yates climbs to his feet, unable to meet his gaze. "Forget you said what?"

"I'm not your teacher, Connor." Yates wipes his fingers on his pants, leaving smudges of white on dark fabric. His eyes dart around the deck. "We're just... just friends."

"That means you can still teach me, right?" Connor scrambles up, reaching out to snag Yates' elbow. Yates' arm is warm and thin, familiar against his palm. "As a friend?"

"I can't be your teacher," Yates snaps, his eyes flashing. "Don't you see? I've molded you into the man you are today. I can't—can't continue to be your mentor. I didn't shape you for myself. That's wrong—"

"So you want me. Admit it." Connor glares. It's so obvious now, when Yates' eyes rake over him, deep blue and anguished. Connor reads the *want* in him, the way Yates leans in despite himself, even as he tries to tug his arm free. "We're just two people, Yates. I'm old enough to lo—"

"I'm ten times your age," Yates cries. "Look at

me, Connor. I've hurt you. I'm an old man—"

"I don't care." Connor hauls him close, so Yates stumbles against him, shoulders bumping into his chest. He smells like rosemary soap. Connor smooths his fingers through his red hair, brushing away the bangs falling into Yates' eyes. He knows all the different facets of this man, knows his habits and fears. "Is that so hard to understand? I don't care how old you are, or whether you're my teacher. I don't care that you've been a bastard. I love you, you idiot."

Yates inhales sharply, sinking closer. "You love me like you would a teacher," he whispers, staring out to sea. "You're just confused. I'm not clever or wonderful. You deserve better. Trust me on that, please."

The wizard tugs himself away, head bowed. He strides back to the cabin and disappears inside.

"Damn you," Connor yells. He's not confused. But he doesn't know how to convince Yates that age doesn't matter, that he can be selfish and love despite who they were. He's spent four years trying to forget Yates. All he wants now is a life with this man. "Just listen to me, damn it."

The door clicks shut. Connor looks around the empty deck, at the glittering sea beyond the ship. The sun inches toward the horizon, bathing the ship in orange, and in the distance, Fort Bragg is a colorful, distant speck.

Connor tucks his hands in his pockets, listening to the gentle splash of waves. *Peace,* the sea says, but he disagrees. It feels like he'll never fill the hollow in his chest.

23
Twenty-Three (Part V)

"DINNER IS mashed fish and boiled pumpkin," Yates says when Connor climbs down into the cargo hold an hour later. While he wandered upstairs, Yates distracted himself by thinking up a menu that would make Connor wince, so Connor would realize that he isn't worth keeping around and step off the ship, his mouth curled in distaste. *I shouldn't be thinking about him.*

"What," Connor says, wrinkling his nose. He deposits his spellbook in the library, then heads over to the kitchen, where Yates prods at boiling fish in another pot. He pulls the spatula out of Yates' hand. "Stop destroying the fish."

Yates chuckles dryly. "I was cooking. Return my spatula."

This close, Connor towers over him, his clothes still damp from washing. He glances sideways at Yates, the weight of his gaze heavy on his skin. Connor isn't his student anymore. Yet some part of his mind still holds on to that relationship, makes him want to teach and correct and help.

In half a day, they'll be headed back to Fort Bragg, where Connor will go home and continue with his life. He shouldn't fixate on Yates. Shouldn't have returned to the ship. But it's too late for that, and the thought of him leaving sends dread rippling through Yates' chest.

"Mashed fish. Really?" Connor pulls the pot off the stove, draining it into the sink. Steam billows up above them. Pot in hand, he checks the pantry, clicking his tongue. "You have dill and pepper in here. Why the hell would you make plain mashed fish?"

"Because it's the last supper?" Yates tries to smile.

Connor rolls his eyes, pulling flour and plastic spice bottles out of the cabinets. "Not funny."

Yates sighs. "It is your last dinner here, though. You're going home tomorrow."

"And so you're making the shittiest food?" Connor's forehead wrinkles. "You taught me to cook."

Yates cringes. He's impacted Connor's life in so many ways—more than he can count. "You have to go home."

"I don't want to go home. Maybe just to check on my dad, but that's it."

"Are you moving out of your father's place?" Yates turns, disappointment echoing in his throat. Where else would he go, if not home? "Away from Fort Bragg?"

"I want to stay with you." Red fans up Connor's neck, to his ears. He drizzles oil over the fish, before cracking pepper over the fillets. "As a friend, or whatever. If you'll have me."

Yates' heart stumbles. He shouldn't like that idea so much. Connor living with him. Connor pressed up against him, kissing him with those full lips, pounding him into the bed. He shakes those thoughts out of his head. "No. You know that."

I love you, Connor had said. The words echo in his head, humming down his spine. When Connor leaves, he'll wrap himself in them and be glad that Connor loved him once. It has to be enough.

Connor purses his lips. He turns the fillets over to give them a light sear, and Yates admires the flick of his wrist, the way his biceps flex. "You know how I feel," Connor says, staring at the sizzling meat. "I just wish you weren't being such an idiot."

"I'm not being an idiot." In fact, Yates is being proper and watching out for him. It shouldn't make him want to kiss that mouth again.

Connor snorts. He drains the pot of boiling pumpkin next, cracking more pepper over the cubed pieces, before throwing on a sprinkle of salt. Watching him, it feels as though Yates has seen this before: Connor making dinner for them both. It feels as though he's looking into the future, at what could happen if he allows Connor to stay. It feels as though they're both standing at a precipice, a decision, and Yates will not let Connor ruin his future by choosing a tired old wizard who has tried to raise the dead.

So he turns away, setting the table with mended plates and glasses. When Connor serves the fish, he fills Yates' plate first, then his own.

"It smells good," Yates says, popping a pumpkin cube into his mouth. It melts over his tongue, sweet with a hint of salt and dill, and he can't help grinning. Connor had taken that recipe card from him a long time ago. "This is a lot tastier than I'd meant it to be."

Connor sits across from him. "You think trying to drive me off with bad food is gonna work?"

"I guess not." He smiles ruefully, hugging himself. "You cook well."

"You just like it 'cause I added dill. Still your favorite herb?"

Yates can't help the heat prickling across his face. It feels a little too intimate, Connor knowing so much about his preferences. "I'm surprised you remembered."

"Yeah."

For a while, neither of them speak. Connor's gaze lingers on Yates, and Yates does his best to avoid it. He chews on fish, focusing on pepper and salt instead of Connor's mouth, the spread of his shoulders, the curl of weathered fingers around his fork. Connor's bath had shoved tempting images into his head. The clean dress shirt he wears fits his frame perfectly, more formal than the T-shirts he used to pull on.

"You're staring," Connor murmurs, sipping from his glass. Yates can't stop looking at the drop of water sliding down his lip, can't help his desire to catch it with his tongue. It makes his mouth go dry.

"I'm just lost in thought," he croaks. All he has to do is lean across the table to touch Connor, kiss him. He tries to remember what their last kiss felt like, years ago, but he can't think of it now when Connor is right here, when Connor is *so willing* to fall into bed with him.

Around them, the ship creaks, a gentle sway

that Yates barely feels. He has a bite of fish halfway to his mouth when a jolt shudders through the floorboards, sending ceramic shards rattling down the scattered piles of debris.

"Something hit the ship?"

Yates frowns. He sets his palm on the table, listening first to the wooden body of the hull. It hums amiably, intact, so he relaxes his senses until he hears the sigh of the sea. *The kraken passed through,* the currents whisper. *It has gone.*

He only thinks to listen for the beast then, wincing. How could he have forgotten? Far beneath the ship, Yates feels the dark, heavy presence of the kraken, the way its coiling tentacles drag its bulk across the seabed. It's moving further away, oddly fast, and Yates can't figure out why. Unease swims in his stomach. "It's the kraken," he says. Connor tenses, scowling. "But it's no longer a threat. It's... in a hurry, maybe?"

"In a hurry?" Connor sets his fork down, studying the floorboards as though he can see through them. "I'll check upstairs."

"I'm not sure there's much to see," Yates says. Pitch-dark stretches far and wide outside the windows. "The ship isn't damaged."

Connor stands anyway, turning. "Still a good idea to look."

As he steps toward the ladder, Yates can't help the relief that washes through him. He's glad that Connor is here. He shouldn't be, but he is. It's calming to hear his rumbling voice after so many years, thrilling to have his gaze slide down his body. He buries his face in his hands, his ears burning. He shouldn't be thinking this.

In his mind, Quagmuth says, *You are a failure.*
Yates knows that he's right.

TWO HOURS after dinner, Connor kneels by the library shelves, holding a lamp up between his chest and the leather spines of spellbooks. Yellow light glints off worn gold lettering: *Herbs of the Fae. Binding Spells. Runes for Daily Life.* By reading *Life Magic in Remains* again, he's discovered that there are other spells the book has hinted at, complex runes involving life magic that he hadn't thought to investigate. So he scans the titles, searching for something he missed years ago.

The circle of lamplight roves over the jumble of titles. Yates would have cringed at their untidiness before the kraken. He likes his books in order, sorted by names and height and subject...

Which is why Connor stares when light falls onto a ragged spine: *Death to Life.*

He reads the words over and over, going still. Through all the times he's browsed these shelves, he's never seen this title, even when he was searching for ways to bring his mother back. How had he not found it before? He slides the tome out silently, glancing over his shoulder, his heart pattering in his chest.

In the shadowy corner of the cargo hold, Yates snores quietly, his bed covers pulled up around his shoulders, his face turned away.

Connor straightens, tucks the book against his chest, and treads soundlessly to the ladder, his bare feet silent on the rungs. He shuts the doors, sits with the cabin to his back and cracks the book open, bringing the lamp close to illuminate the pages. He freezes.

In every spellbook he's read, the pages are clean, inked writing printed neatly like textbooks from school, read but not touched. Sterile. Like Yates had merely collected them as a hobby. In *Death to Life*, the pages crinkle as he flips them, a familiar looping script crammed between lines of text. Connor can recognize that handwriting anywhere—he's read it for years, followed it on recipe cards while he baked cookies and meat pies and lasagna.

Avoid caraway root. Tangles up ashes. Do not use rune for 'store'. I am so weary. Success is elusive. I'm sorry.

Connor thumbs through the book, bereft of words. On some pages, all Yates writes are potion ingredients and methods of casting. On others, he writes, *I wish you were here. I'm sorry this is taking so long. Your ashes sit by my side, and I'm terrified of failing you.*

Connor struggles to breathe. Yates tried to bring someone back to life. Yates wanted the same thing he did, and Connor had no idea. *Who is it?* he wants to know. At the same time, he's afraid to find out. It could be a lover. Connor shoves that thought out of his mind, because it sends envy snarling through his gut. He flips through the pages instead, watching as the dates hop between 1829 and 1858.

Toward the end of the book, Yates' handwriting grows scratchy, illegible. *I brought a rabbit back to life. It breathed for two minutes. I'm getting there, Wesley. Please don't hate me.*

Connor flips to the end of the book. All that is left of the last few pages are jagged, ugly stubs, sheets that have been ripped out with no care for their contents. He studies them for a long moment, tracing their edges with his fingertips. He imagines Yates in his youth, hair a mess, eyes wild and helpless when his resurrection failed. His heart aches. This has to be why Yates never discussed revival, why he was so quick to shut Connor down whenever he mentioned his mother. And Connor never *knew*.

He clenches his teeth, glaring at the torn pages. Yates had kept this from him. It had mattered so much to the wizard, and it matters to Connor, too, because they had the same goals. If Yates had a hundred years to practice his spellwork, how did he fail to revive Wesley?

Connor flips back to the first page, reading first the text, then Yates' notes. Tiny writing marches across the page, a strain on his eyes. By the fifth page, the words begin to swim. He tucks the book under his arm and stumbles back down the ladder. At the library, he pauses, pulling out a handful of books from the lowest shelf. He tucks *Death to Life* flat against the back wall, then replaces the books.

"Night," he mutters at the blue urn sitting behind the beanbag chairs. It doesn't answer.

Next to the bed, Connor kicks off his shoes. He sets the lamp on the floor and slips gingerly under the covers, easing into the space Yates has left for him. In his sleep, Yates doesn't frown. He looks peaceful. Carefully, Connor reaches over, brushing fine strands of hair from his face. When the wizard doesn't stir, he slides further down the bed and leans in, pressing his lips to Yates' forehead.

"Sorry you were hurting so much," he whispers. He wraps an arm around Yates' back, drawing him closer. "You aren't a failure. I won't hate you."

Still asleep, Yates tucks his face into Connor's neck. His breathes in slow, and Connor inhales with him, until the lamp flickers off, plunging them into inky darkness.

For his twenty-third birthday, he wishes for Yates to have him the rest of their lives.

24
Twenty-Three (Part VI)

YATES WAKES to soothing heat wrapped around him. For a long moment, he thinks he's burrowed in sun-warmed blankets, albeit sturdier and more snug. Something tickles his nose. He opens his eyes, staring when he finds a mess of chestnut hair in his face. He knows the accompanying strong jaw and full lips, and it's *Connor* asleep next to him. His heart slams into his ribs.

"Suck it," he yelps. What's Connor doing in his bed? How did he get here? Why does he have to feel comforting and solid and warm against Yates' skin?

Connor stirs, eyes fluttering open. "Hmm?"

"What—How? You aren't supposed to be here," Yates splutters. He doesn't dare move, in case he's still dreaming. He doesn't want Connor to leave. He's been dreaming about him in his bed for years, and this has to be a trick of his mind.

Connor stares at Yates like he can't believe it either, but he doesn't panic. With a rustle of fabric, Connor leans over and kisses him, soft lips meshing with his, languid like he wants to savor this. It feels real. Yates can't be imagining his stubble and morning breath. Connor sets a large hand on his waist, calloused fingers catching on exposed skin, and Yates' breath snags in his throat.

"Morning," Connor murmurs against his lips. He licks at Yates. Yates lets him in, stunned, and Connor sweeps into his mouth, hand sliding under his shirt, up his side. All his blood rushes south. Connor slings his thigh heavily across Yates' hips, right over his growing cock.

"Connor," he gasps, rocking into his thigh. Connor groans, his own cock grinding into Yates' leg. Yates' throat goes dry. Connor wants him, wants him right now, and Yates pushes his hand down between them, into Connor's pants, taking his hard, silky cock in his fingers. Connor ruts into his palm, a firm, demanding weight.

Why haven't they done this earlier? Why hasn't he dragged Connor deep into him? Why —

Connor was his *student*, and here Yates is, feeling him up, tasting him, fantasizing about riding him until he comes. What in the *blazes* is he thinking?

"No," he gasps, jerking back. Connor's limbs are wrapped around him, and Yates wants him far away, wants him off his ship. He shoves at Connor, trying to pry himself out of sheets and arms and legs. "Suck my — No. I didn't say that."

Connor glares, easing back, his chest heaving. "Two minutes ago, you would've begged for it."

He refuses to admit that Connor is right. Yates scrambles across the bed until his back hits the wall. His cock throbs. "We're heading back to Fort Bragg soon. Please stay on deck. I'll make breakfast."

Connor narrows his eyes. It's a relief to have him at a distance, even if Yates needs him far closer. Yates stares at the rumpled sheets, heart pounding. He needs to calm down. The pressure at his groin demands attention, and he grasps at the strands of his logic, trying to convince himself that straddling Connor is *not* the better option. Even when Connor's gaze trails over him, reading all the things he cannot hide.

Connor watches him for a moment longer before sighing. "Fine," he says, swinging his legs off the bed. He pauses for a heartbeat. "Who was Wesley?"

The buzzing clamor in his head muffles. Yates freezes, flashes of red hair and glowing runes and *death* ripping through his mind. He's never told Connor about Wesley. "How—How did you find that name?"

Connor shrugs, looking away. "I can have secrets too."

"You aren't supposed to know that," Yates says, wracking his mind. He's kept pictures of Wesley lying around, old letters tucked away in drawers. And the spellbook. Connor couldn't have found it... could he? Yates glances at the library, at the mess of books crammed on the shelves. His stomach plummets. The kraken must have shaken the book off the top shelf. "Tell me you didn't."

"I don't lie, Yates." Connor narrows his eyes. "What went wrong?"

Shame floods his cheeks, hot and damning. He never wanted Connor to learn about his failures. How much of *Death to Life* has he read? Where is it now? "Return that book."

Connor holds his gaze. "No. I want to know what you did wrong."

Yates stares at the worn flower print of the bed covers. He doesn't want to remember the revival. It floats to the top of his mind anyway, like a bloated corpse, and he sees the circles he's second-guessed repeatedly, the walls of complex runes he'd checked ten times over. He remembers the rabbit's fern spores and the twisted elk horn, the chilling green glow shining through chalk lines. Remembers fresh carcasses melting into pieces of bone, the shimmer of Wesley's body forming in the circles.

Wesley had returned for half a second, rising to his feet before his flesh sloughed off his face in chunks, like a cliff collapsing into the sea. The memory sends a surge of nausea through Yates' gut, dizzying and oily. He stumbles across the cargo hold, bends double over a bucket by the tub, and heaves out the contents of his stomach.

Connor drops to his knees next to him, brushing hair out of his face. "Shit. Yates. I'm sorry. I didn't—didn't think. I'm sorry."

Yates squeezes his eyes shut, struggling to breathe: one gulp of air, then another. This is pathetic. He can't even think about the revival without his body rebelling against him. Disgust wells in his stomach. Why would Connor stay for this? "Go away. Just go."

"I—I thought I could figure out what went wrong if I asked you." Connor leans in despite the smell, rubbing a soothing hand over his back. Yates doesn't deserve this kindness, doesn't deserve this patience. "I'm not gonna ask again. I don't have to know."

Yates shakes his head. Connor can't still be sitting next to him, even now. Yates is a failure of a student, a disappointment of a brother. Connor should be muttering like Quagmuth did, ready to turn away at Yates' smallest mistakes. He should hurt Yates like Yates has hurt him. And so Yates talks, because Connor needs to know how terrible a person he is. "Wesley... He was my brother, younger by a year. He drowned in the sea last century. I couldn't save him."

Connor tenses. "Oh."

"It's why I bury the bodies on the shore. To remember." Yates spits to rid the taste from his mouth, pushing the bucket aside. He shouldn't let Connor any closer. Should be pushing him away.

"But you can save them," Connor says, his hand moving in a slow circle on Yates' back. Then he pulls off, heading to the kitchen.

Yates concentrates on breathing, on where he is right now. He's in northern California, not the coast of Washington. He's at home, in his own ship. He has Connor with him. Things are okay.

When Connor returns with a mug of water, he says, "The kraken's the one killing those people. We can stop it, right?"

Yates accepts the water gratefully, leaning against the side of the bathtub. "There's no end to the krakens. If we kill this one, another will move in. They live in vast colonies further out in the ocean."

"There's more than one?" Connor winces, digesting the thought. "How do you know another will come? You've killed one?"

"I did." Yates doesn't want to think about it, but Connor should know the rest of the story. "I was having trouble with it—magic doesn't harm the kraken permanently. Wesley tried to help, firing heat spells from behind, but the kraken capsized his boat and pulled him under. I didn't see where he'd gone until it was too late."

"Fuck." Connor pulls him into a tight hug, and Yates allows himself a moment of comfort. Connor still isn't leaving. Yates needs him more than he's needed anything else, and Connor doesn't deserve to deal with the mess his ex-mentor is. Connor kisses his neck. It sends a thrill down his spine. "When I get stronger, I'll deal with this."

"Deal with what?"

"A better revival technique," Connor says. "There has to be one."

Yates tenses then, ice shooting down his nerves. He can't possibly be thinking about resurrection. "No. No, Connor. I've told you this before, and you know it. People can't be brought back to life."

"You can help me with it." Connor studies him, considering.

"No! You can't... can't be serious." But that's why Connor read that book, isn't it? Why he practiced the circles of three. Why his mother's ashes are on board with them. Connor's thinking of reviving his mother. Horror oozes up his throat. "No one has the power to bring something back to life."

Connor scowls. "Fine."

But it isn't fine. Connor has always had an interest in life magic. It's why he draws his runes with such familiarity now, even when Yates hasn't spoken to him in four years. "Please don't," Yates says, grabbing his arm. "If I couldn't do it, I don't think you can."

"It'll help people everywhere," Connor says. "It's not just for me. I figured... if it'll help other people hurt less..."

"We should let go of certain things in life," Yates says, his heart thudding slowly in his chest. How could he not have foreseen all this happening, teaching Connor through the years? "Death is a natural process. We cannot reverse it."

"Maybe you can't." Connor looks toward the library, his gaze contemplative.

It stings like a slap, and Yates bristles, anxiety sparking through his gut. He wishes he had enough energy to get up and hide the library from Connor. "We have to move on. Nothing ever stays the same. Don't you see?"

"Nothing stays the same? Like how you'll always be my mentor? I don't care if you don't teach me anything, Yates. I want more. So do you." Connor narrows his eyes, standing. He towers over Yates. "Listen to your own bullshit, and then tell me what to do."

Yates flinches. Connor turns on his heels, stalking toward the ladder, his footsteps thumping across the floorboards. He'll let go of this. They'll return to Fort Bragg, and then part ways.

It's the only solution Yates can think of at this point. He wishes he didn't regret it so much.

CONNOR STALKS around the deck for what feels

like an hour. The wizard consumes all his thoughts—Wesley, the revival, Yates throwing up at the thought of the resurrection.

Secretly, he's glad that Wesley wasn't a lover. That Yates hadn't spent so much effort trying to bring back someone he loved more than Connor, even if Connor knows he shouldn't worry about stupid things like that. It isn't as though Yates has agreed to be his lover, anyway.

But he hadn't expected Yates to bolt across the room, hadn't expected the terror in his eyes. It makes him want to hold the wizard close, protect him from his memories.

Yates loathes resurrections. Part of Connor has always wanted to bring his mother back. With the wizard so close, it's no longer a priority, but the thought nags at him when he needs a confidant. He needs to know that it's something he'll be able to do. If Yates has done research on it; Connor should be able to do the same.

He reaches into his pocket for some chalk, thinking about his father. If he brought his mother back, there wouldn't be space in his dad's life for her, and he can't do that to either of them. He doesn't even know if his dad is really okay. And if Dad is, he's going to be so damned worried about Connor disappearing. With a wince, Connor looks up, searching for land and a colorful speck in the distance.

The horizon is a flat, calm line to one side of the ship. On the other side, flat green land stretches down the coast, forest for miles on end. No town, no pastel houses beckoning him home. Connor checks the shoreline again. Fort Bragg is missing.

The coast shouldn't even be dipping inland. Another tidal wave? No, there would have been destruction left behind.

What the hell's going on? Connor strides along the railings, thinking. Then it strikes him, and he swears. They've been swept away by the ocean current.

He jogs back to the cabin, throwing its door open. "Yates," he says. "We drifted south along the coast. I don't know how far."

Below-deck, Yates curses. When he steps into view, he seems calmer than before, lips in a thin line. "We dropped the anchor, didn't we?"

"Yeah." Connor jogs to the bow of the ship. Most of the anchor chain is deployed; the windlass is near empty. But how can the ship drift, if they're anchored to the seabed? Connor pushes energy into his arms, grabs the windlass handle, and turns. The anchor chain reels in too easily, glinting steel rings hissing up over the railings with no resistance all. It isn't right. The anchor should be weighing it down. Connor pushes down on the handle, winding it faster.

The last of the chain arcs up, a silver snake clattering onto the deck, and Connor swears. The anchor is gone.

"Suck it," Yates says behind him. He strides to the side of the ship, gazing out over the sea. "How far did we drift?"

"Ship's moving at less than half a knot. If we sailed through the night, maybe ten miles down the coast. How did we even drift?" Connor thinks back to the night before, after he'd dropped the anchor. He knows these waters like he knows Yates—he's anchored the fishing boat a thousand times. The only difference... The ship had jolted last night. "That damned kraken! I thought it was leaving!"

"Maybe it was the other way around. Maybe the ship drifted away from it." Yates strides away, avoiding his gaze. "We'll sail to shore. From there, you can hitch a ride from the nearest town."

His stomach turns. Leaving Yates means he'll never see him smile again. "No. I'm not leaving."

Yates picks at his shirt hem. "Your father's still in Fort Bragg. Aren't you concerned?"

"Of fucking course I am," he snaps. Yates refuses to meet his eyes, and it hurts. "But I'm not leaving this ship, damn you."

The wizard sighs. "We'll have to drag it out of the current. I'm not sure I have the strength to get us all the way back to town."

"I'll help."

Yates hesitates, then nods. Looking at him, Connor feels a pang of sympathy; the wizard's belongings have shattered, his home washed out to sea. They can't return to Fort Bragg by tonight. Connor wants to stay close, lending warmth until he recovers.

They sit side-by-side on the deck, pushing energy through their palms into the propeller of the ship. It takes them two hours to coax the ship out of the current and turn it northward.

Three hours after that, Yates runs them aground further up the coast, on a beach with fir forests to either side. He turns and heads back to the cargo hold without a word. Connor wants to swear. He watches the wizard wistfully instead, his body aching and wrung of energy.

The man he loves is an idiot. They are both idiots.

25
Twenty-Three (Part VII)

FOUR DAYS later, they're halfway to Fort Bragg and still not talking. The food supplies have dwindled: the cake is gone, the potato baskets are empty, and they're starting to see the bottom of Yates' dried fish tub.

During the day, Connor casts fishing lines, snaring perch, trout, and snapper. At night, when Yates falls asleep, he pulls *Death to Life* from its hiding place, reading Yates' secret thoughts until his vision blurs.

Tonight, his mind lingers on *I wish Quagmuth were proud of me.* As Connor draws the largest chalk circles he can on the deck, he thinks about Yates trying to be a good teacher, trying to follow the rules he set for himself. Connor had no idea that Quagmuth was Yates' mentor — the name appeared in various texts, but he'd never connected them until he found *Death to Life* and seen Yates' fears scrawled in tiny words between large, bold print. How much has Quagmuth influenced him? Is this why he refuses to love Connor the way he wants to?

He shifts on his knees, throwing his drawing

arm out in an arc. White chalk runs stark against the shadowy planks. His circles aren't perfect. Neither are the lines joining them — is it four lines, or five? He frowns, keeping the concentric circles as close together as he can.

Overhead, lightning flashes in the purple-gray clouds, followed by a rumble of thunder. Connor barely glances up. Instead, he brings his lamp closer, leaning in to carve tiny runes on the deck. For a barrier wider than he is tall, how much magic would it contain? How strong would it be if it were six circles deep? Could he revive a fish? Could he trap the kraken?

He scribbles runes for *barrier* and *bind* and *life* between the circles, standing to assess its shape. The circles are lopsided, bumpy where the floorboards don't line up right. *Will this work?* He hasn't pushed magic through his recent circles, for fear of their power jolting Yates from sleep.

Connor kneels, imagining Yates in his past. How had he done the barrier for Wesley's revival? What had gone wrong?

With his brother gone, had Yates ached for some company? Because Connor damned well does, not talking to him. It hurts. Over the past few days, Yates has stared at his food at dinner, turned to the furthest end of the bed when Connor goes to sleep. He's kept to his side of the ship, repairing broken teapots and magnifying glasses as though Connor weren't on board.

It feels like he's nineteen all over again, Yates banishing him from his life like he doesn't fucking care. Connor misses the wizard, wishes he could touch Yates and hold him and tell him things will be fine. He wants someone to fill that space in his heart, someone he can rant to, who will listen with kind eyes and an easy smile. He wants a friend who won't ignore him, someone who will be *there,* like his dad or his mom.

Connor wants to talk to his mom suddenly, wants to hear the excitement in her voice when she asks about Yates. He wants to see her eyes sparkle, wants to see delight flood through her face when he introduces the wizard and says, *This is Yates. He taught me magic, and I love him.* She would hug Yates, welcome him to the family. She would appreciate all the things Connor likes about him.

His heart splinters, and the night's chill eats into his skin.

He has a book now, has instructions on how to draw the spell. Connor runs his hand along the ship's railings, the sturdy, dense frame of *lignum vitae*. The thunderclouds hang above, electricity sharp in the air, waiting for *something*.

A flare of hope unfurls in his chest. Connor's breath hitches. He flips the book open to the ten-circle barrier, scrubbing off the previous runes and adding another four circles. He needs the complex shapes, the herbs in Yates' lab. He needs a stick of *lignum vitae*.

The wind picks up around the ship. The waves crash harder on the shore, and Connor is glad that they've run aground for the night, so the storm waves will not wash them away. With most of the hull made of *lignum vitae*, the ship can withstand far greater impacts than the average boat would.

He hunches his shoulders and copies the runes in the book, his heart hammering in his ears. *This is stupid*. Yates will banish him if he discovers this, cut him off for years because he's an idiot. Connor doesn't want to hurt all over again. He hesitates, fingernail digging into chalk. Then, he finishes the first block of runes. *I can do this without you,* he thinks bitterly. *I don't need you for everything.*

Thunder roars overhead, and lightning bursts through the purple sky. Connor grits his teeth, hoping the sound doesn't wake the wizard. He hurries down the ladder with the lamp, gathering the spell ingredients: pike's tooth, bear's spleen, elfroot powder. He sets all the ingredients in two large mixing bowls from the lab, bites the lamp handle between his teeth, and climbs back upstairs.

A gale whips around him the moment he steps onto the deck. Powder from the bowls puffs up into his eyes, making them water. He swears. He sets the herbs and spellbook down in the cabin, then hurries back out to the circles. A raindrop patters on his arm.

He winces, holding the lamp up to scan the barrier. Did the rain erase any part of his spell? The lines sprawl out before him, too wide an area for him to inspect closely, so he sets a finger on the edge of the largest circle, sending a gentle pulse of magic through. The spell hums like a purring boat engine — still intact.

For a long moment, he stands still, listening. But the wizard doesn't climb through the trapdoor. He scatters the spell ingredients in the circle, making sure to keep pike's tooth on the edges of the innermost barrier to strengthen it, and bear's spleen scattered throughout to even the spread of energy.

He's ducking into the cabin for the other ingredients when the ship shudders and creaks, although they've already run aground. Thunder rumbles closer. Connor glances up, scanning the sea. Past the railings of the ship, waves churn along the shore, and only then does lightning explode through the sky.

A hulking shadow towers over the ship, three yards from the stern. Connor doesn't need light to identify it. Thick tentacles sweep slowly out of the water, mirroring the wicked, twisted horns protruding from the kraken's head, its maw gaping open.

"Shit," he whispers.

SLEEP EVADES Yates. The cargo hold yawns dark and empty around him, light bursting sporadically through the windows to illuminate the debris, and thunder vibrates through the ship.

He's been lying in bed for an hour, waiting for Connor. He shouldn't have let him share the space. Now that he knows Connor will return at some point, Yates wants him here, wants him closer. He should have spoken to Connor three days ago, four years ago, because he needs to hear his voice, but he can't. He shouldn't.

He groans, pulling the covers over his head. He has fantasized too much over the past week, about Connor's mouth on his, Connor cooking with him in the kitchen, Connor waking up with him in the mornings. His hand trailing down the smooth length of Connor's cock, guiding him inside. He shouldn't be thinking about any of this.

Thunder booms again, and it sounds more menacing, somehow.

"Shut up," Yates mumbles, burrowing his head under the pillow.

A jolt shudders through the ship.

He freezes then, listening. Where there was only calm before, a familiar, ominous darkness lurks. The kraken? But it never comes this close to shore, and it moves only when ships sail over its home. Yates frowns, setting a hand on the wall.

He feels a prickle of magic then, a faint tingle that fades away. Was that from Connor?

The ship vibrates. The dark presence creeps closer, and Yates swears, fumbling for a light. He can't see through the inky shadows. Connor is too far for him to protect, and the kraken has returned.

FIND A *weapon*. Connor ducks further into the cabin, its windows smashed. He doesn't have enough magic... but the ship does. The waves and the storm contain energy. A slim, flat stick catches his eye next to jagged glass, and he grabs it, pausing at its familiar weight. It's a wooden shaft bearing. In his mind, he sees tropical forests further south, large cats prowling between yellow-wood trees, mist sweeping through their canopies.

They insist Merlin's wand was made of this very wood, a voice in his head murmurs, and Connor tightens his fingers around the stick, heart galloping. He can do this. Yates has taught him how to wield his magic. Maybe not in the face of a creature standing three stories over him, but he can try.

Connor darts out of the cabin, dodging as a shoulder-wide tentacle whips over his head. Three inches lower, and it could have knocked him unconscious. *No time to worry.* As the kraken roars, he drops into a crouch, scratching out runes for *heat* and *knife*, then the directional arrows, to aim the energy at the beast. His chalk darts over the floorboards, weak taps next to the beast's roar. Will the spell work? Connor pushes magic through the runes. The lines glow bright blue, and heat blasts toward the creature, into the base of a limb.

The kraken bellows. A broad tentacle sails toward him. He throws himself to the side, swearing when more limbs swarm up around the ship. The tentacles constrict and bulge, and the ship lurches, creaking in protest. But the kraken stays uninjured. Simple runes will have no impact. He needs powerful shapes, but drawing them will leave him defenseless. Can he really defeat this monster?

The tip of a tentacle flies out from nowhere and lashes across his arm. His bicep throbs. He throws himself away from more whipping limbs, grimacing when the kraken heaves on the ship, shoving its stern down. He stumbles across the deck, his foot smudging the outer chalk circles. "Damn it!"

The kraken releases the ship. The hull crashes back onto the sandy shore. Below deck, crockery smashes, time and effort nullified at the creature's whim.

Furious, Connor kneels. He can't let this beast

wreck Yates' home a second time. His chalk scrapes against the floorboards. He needs energy to defeat the kraken, something that will pierce its chest. What if he traps it within the barrier? The runes for resurrection are already there. Would they create another monster?

A sweeping tentacle swipes at him before he can complete the spell. Connor swears and ducks, his heart pounding when air rushes over his back, the limb missing him by inches. He finishes the circle, an imperfect arc. It's not ready.

When the tentacle comes swooping back, Connor throws himself to the side. The limb thumps solidly in the middle of the barrier, smudging chalk. *No time.*

Connor drops to his knees, slams his palms on the floorboards, and pushes magic through all ten circles.

26
Twenty-Three (Part VIII)

A SHADOW sweeps past Yates' window, and only then does he realize how very close the beast is. He should have noticed it sooner. Thunder rumbles. A shudder runs through the ship again, then another, and another. Then the ship cants forward, throwing him over in bed, and Yates' stomach plummets when the ship crashes back down, plates shattering in the cargo hold.

He leaps out of bed, feet skidding on a pile of sharp clay shards, and swears, wobbling through the darkness. Where's the lamp? He stumbles to the wall, feeling around for a sconce. All he finds is smooth paneling.

With a grimace, he draws the rune for *light* on his palm, wincing when it burns his skin. But golden light gleams from the rune, and Yates holds it above his head, hurrying through the cargo hold. Connor knows better than to aggravate the kraken. The beast roars. Yates scrawls the runes on his throat to listen, his pulse racing.

"Foolish human," the kraken snarls. *"You think you can lure me close with magic."* The ship shudders with each slamming tentacle, and Yates swears,

hooking his hands on the ladder rungs. Was Connor baiting it? *"You dare threaten me with your spell, weakling? You worthless fool — "*

Magic flares to life above, a pulse of taut energy that crashes through the ship like a tidal wave. The force of it punches the breath from his lungs, leaves the taste of ozone bitter on his tongue. What is Connor doing? What kind of — What can possibly thrum like a circle of ten? Horror curls through his veins. Connor has been reading *Death to Life.* It *is* a ten-circle spell. There's a blazing ten-circle spell on his ship, and *Connor* activated it.

"No," Yates breathes, ice spiking through his chest. He knows that spell. They don't have the resources to sustain it, and it will drain all the magic it needs. "Connor, no."

ON THE deck, an unearthly green brilliance sears through the outermost circle. The next circle begins to glow, then the next, until the ten-circle barrier banishes the shadows on the entire deck. Then, the glow sweeps into the runes, blocks of spellwork lighting up one by one.

Pain spears through Connor's arms. His magic pours out of him, torn from beneath his skin like ripping fabric, and he doubles over, agony crackling through his nerves, down into his ribs. His ears buzz. He can't breathe, can't move. His limbs hang weakly from his body.

The kraken slams its trapped tentacle down, dragging it against the invisible barrier. Its other tentacles squirm across the deck, pushing the kraken away from the stern, but the barriers cage its limb within. *Shit, it worked.* And as Connor gasps in pain, the skin on the trapped tentacle begins to peel. Maroon muscles gleam beneath leathery skin. The beast bellows. A spike of blackened flesh pushes out of the broken hide, one tapered rod at first, until it begins to split at the ends, like the skeleton of a tree reaching toward the sky.

Connor's mind whirls. How the fuck did that happen? How does a charred tree grow from a kraken? But none of its other tentacles are cracking, only the one in the circle. It's the damned revival spell doing this. The branches of the tree spread out, scraping against the wall of the innermost barrier.

This isn't supposed to happen.

The kraken shrieks, its grating cry piercing his ears. Connor tugs on his magic. He has to fight the creature some other way, not with a spell gone wrong. Is this what the revival spell actually is? Would this happen to his mother's ashes?

He can't pull his hands off the deck. Horror claws up his throat. He tenses his arms, concentrating on the thrum of his energy in the circles. But magic rips out of his body, tearing from his feet and stomach and skin, and it feels like there's a beast inside him, shredding his insides open.

Connor coughs, yanking uselessly on his arms. He has to get the kraken away from the ship. The life in his body washes out like the tide, and he can't breathe. He sways on his arms, his vision fading around the edges. He's going to die. He hasn't even said goodbye to Yates.

I've disappointed you, he thinks, dizzy and sick with dread. Crestfallen blue eyes flash through his mind. He should have listened to Yates. Shouldn't have doubted him. Shouldn't have thought he could walk away from this unscathed, when Yates has tried and failed. He should have spent more time with the wizard, teased laughter from him, held him close and told him how important he is.

Something flickers to his side: a flash of red hair. The kraken thrashes around the ship, its limbs flailing, and all Connor can see is the ground slanting closer, Yates face hovering above his. He sees the whites of Yates' eyes, the way his lips move soundlessly.

"Sorry," Connor mutters, before the world around him goes dark.

YATES BURSTS through the trapdoor. The kraken bellows, its words dissolving into screeches of agony.

Past the cabin doorway, radiant green light burns from ten imperfect, concentric circles, pulsing with malignant energy. Within, a tentacle flails, cracking, blackened flesh growing from its skin like a parasite. Yates stops breathing. In his own circles, bodies had fallen apart, stayed dead. None grew inexplicable projections from their own limbs.

Had Connor done that? Does he know that the ten circles require a base amount of energy? They'll siphon magic from the spell-caster first, and Yates can feel the ship brimming with life beneath his feet, can feel the electric sharpness of the approaching storm. The circles aren't connected to either. They're sucking energy from Connor like a dry sponge, strengthening the barriers around the kraken's limb.

Ice in his chest, Yates bursts out of the cabin, glancing around. He needs to halt the spell. Connor slumps to the side, gasping, his skin pale. The faint heat of his magic flickers.

He has a minute to live, maybe. One minute, and Connor will be dead, gone, and Yates won't see him grin ever again. His throat closes. He can't breathe. Can't think. He can't lose this man.

Yates ducks from the twisting tentacles, falling to his knees next to Connor. Connor's chest barely rises, and it makes his heart constrict. The magical drain must stop. But there's no way to halt the flow until the spell takes what it requires, and it *will not* take Connor from him.

"Connor," he cries, grasping his shoulders. "Hold on!"

Connor stares up at him, his eyes glazed over. Yates sets a trembling hand to his neck, feels his weak, fluttering pulse. *No time for chalk.*

Yates pushes energy through his fingertip, scrawling runes into the floorboard to change the flow of magic. There's plenty of life magic in the ship. He can lose his home, but not Connor. His fingers tremble and fly over wood, and halfway through the spell, the air around them prickles. Rain patters down.

He completes the final rune. The circles begin to draw energy from the ship, turning the floorboards a dull gray. He snatches the stick of *lignum vitae* from Connor's hand, throws his arm into the air. Yates pushes energy into wood to charge it, and all he can think is *Please don't die. Please stay with me. I need you so much.*

Lightning crashes down a heartbeat later, lighting the grotesque countenance of the kraken: dripping beard, beady eyes, spiny teeth. Energy scorches into the shaft bearing in Yates' hand: powerful, blazing, *alive.* He plunges the stick into the outermost circle, shoves his own magic through wood to discharge it. In the next second, the ten circles rip the energy from the shaft bearing and the ship, and a good half of Yates' magic along with it, as though it's tearing his soul right out of his body.

Then, the magic stops flowing. The link between Connor and the circle dwindles and snaps. Connor slumps. Pain sluicing through his body, Yates lurches under the flailing tentacles and staggers back to him, collapsing to his knees. Life flickers in Connor, a barely-there flame that makes Yates' breath catch. He's alive.

He draws a barrier around them, his fingers shaking, then draws a second one because he can't draw a blazing *circle* right. Connor's barely hanging on and he—he needs to calm down. Needs to secure a space for them first.

Yards away, the kraken jerks and roars, its bloodied tentacle thumping behind the ten-circle barrier, its trapped limb blackened and encased in a web of spines, and all Yates can see is Connor.

He flattens his palm against Connor's chest, feels the flutter of his heart, the erratic flicker of his magic. Then, he pushes his own gently forward, teasing it against Connor's, until it melds with the edges of his magic and sighs into his body. This wouldn't be possible if they weren't close, if Connor's magic hadn't spent years adjusting to his.

For minutes, Connor stays pale, his breathing shallow. He can't die. Yates' heart thumps slow with dread, and he pushes his magic steadily into Connor, feeling it seep into his heart, into his chest and arms and legs.

Connor draws a deeper breath. His cheeks gain color as Yates' magic flows into his veins, and Yates presses their foreheads together, hot tears welling in his eyes. Connor will be okay. He'll live through this, and Yates will see him smile another day, hopefully for the rest of his life.

"Hey," he whispers, wrapping a shaky arm around him. Connor is alive. His voice breaks. "Connor."

Slowly, he slides a hand under Connor's back, heaving him close. Connor's eyes are shut, dark lashes fluttering against his cheek, his skin smudged with herbs and chalk. Yates sucks in a slow breath, just watching his chest rise and fall, his magic still trickling into Connor's body.

Across the deck, the energy in the circles fades. The binding spell breaks. The kraken roars in agony, its limb trembling and blackened, and Yates can only wince as it shudders, heaving itself back into the sea. In moments, it disappears under the waves, leaving the night sky open once more.

"I'm sorry," Yates whispers. Both to the kraken, and to Connor. He stops the energy transfer when his magic burns brighter in Connor's body than his own, and leans in close, hugging Connor to himself. "I'm glad you're alive."

Connor doesn't answer. But he breathes, safe in Yates' arms, and Yates can't ask for more.

In the pouring rain, he smooths Connor's hair away from his face, brushing a kiss over his forehead. It's taken him Connor almost dying to realize what he wants, what he isn't willing to lose. Whoever he was before this—Quagmuth's student, Connor's mentor, an abject failure—it no longer matters. He can't deny this bond anymore.

And so he has an answer for Connor when he wakes. He can only hope that Connor will feel the same.

27
Twenty-Three (Part IX)

WHEN CONNOR opens his eyes, it takes him long seconds to remember where he is. Faint light shines through the portholes above. Shadows cluster around him: across the rafters, along the wood-plank walls, darker to one side of the sprawling room.

He's in the cargo hold, in Yates' bed. Yates' rosemary scent lingers in the warm covers around him, like an embrace, and it feels like home.

"You're awake," Yates murmurs, looking up from the bedside table. Connor glimpses a half-mended hourglass on the table's surface and the chalk circle around it. But that's not important, when Yates sits in a chair just a few inches away, blue eyes lit by a lamp on the wall. Connor's heart quickens. "How do you feel?"

He clears his throat, testing his body. His limbs move easily, though they're a little bruised, and — the kraken. What happened last night? Is the ship damaged? "'M fine," he says. He pushes himself upright. "Kraken was here. I couldn't stop it."

"Don't worry about it." Yates sets a firm hand

on his shoulder, easing him back down.

The covers slip a little, over his bare pectorals, and only then does Connor realize he's dressed in just his underwear. He glances down, then at Yates. A hint of red sweeps through the wizard's cheeks. He turns to fiddle with the hourglass. Connor can count five times he's seen him blush, and it makes him want to pull Yates close.

"You were covered in powders and brine. I thought I'd clean you up, see if you were injured." Yates nudges the glass pieces around on the table. Then he sighs, handing over a mug of water. Connor props himself up on an elbow and drains it all. "But we'll have to talk about last night."

He winces. It's not as though he can keep his research from Yates forever, especially after that ten-circle spell. And because it's so unlike Yates to discuss resurrection, Connor doesn't try to change the subject. "I slept through the night?"

"And most of the day. It's evening now." Yates glances at the window. "While you were unconscious, I sailed us back up north. Fort Bragg is still intact—people are moving about in town. I think your father is fine."

Relief filters through his body. Connor sags back into the pillows, exhaling. Whether the townsfolk are fine because of their spell, or because the rocks around town weakened the waves, he doesn't know. It doesn't matter, though. His dad is fine. Sheila too, probably. And maybe he's kind of glad that Sheila is around with his father, providing the support that Connor was never able to. "Okay."

Yates reaches over, pressing his fingertips to

Connor's neck to take his pulse. "We should probably return soon. I think they'd be worried about you."

"Yeah, well." Connor doesn't know about seeing Sheila again, but he should check in with his dad. *He's probably damned worried.* "Today?"

"Tomorrow, I think." Yates doesn't pull his hand away. Instead, he brushes his knuckles along Connor's jaw, tracing up along his ear.

Connor shivers. Yates has never done this before, has never just *looked* at him, eyes soft, his lips curved in a wistful smile. It makes his heart pound. "What are we doing tonight?"

"We'll talk tonight." Yates licks his lips, his gaze darting to the bed. "And maybe... Well, we need to talk. About the circle of ten."

Connor grimaces. Yeah, he shouldn't have done that. He had no idea those circles would anchor him down, drag his magic out of his body. For painful, terrifying minutes, he had thought he was going to die right there, on the deck of Yates' ship. "I won't do it again."

Yates' fingers still midway through a caress. "Why? I thought... I'm not saying I approve, but you did always want to bring your mother back, didn't you?"

"It's not right," he says, remembering split flesh and growing black spikes. If that was what Yates had seen when he'd tried to revive his brother, Connor can understand why he'd thrown up. "I know why you're against it now."

Skin itching from just lying down, he pushes himself into a sitting position, running his fingers through his hair. Yates' attention flickers to his arms, then his chest.

"I just... don't want to see my mom like that." The urn still sits by the library shelves, anchored to the floor with runes. His stomach had turned when he watched the kraken's tentacle mutate. Yates reaches over, setting his hand in his. Connor curls his fingers around Yates', rubbing his thumb over his skin. "Anything can go wrong and she'll... I can't do that to her. I mean, that wasn't a complete spell, but the risks are too high. I can't bring her back and die doing it. I can't desecrate her ashes. It's stupid."

Yates' gaze drifts into the distance. "I did everything right," he murmurs. "He fell apart anyway."

Connor squeezes his hand. It isn't enough to break him from the memory, so he shuffles further along the headboard, patting the mattress next to his thigh. Yates stares. "C'mon," Connor says. "Don't make me wait."

The wizard chuckles. He rises from his chair, crawls onto the bed, and Connor slips an arm around his waist, leaning in to nuzzle his ear. Yates shivers. But he stays, his warmth seeping into Connor's side. This is new. Yates hasn't accepted affection like this before. "So... you no longer want the revival spell," Yates says. He sets his hand carefully over Connor's leg, on top of the bed covers. "What will you do now?"

"I have to let my mom go." Connor hasn't had the chance to think about it. The moment the words leave his lips, though, he knows it's the right decision. The thought of never seeing his mom again hurts, like he's giving up on a childhood dream. "I can't... hold on to her and hope she'll return."

"You have me." Yates looks down. "I'm here."

He can't hear past the blood rushing in his ears. "Really?"

Yates nods, his fingers curling into the covers, soft points of pressure on Connor's thigh. "You almost—You almost died last night." Yates sucks in a slow breath, then releases it. "I can't... I don't want to regret. There are voices in my head that say it's wrong, and I hear them all the time."

"Quagmuth?" Connor curls his fingers around Yates' hand, lifting it to kiss his knuckles. Yates still hasn't fled. It speaks of a new, precious thing between them, something that steals the breath from his lungs.

Yates sighs. "I guess you've read about that. Yes. He... I was never good enough. Did you know? I was so amazed when you became my student, because I believed that I'd failed his teachings all along."

"You need to let that go," Connor says, meeting his eyes. "I'll love you no matter what."

Yates' mouth falls open. Tears well in his eyes, and Connor releases his hand to hold his face. It takes Yates a few moments to find his voice. "Why... Why would you love me? I've hurt you. I've been such a coward, Connor."

Slowly, he says, "You're the only person I ever wanted."

Yates breathes in sharply. Connor shifts on the mattress to face him, brushing the tears from his eyes. It's the truth. He's known this for years, has hidden it in his heart. It's a relief to say it now, a secret finally out in the open. Yates leans in, and Connor kisses him gently on the lips. His mouth is soft and pliant, his breath brushing warm on his skin. It feels *right.*

"You're everything to me," Connor says, even though it's cheesy as hell. It's what he feels. "You were my best friend. You were there for me, Yates, even if you were a bastard the past four years."

Yates flinches, lowering his gaze. "I guess I was afraid. And confused."

He holds his breath. "Are you still...?"

The wizard shakes his head, the teardrops on his eyelashes catching the lamplight. "No. I don't want to regret letting you go. I have to be brave. Quagmuth may have been my mentor, but he's gone, and I'm not answerable to him. I trust this feeling in my heart."

Connor leans in, tracing Yates' bottom lip with his thumb. He needs Yates to be sure about this. For so long, he's been selfish, wanting Yates to love him, even forcing him into a decision to gain his touch. But Yates' choice weighs as much as his own, and it's something he's learned not to manipulate. "What feeling?"

"I love you," Yates whispers, taking Connor's hand and setting it on his chest, where his heart beats against Connor's skin. "I'm not running anymore, Connor. I'm yours to have."

It feels like Connor's chest is too small for his heart when he leans in, kissing him hard. "Love you," he murmurs. "Thank you."

28
Twenty-Three (Part X)

YATES BLINKS away his tears. Connor accepts him despite what he's done. Connor's moving on from his past. Connor's mouth is on his, hot and hungry, his callused hand slipping under Yates' shirt, sliding up his stomach to his ribs.

"Been waiting," Connor whispers against his lips, pushing his tongue inside. Yates groans, sucking on him until Connor cups his ass, heaving him up and forward. Yates sprawls onto his lap in a mess of limbs, his thighs spreading as Connor drags him close.

His fingers dart over Connor's tanned skin, the broad spread of his shoulder blades, the curves of his biceps, the discs of his nipples. Yates doesn't remember how long he's wanted this, how many times he's imagined touching him. Having him to himself. Connor licks slowly into his mouth, and Yates doesn't want to know where he learned to kiss. Instead, he slides their tongues together, then nuzzles along Connor's jaw, the musk of sweat faint on his skin.

And there's so much skin: the smooth expanse of his chest, the flat muscles of his abdomen, the sprawl of his thighs. Yates kisses down his throat. Connor's pulse flutters against his tongue, quickening when Yates grinds into him. Connor pushes him backward, pins him to the bed, one heavy hand sliding between his legs.

"Missed tasting you," he growls against Yates' throat, squeezing his balls through his clothes, and Yates is already hard, pushing up into the heat of his hand.

"Tasting me where?" he gasps, leaning close to lick down his chest. Connor's groan rumbles against his lips. With deft fingers, he undoes Yates' pants and tugs them off his legs so his cock springs free, jutting up between them. Connor glances down. It makes Yates shiver, having him stare at his arousal. But he parts his legs wider, inviting, and Connor ducks his head, lapping over his tip. Pleasure unfurls through his nerves like a bird's wings. Yates swears, rocking up, pushing into his mouth. Connor takes him halfway in, hot and wet, and Yates forgets to breathe. "You're—you're impatient. I thought you would have... gone slow."

Connor laps around his head, tongue flicking against Yates' slit, and Yates arches off the bed. "This is slow," Connor says, pulling away by a hairsbreadth, dragging his lips down Yates' cock. The light pressure isn't enough. He grinds his cock over Connor's mouth, trying to tempt him into more. "Or do you want it slower?"

Yates squirms. "This is too slow!"

But all Connor does is kiss his way down to Yates' balls, sniffing at his skin. Heat creeps up Yates' cheeks. He wants to taste Connor, wants him sucking on his cock, wants too many things to put them all into words.

"Suck it," he hisses. "Connor."

Connor smirks. "You sure?" he asks, pushing Yates' legs flat against the bed, kissing along his inner thigh instead, his stubble scraping Yates' skin. "You're not just swearing?"

"Suck—Oh, blazes, Connor," he mutters, rocking his hips, feeling so very exposed. Connor looks appreciatively at the way his cock jumps, before dropping kisses on Yates' knee. "Please!"

"Fine," Connor says, nipping at his skin, up his thigh. Then he takes Yates' tip back into his mouth, sucks on him, slow and languid, rubbing his palm under Yates' balls, until Yates pulses, his legs trembling, his cock so taut it aches.

"I need—" he gasps, hips rocking up, his cock leaking into Connor's mouth.

Connor pulls away. Wipes off his glistening lips with the back of his hand, and Yates cries out in frustration, reaching down to seek his release. Connor grabs his wrists, pins them to the bed. Yates whines. He bucks his hips, trying to grind his cock on something, anything. But Connor leaves his cock pulsing and bereft of touch. The wave of urgent need passes. He bristles, panting, his body tense with arousal.

The moment Connor releases him, Yates lunges up, grabbing his shoulders and shoving him down until his back hits the mattress. Connor's eyebrows dart up. But his mouth curls into a knowing smirk, and Yates glares, straddling his waist. He's wanted to see Connor beneath him for years, see this beast of a man pinned beneath him, his strength caught in Yates' control.

Watching him, Yates shrugs out of his shirt. Connor's gaze wanders down his chest, to his abdomen and his flushed, dripping cock. It makes him tremble with anticipation. He sits on the hard line of Connor's boxers, grinding down, groaning at the press of Connor's cock against his ass. Connor growls beneath him, rocking upward.

The idea flickers into his mind. Yates leans forward, capturing one of Connor's hands, before pinning it above his head. He pushes magic into his fingertip, burning first a circle, then runes for a binding spell into the mattress. Then, he snares Connor's other wrist, shoves both his hands within the circle, and activates the spell.

Connor tugs on his wrists. When they don't budge, he barks a laugh, watching Yates. "You kinky little bastard."

"I'm not little," Yates says. He has Connor pinned beneath him, all six feet of his muscular frame, and it makes his pulse race. Yates slips his fingers into the waistband of Connor's underwear, pulling it down so his cock juts free, thick and damp. It makes his mouth go dry.

Yates straddles him again, pushing their bare cocks together like Connor did four years ago, and Connor's eyes darken, his lips curving up.

"It'll be different this time," Yates whispers.

"Yeah?"

He slides their cocks together, feeling the hot length of Connor's cock, the way it jumps against his own, heavy and hard, smearing his wetness between their skin. Connor's breath hitches. Yates smiles.

But that isn't all he wants from the spell. He

climbs off Connor's hips, flings his boxers onto the floor, and binds Connor's ankles to the bed. Connor strains at his wrists, muscles flexing.

"I have plans," Yates says, settling between his legs. Connor grins, handsome and perfect, and Yates leans in first, kissing his forehead, then his eyelids, and the tip of his nose. When he seals their mouths together, slow and lingering, Connor parts his lips for him, his tongue sliding against Yates'. He shivers at its intimacy. He's always wanted this, and Connor has always been so willing to give this to him. And they're here now, pressed skin to skin, and Connor watches him with those hungry eyes, full of love and anticipation.

Yates kisses him sweet and slow on his lips. Then he moves down, dropping kisses along Connor's chest, sucking on his hard nipples, then down the fine line of hair between his abs. Connor's breath hitches. When he reaches Connor's cock, he sniffs at it first, enjoying its musk, the way it jumps. He's wanted this for too long, wanted to taste his skin.

He plays with Connor then, sucking on him steady and slow, flicking his tongue over the sensitive spot just beneath the head. Connor swears, his breathing growing ragged as Yates teases him, until sweat prickles along his groin, and his thighs tremble. Yates pulls away from his cock with a wet *pop*, a trail of slick stretching between Connor's tip and his mouth.

Connor's hips snap up, his cock flushed with need. "Fuck!"

Yates pushes him back onto the mattress, grinning when he glares. "I said it would be different."

"Damn you," Connor says, thrusting up. Yates kisses his tip.

He blows on Connor's cock with puffs of hot breath, sliding his fist down around it, then up again. Connor gasps. He fucks up into Yates' hand, leaving a smear of wet, the head of his cock pushing slickly out of his grasp, and Yates pulls away. Connor swears. And Yates does it again: lapping around his head, sucking on his balls, one thumb stroking his too-sensitive tip, until Connor roars, his body taut, and Yates relaxes his grip. Teases him again.

Connor thrashes in his bindings, sweat gleaming on his body, his cock standing thick and red. He watches Yates with predatory eyes, arms straining so hard that the heavy mattress beneath them groans and bends under his frustration.

"I should set you free," Yates says, his voice rasping with hunger, his ass aching to be filled. He rests one hand on Connor's ankle, where the magical binding is. "What would you do?"

"Fuck you through the bed," Connor growls, yanking on his restraints again. Yates throbs, hearing that. He craves it. Has been craving it the whole time he kept Connor hovering at the edge. So he straddles his chest, rubs the tip of his cock on Connor's lips while he reaches into the bedside drawer for some sunflower oil.

Connor takes him into his mouth, touches him with the point of his tongue, sucks on him light and slow. Yates almost drops the vial. And Connor smirks, pushing his tongue under his skin, licking around his tip. He parts his lips, and Yates sees the way his skin clings to Connor's tongue, trapping him right against the tip of his cock, and Connor pushes his skin down with his lips, exposing his ruddy head. Pleasure whispers through his body, and Yates shivers, his thighs weak. His tip skims along Connor's lips, and he rolls his hips forward, filling Connor's mouth with his cock just to see himself inside Connor, just to see Connor taking his cock, his lips wrapped around it. Connor groans, and Yates' breath shudders out of him.

Connor sucks on him, lightly at first, and Yates' thighs shake. Then he hollows his cheeks, and Yates almost comes right then, his cock throbbing hard, his balls tight.

When he pulls away, he leaves a trail of wetness between Connor's lips and his cock. Connor looks up at him, his pupils dilated, and Yates gulps. He pours oil onto his palm and slicks Connor with it, from his base to his tip. It makes Yates shiver, just feeling the heat of that cock in his palm, the heft of it. He wants Connor inside, has craved for him for years.

He releases all four bindings.

With a bellow, Connor rears up like a beast, toppling Yates onto the bed. He pins him down with an arm across his chest, grinding his cock against Yates', rough and demanding, pushing Yates' cock right against his abdomen. It sends a thrill shooting through him; Connor bares his teeth. Then, he points his cock down, sliding between Yates' cheeks to spread them. He gasps. Connor pushes against his hole, and Yates feels every blunt, solid stroke.

So he ruts back at Connor, spreads his legs

open. With a groan, Connor splashes oil onto his fingers, slicks them up, and pushes two into Yates. The intrusion is sudden but welcome, opening him up, and Yates throws his head back, tugging on Connor's hips to pull him closer. Then those fingers crook inside him, and pleasure jolts through his body, yanking the breath from his lungs.

Connor leans over him, arms on either side of Yates' head, and kisses him hungrily, sliding into his mouth, the point of his cock dragging a line up Yates' stomach. Yates moans, sucks on his tongue. It draws a low rumble from Connor's throat, makes him drag his hand down Yates' abdomen, push his fingers deep into his ass. His fingers curl and slide inside, circles his prostate until he jerks and shudders, grinding down on it with his fingers, nudging at it. Pleasure hums in his body. Yates mewls, rocking up at him, his cock dribbling shamelessly at the torment.

He whines when Connor pulls his fingers out. He needs him inside, needs to be ridden hard. Connor kisses him again, pushes his wet, blunt tip against his hole, nudging at it until Yates opens for him, and he slides in slow and deep. Yates groans, his body stretching around him, taking him in. Connor thrusts in shallowly, his breathing restrained, as though he's trying to hold himself back. "Fuck," he whispers, rocking into Yates. Yates feels every inch, feels him *inside,* and that's all he wants right now. "You're tight."

"Haven't had anyone in a while," Yates pants. Connor's eyes gleam. "Go harder. I want you."

And Connor's restraint breaks. He plunges into Yates, hard and fast, sending jolts of pleasure through his body. Yates grasps at the sheets, trying to hang on. But he can't, when all he can feel is Connor inside him, a welcome, forceful heat. Connor kisses him sloppily, panting against his lips, filling him with every stroke, sinking to the hilt.

Connor wraps a hand around his cock. He slides Yates' skin down his tip, exposing him, and Yates thrusts messily into his hand, overwhelmed by Connor on him and in him and around him. Connor's cock grinding up against his prostate, sending jolts through his body. Connor's hand squeezing around him, his cock sinking home.

Pleasure crashes through Yates' body, his back arching and his toes curling, breath caught in his lungs. He comes all over his own chest, streaks of white smearing between them, and Connor swears. His strokes turn erratic. His hips snap sharply forward, and he roars, burying himself deep inside Yates, spilling into him.

When their panting evens out, Connor pulls away, rolling onto his side. But he doesn't leave, instead draping a sweaty arm across Yates' waist, dragging his nose along his shoulder. Yates sighs and leans in, his limbs loose, his mind hazy. "That was good," he mumbles. "I've been needing that for years."

"Yeah?" Connor draws him closer, until they're pressed skin to skin, a mess of fluids between them. "For years?"

It seems like such a pointless ordeal when he thinks back on their history, on all the years of aching and separation. Yates buries his face in Connor's shoulder. He's been such an idiot. "Don't make fun of me. I know."

Instead of a gibe, Connor kisses his temple, then his ear. "Glad you're here now. I've been waiting a while."

"You're so much more than I deserve," Yates whispers, sliding his palm over Connor's damp hip, relishing his proximity.

He never truly believed that Connor would forgive him for sending him away all those years ago. He's broken his trust, and Connor had simmered with fury. Now, Connor cradles him against his chest, his chin tucked over Yates' head, and it feels as though something has quieted in his heart.

"I'm... still not sure what to think of all this," he says. "It feels like I've maybe raised you somehow."

"Maybe. But you were also my best friend. I want us to be best friends again." Connor pulls away to meet his eyes. A hint of uncertainty lingers in his gaze; it makes Yates' breath catch. He needs to stop making Connor doubt himself. Needs to stop dragging Connor through all his problems. Connor squeezes his flank. "I want to be in your life again. I want... everything. You."

"And I'm here," Yates says. He slips his fingers into Connor's hand, coaxing a trickle of magic into his skin. Connor's eyes widen. But he accepts it, taking Yates' magic into his body. Then, he pushes back with some of his own, his energy a dancing warmth sliding under Yates' skin. Yates smiles. "I promise I'll always be here."

Connor presses his forehead to Yates' with a sigh. "Thank you."

"Thank *you*. For showing me that I don't... don't have to be what someone else thinks I am. Thank you for waiting. For loving me." It resonates in Yates' chest as he says it, and it makes gratitude and relief well up in his throat.

Connor brushes callused fingers over his cheek. "You've always deserved it," he says. "You just needed to believe it yourself."

If Connor can see something worthwhile in him, and if he trusts in Connor's judgment, then he should believe that, too. Yates leans into Connor's chest, taking comfort in his heat and safety. "I love you."

Connor hugs him close, his eyes warm. "Love you, too."

29
Twenty-Three (Part XI)

"I WANT you to meet my dad," Connor says as they descend from the ship, splashing through shallow waves onto the shore. Above, the sun crawls ever higher in the sky, lighting the eroded beach. Connor stretches his arms over his head, breathing in briny air. He's glad to have land beneath his feet again. "He mentioned having dinner with you."

Yates catches up with him on the sand. "You've talked about me?"

He rolls his eyes, wondering if his dad still remembers Yates. He hasn't mentioned the wizard in years, and now... this. They've made up. They've more than made up. So much has happened over the past few days. "Yeah. I used to talk about you all the time."

"Oh." The wizard blushes.

In the distance, the cormorants soar on an updraft, unconcerned by the destruction of the tidal wave. It feels as though he and Yates have been sailing for weeks instead of days. Right now, Connor doesn't know what he'll do after this. Before the tidal wave, he'd been fishing with his dad every morning. Having Yates back in his life doesn't change that. But Yates trails behind on the shore, a wrinkle on his brow. Connor hesitates. He hadn't thought that Yates might regret this. "You're going to be part of my family, right?"

The wizard slows to a halt on wet sand, red flooding his cheeks. "It hadn't occurred to me. Being part of your family," he says, wringing his hands. "I guess I've been living alone for too long." Yates catches the expression on his face, shaking his head. "No, no. Please don't misunderstand. I think... Well, I know we'll get along fine if we married. I've seen the pastor at the church marrying men before. It's unusual and not legally binding, but still very nice of him. It's just... me having relatives again."

It's been less than a day since they first made love on Yates' bed, and perhaps it's too soon to talk about marriage. They've been apart four years. But Connor can't see wanting anyone else more than the wizard, even after all this time. "So you'll marry me?"

"If you'll have me." Yates dips his chin, suddenly shy, and Connor can't help the rush of relief and affection in his chest.

"Yeah. I'll have you for the next three centuries." He grins as he says it, his heart thumping when a tiny, disbelieving smile grows on Yates' face.

"What happens after three centuries?"

"We'll get married again."

Yates laughs, his eyes gleaming with delight. "We'll need rings," he says. He can't stop smiling. "Any sort. But I prefer simple ones."

"There should be a jeweler open in town. We'll go after we see how my dad's doing. And Sheila—that's her name. Dad's wife." Connor quells the slight discomfort that whispers in his mind. He shouldn't have walked out so soon after the ceremony. But he doesn't regret it, when it's brought him back to Yates.

Yates nods. He drifts closer to Connor as they stroll along the shore, tangling their fingers together. "Okay. So we'll get rings. Remember how we met around here? Oh, heavens. That was a while ago."

"A damned long time ago," Connor says. "Thirteen years."

"I guess that's not such a long time." Yates surveys the beach, his gaze lingering on the driftwood and seaweed strewn everywhere. The sand dunes are gone, and most of the cemetery mounds have flattened. Further in the forest, he glimpses clumps of seaweed around the firs.

"It's long when you've only been alive twenty-three years."

"You're so young," Yates murmurs, his shoulders sagging. "They call people like me cradle robbers."

Connor glares. "Don't say that. 'Sides, you look about as old as me."

"I guess." The wizard glances away, lifting Connor's hand to kiss his fingertips.

Connor leads them onward. He can't change the difference in their ages, but he's willing to help Yates think better of himself, no matter how long it'll take.

In town, sand and rocks pepper the roads,

scattered across streets and boulevards. Puddles stretch through the intersections, spray scattering across the sidewalks when cars roll through them. But the buildings are intact, watermarks a few feet high, and little has been washed away. Connor keeps his hand firmly in Yates'. Not much has changed. The people in town stroll by the shops, drive off in their cars, and no one gives them a second look. After a while, Yates relaxes.

Connor slows when he approaches his father's house, its pastel-blue siding familiar and strange at the same time. It's not exactly home anymore. Dad lives with Sheila there, and he doesn't want to stay with them. He wants to be home with Yates in the ship, deep in the forest where it's just the two of them.

He presses the doorbell.

The conversation trickling through the windows cuts off. There's a pause, and footsteps sound from inside. The door pulls open.

"Connor!" his dad says, tired eyes lighting up. Before Connor can move, Dad's stepping forward, yanking him into a tight hug. Dad seems uninjured, since he's moving easily. Connor wraps his arms around him, feeling the sturdiness that is *love* and *Dad*. "Sheila and I have been searching for you for days! Where the hell have you been?"

Over his shoulder, Connor meets Sheila's eyes. She grins hesitantly at him, wriggling her fingers. He smiles awkwardly back. The living room is free of water damage; no stains on the walls, and the stack of newspapers in the corner sits crisp and dry. The house perches on a small hill, and he's glad that his dad doesn't have to deal with consequences from the flood. "I've been sailing. Long story. Glad you're fine, though," he says when his dad pulls away. Connor steps closer to his wizard, setting a hand on the small of his back. Dad raises an eyebrow. "This is Yates."

"Hello," Yates says, beaming. It's the expression he pulls on when he wants to hide his nerves. Connor wants to remind him that he's two centuries old.

Recognition flickers in his father's eyes. He studies the wizard shrewdly, then glances between them. "Yates, huh? You don't look forty... eight, was it?"

Yates turns, the question stark in his gaze. *Forty-eight?*

Connor sighs. He can't keep lying to his dad anymore, not when he's been talking about marriage with Yates. They'll all be family at some point. "Two-hundred and fifty-three, actually. Yates is a wizard."

Yates raises his eyebrows. Sheila gasps, and Dad curses. "You're kidding," Dad says. "I don't believe this."

"Pleased to offer my services," Yates says, bowing. Connor wants to kiss him again.

Dad's forehead wrinkles. "The hell are you doing with a wizard?"

"I found him," Connor says. It stings, though. He'd been hoping for his dad to accept the man he loves. "Thirteen years ago."

Silence stretches long and loud between them.

"Thirteen years ago. You were ten," Dad says. He stares at Yates, then Connor, lips twisting. "The fuck are you doing with those people? You never said he was a damned wizard. The hell?"

Yates opens his mouth, ready to intervene, but Connor shakes his head. "He was my mentor. I told you years ago when you were drunk, but I guess you don't remember: I'm magic, Dad."

"Fuck," his father says, massaging his temple. "Fuck. I don't even—You're magic? I thought I..."

"Bradan," Sheila says, stepping forward to touch his shoulder. "Connor's back. You shouldn't be yelling at him."

Dad scowls, and Connor sighs. But Sheila doesn't seem to share his dad's hostility toward magic, and he's grateful for that.

"Perhaps we should take a seat," Sheila says. She steers Connor's dad into the living room, smiling apologetically at Connor and Yates. Dad shakes his head.

When the door's shut and they're all seated around the coffee table, Dad says, "This is crazy."

"Were you in the church when the wave hit Fort Bragg?" Connor asks. Dad's still scowling at the table, so he looks to Sheila for an answer.

"We were. Someone shouted warnings," she says, leaning into his dad. "All of us went upstairs. We couldn't find you, though. Your dad was so worried. One of the fishermen—I think it was John—said he saw you leave, so we organized a search for you after the wave subsided. It flooded the ground floor, about three feet. I felt really bad that you thought you had to leave." Sheila winces.

"Sorry," he says, grimacing. Sheila and his dad seem decent as a pair. He's watched them together before, but that was when he couldn't accept his father loving anyone aside from his mom. Now, he understands better, knows to let his father seek happiness where he can find it. "Congrats, by the way. On getting married."

"Thank you." Sheila brightens, her shoulders sagging in relief. She seems more youthful without the worry lines on her face. Connor can appreciate her now, too, appreciate that she isn't trying to replace his mom.

Dad huffs, still glowering. "Where were you when the wave hit?"

"On the shore," Connor says. "The sea pulled back. I realized a huge wave was coming in, bad enough to flood, so I went to Yates."

Yates meets his eyes, grinning crookedly. "I guess I could only avoid you for so long."

"Idiot," Connor mutters, but his heart swells with warmth. In a louder voice, he says, "We tried shielding the town with magic. Not sure if it worked, but we tried."

"I heard there was an invisible wall," Sheila says. She leans forward on the armrest of his father's couch, curiosity gleaming in her eyes. "It held most of the waves back. Was that from you?"

"We didn't have much time to set up a barrier." Yates dips his chin in apology. His gaze darkens, as though he wishes he could have done more. "From all the way in the forest, it was a feat."

"You did most of it," Connor says, squeezing his hand. He's proud of the wizard. Proud that they've managed to protect the town, that their spellwork hadn't been for nothing.

Yates' mouth curves into a smile. "You helped. I'm glad you remembered your runes."

Connor shrugs. He'd practiced them as a

distraction, thinking about Yates and trying to forget him at the same time. It doesn't matter now, though. Briefly, he explains Yates' ship floating through the forest, the kraken surfacing, being flung across the ocean, and drifting down the coast on a current. He doesn't mention the failed resurrection spell, though, or his mom's ashes still sitting in the ship.

"Damn," his father says. "Krakens are real?"

"My grandpa's seen one before," Sheila says, nudging him in the side. "So yes, they're real. But I've never met a wizard."

Her eyes sparkle. Yates beams at her, and Connor thinks maybe he can like Sheila.

"So you left our wedding six days ago, right before it flooded," his dad says, face pinched. "Then you found your wizard, tried to stop the tidal wave, and it swept you out into the ocean. In a ship. Then you met a fucking kraken."

"That's about right," Connor says, watching him warily. Dad's taking all this really well, even if Sheila keeps elbowing him to make him listen. "And we tried to save the town. Didn't work out the way we wanted, though."

"Goddamn," Dad says.

What's more insane, to Connor, is that he has Yates now, that Yates is sitting with him, holding his hand. He still can't believe it. "Anyway, I'm moving out," Connor says. "I'll be back in the mornings to fish, though."

Dad's forehead furrows, but his scowl eases. "Fine. If you want."

"You need all the help you can get, old man," Connor says, and his dad cracks a smile, relaxing slightly. It makes the tightness in Connor's shoulders ease, too.

They make small talk about the rest of the town, the flood, and the wedding. Sheila dishes out fresh pecan cookies, and the tension in Dad's posture falls away.

Later, as they're getting ready to leave, Dad pulls him back into another hug. Yates turns to watch from the corner of the porch, bundles of Connor's things under his arms. Connor waves him on.

"Look, I may not agree with magic and all that," Dad says. "But I know how you feel about Yates. I've heard you talk on and on about him. He's not that bad in person."

Which is a compliment, with all his prejudices. Connor grins, the knot in his chest unraveling. "Thanks."

"Take care," his dad says, clapping him on the shoulder. "See you in the morning."

"See you."

As Connor sets off with Yates, his belongings tucked into backpacks, and his dad and Sheila watching from the porch, it feels as though he's leaving behind his old life.

He's ready for it. He's been ready for a future with Yates for a long time.

Epilogue

"ARE YOU sure about this?" Connor asks. They've finally pushed the ship into the forest, rolling it on logs over mushy ground. Since their return from town, they've been securing the ship back in the old clearing, binding it down with spells and ropes so it won't be washed away again. "Me moving in with you?"

Yates pushes magic through an anchoring spell, watching as blue light glows around the ship supports. "Are *you* sure about living with me?"

Connor rolls his eyes, but the wizard looks so earnest that he sighs, setting down his mooring ropes. "Are you only going to believe me when I shove my clothes into your closet?"

"If that's a euphemism, you'll have to do better." But Yates brightens, wandering over to slip his arms around Connor's waist. He presses himself to Connor's back, warm and pliant, his eyes lit with quiet humor. Connor breathes it all in. The ground may be soggy beneath his feet, and the air may be cool and heavy with damp, but he's back in the forest again, with the wizard he's spent a decade with.

"You're the one who swears about sucking dicks," he says. "Not me."

Yates buries his face in Connor's shoulder, his breath puffing through his shirt. "It doesn't have to be swearing. Suck my dick."

Connor snorts, picking up his ropes again. They have an hour before sunset, and the ship still has to be tied down. "I'm busy."

The wizard wriggles. "Really?" he whines. "You can't take a second off?"

"I'll be away fishing half the day tomorrow. Unless you wanna tie the ropes yourself, let me finish this first."

Yates sags against him, his body warm, his cheek soft on Connor's arm. "It's starting to sound like we're married, you know. Doing things around the ship."

Connor laughs. "The rings aren't even ready yet."

Yates perks up. "I think yours will look lovely on you." Light glints off his flame-red hair, and Connor dips his head to sniff at him. He smells like fresh sweat, like rosemary and fir. Connor can't have enough of this, of touching and talking and being with him. The wizard kisses his throat. "Are you excited about the rings?"

"I have you," Connor says. "That's plenty."

Yates beams. He trails his fingers down Connor's abdomen, voice dipping into a purr. "What about later?"

Connor's breath hitches, heat shooting down to his groin. He tries to focus on tying the ship down, but he can't stop thinking about Yates' mouth now.

"Yeah, later."

Yates laughs. He reaches further south, between Connor's legs, and squeezes. Then he pulls away, walking off, and Connor gives up on the ropes. Yates can't tease him and leave and think he'll ignore it. So he turns, catching up with Yates, grabbing him by the elbow.

"Damn you," Connor growls.

The wizard smirks, a promise in his eyes, and they forget about the ship for a while.

HE FINDS Yates on a bench the next week, surrounded by his customers from the previous visit. The crowd is smaller this time, collecting mended crockery and snow globes instead of explaining what needs to be fixed, so Connor leans on a nearby tree, waiting for the people to disperse.

When the last customer has gone, Yates hefts his leather pouch in his palm. "I think I have enough to pay for the rings."

"I'm paying for them," Connor says. He pushes away from the tree, taking a crate of jars and watches from Yates: more things to be repaired.

Yates sighs, nudging him as they fall into step along the sidewalk. They pass trees and bus stops, newspaper stands and florists. "We can't keep arguing over who pays for what if we're getting married, you know."

"So it all goes into a coin bank?" Connor grins, heart lifting at the thought of them stitching their lives together.

"We'll have a hoard." Yates matches his smile.

"Like a kraken's, but with actual money."

"Had no idea krakens hoard."

"They do, in the deep sea. I've only seen it once—it was blazingly dangerous to get so close." Yates hefts his own bag on his shoulder, slipping his hand into Connor's. "Mostly, they collect shells and metal pipes. I've seen one with stone busts from Atlantis."

"Yeah?"

"Of course, I wasn't going to steal any of that."

"What about the one that attacked us?" Connor frowns, feeling a pang of regret. "I hurt it."

Yates squeezes his hand. "It'll lose that tentacle and grow another. Don't worry too much about it."

They turn into the jeweler's, a quaint shop with potted sunflowers and a set of bronze armor in one corner. Yates waves at the sprightly old man behind the counter, beaming. "We're here for our rings," he says. "You measured us last week."

The jeweler straightens, eyes crinkling. "Yates and Connor?"

"That's us."

"Just a heartbeat. Your rings are in the back." He disappears through the heavy velvet drapes at the back of the store, then emerges a moment later, cloth pouch in hand.

The rings tinkle out into Yates' palm: gleaming white-gold, carved on the inside with protective runes. The wizard turns them over, his eyes bright and filled with wonder. Connor picks up the smaller one. Slides it onto Yates' ring finger. It fits perfectly, cool metal on pale skin. Yates stares at it, then up at Connor, his mouth agape. "You didn't even propose."

Connor sighs, hating the heat that sweeps through his cheeks. "But we agreed to have rings. We talked about getting married. Isn't that the same?"

"It's not the same," Yates says. His lips curve up. "You should be on a knee."

"If I have to be on a knee, then so do you," Connor retorts, grinning back. "You can't not ask me."

They both get on their knees. Yates laughs. "I haven't seen a proposal like this."

"Are you asking, or not?" Connor lifts his brows, glancing around the cramped shop. It's a weekday afternoon, so everyone else passes by, save for the jeweler behind the counters. The old man twiddles his thumbs and looks up at the ceiling, smiling. "I'm not kneeling here all day."

"But you would if I asked. You're romantic like that." Yates trails his knuckles over Connor's forearm, his touch a reminder: *I'm here.*

Connor shivers. He wants to glare, but Yates is right. And he doesn't want to wait. "Well?"

Yates takes the ring off his finger, pressing it back into Connor's palm. With his hands tucked into Connor's, he murmurs, "Connor, son of Bradan, will you marry me, and stay by my side for the rest of our lives?"

It's different when Yates is inches away from him, his eyes warm and hopeful, his mouth curled up at the corners. Connor hasn't seen a proposal like this, but it speaks of age and tradition, of timelessness and gravity. He can imagine decades with Yates, his entire life with this man, with them cooking and learning and living together. So he says, "Yes."

Joy lights Yates up from within. He traces the circle of gold in his hand, and his eyes glow with love. It makes Connor's breath catch.

"Yates," he says, trying to find his voice. He wants to pull Yates close, but this has to come first, and he's half-afraid that he'll mess it up. He's been practicing it in his head the whole week. "Son of Donarad, will you marry me, and stay by my side for the rest of our lives?"

"Yes," Yates whispers, leaning in. "Yes, I will."

And Connor lets Yates slide his ring on first, silvery band warm against his skin. It feels like an oath. With a shaky hand, Connor presses the smaller ring back onto Yates' finger, marveling at the way it fits, the way their bands match. He brings Yates' hand to his lips, kissing his fingers. "Mine," he says.

"Yours." Yates ducks his head, a flush spreading through his cheeks.

In that moment, it feels like there's only the two of them in the world, and he's never wanted anything more than this.

THE RING gleams on Connor's finger, catching light whenever he does the littlest things: cooking with Yates, folding the laundry, practicing his magic. Dad sees it the day after they put the rings on each other, right after the first net goes out to sea. He eyes the ring contemplatively. "You're sure about him, huh?"

"Yeah." Connor revs the boat engine so they

begin their trawl. "It's always been him."

"I've thought about it," his dad says carefully, looking at him sideways. His mouth stays a flat line, and it makes Connor tense. Dad still has hang-ups about magic. "Just wondered if it would've been different if I hadn't been so drunk back then. Whether I could have changed this. You were a minor when you were hanging out with him."

Connor shrugs. "Nothing happened back then. He was just teaching me magic."

His dad scowls. "But he could have influenced you."

"Not directly, no. I've thought about it, too." Connor sighs, sitting back in one of their plastic chairs, checking their iceboxes to make sure they're ready for fish. "I kissed him when I was sixteen. He rejected me. Remember?"

"Huh."

But his dad still frowns, sipping from a tumbler of coffee, so Connor keeps talking. "If all he wanted was to sleep with me, he wouldn't have kicked me out right after we did. I was nineteen."

Dad winces. "I didn't need to know that."

He falls silent, though, and Connor listens to the waves as they splash against the boat. Understanding Yates' actions doesn't make the past sting any less, but he's grateful that it's behind them now. Grateful that he has Yates to go home to.

"Still can't believe you hid your magic from me," his dad says.

Connor watches the pelicans soar above them, thinking about a shadowy kitchen a decade ago, when he'd conjured a fire in his palm, and his dad had smacked his hand away. That memory still hurts. *You don't even remember doing that.* "You would've thrown a fit. Don't deny it."

"Yeah, I guess." Dad sighs. He sharpens their gutting knives on flat polishing stones, rinsing them off with clean water. After a moment's hesitation, he says, "But you haven't used it around me."

I guess I haven't. It's a habit. He's used to solving things without magic when his father is nearby. "You want me to?" He twists the ring around his finger, wondering what spells he could possibly demonstrate. Most of the runes he's learned have invisible results, like increasing his strength, or improving the health of plants. "But I'm not using it to fish. That's cheating."

His father nods. "That something you came up with by yourself, or did Yates say that?"

"Yates did."

"He's an odd one." Dad wanders over to the fishing net, his eyes downcast. "I guess he's not so bad. He doesn't remind me of my parents. Doesn't get all arrogant next to non-magic people. Guess it'll just take a bit of getting used to."

"Okay." Connor relaxes. He wants his dad to accept Yates, so Yates will have more people he can count on. He nudges at his ring again, thinking about the runes on its inner surface. "Hey, how about I write a protection spell for the boat? Just a bit to ward against rocks and lightning."

His father thinks on it for a bit, then cracks a smile. "Guess you could. The boat won't catch fire or anything?"

"Hell, no." It's a step forward, and as Connor

burns his runes into the side of the boat, he can't help grinning.

LATER THAT night, Yates cradles Connor's old sailboat, tracing the fishing lines holding tiny canvas sails in place. Connor watches as his eyes gleam. "I got that boat when I was twelve," he says. "I gave you soggy cake the next day."

Yates laughs, setting the boat back on the library table. "I remember that cake. My mouth was full of sand afterward."

"Sand?" Connor riffles through his memories, confused. "I didn't trip or anything."

"I had to eat with my hands, and they were sandy. Neither of us had a fork." Yates wanders over, slipping his arms around Connor's waist. He fits easily against Connor's body, and Connor pulls him close, smelling the shampoo in his hair. "I was touched that you remembered me."

"I've always remembered you," Connor says. "The boat was the last birthday present I got from my mom."

Yates stills, breathing in deeply. "I'm sorry."

"It's fine. I've just..." In his youth, he had looked at the boat and dreamed about adventures and magic. Now, he shares a ship with Yates, and that's enough. Home is right here with his wizard. "I wanted to see the world when I was a kid. I told my mom I was going to live on a ship."

Yates' gaze softens. "We can go sailing," he says. "After we repair the engine mechanisms. I'm not sailing with my magic—it's too tiring."

"Just means you have to work harder," Connor says, grinning when Yates' mouth pulls down in an exaggerated pout. "I'm kidding. Maybe when Dad retires and I don't have to help him fish."

"We'll be old and married by then," Yates says. His eyes light up, and Connor's pulse quickens. He wants to marry Yates. Wants to have him forever.

"Yeah," he says thickly, throat tight. "I want that."

The wizard hears the lowering of his voice, the words he doesn't say, and he leans in, his eyes soft. He's beautiful. "I'm yours," Yates whispers. "Always."

Connor pulls him close, wrapping him in his arms. "I'm yours, too."

THEY GATHER on Connor's favorite clifftop a month later, on a balmy day with a light breeze. Standing amidst swaying grass, Connor remembers: Yates living through a lightning strike years ago, them watching the forest burn, lying down and feeling rain patter on their faces.

"It's a good idea," Connor's dad says, staring wistfully out to sea. "I think Mags will like it."

Connor nods, glancing sidelong at Yates. The wizard squeezes his hand. Connor returns it, before taking the pastel-blue urn from his father. He holds his breath, twists the lid open, and exhales. Yates was the one to suggest it. Connor hadn't thought of how he wanted to let his mother go, until they strolled along the shore and glanced up at the cliffs.

"Guess this is goodbye," Connor murmurs. He

dips his hand into the ashes and scatters some out over the cliff, watching as the wind takes his mother away. He thinks about her laugh, about her twirling around the kitchen with his father. He thinks about her asking questions when he talked about magic. She'd have loved to meet Yates.

Next to him, his dad releases the next handful into the wind.

His chest feels heavier than he expected. There's no undoing this, no bringing his mom to life. He thinks she'll like it better this way, just the untouched remains of her body drifting out to sea. She's always loved the ocean.

In silence, Connor and his father take turns emptying the urn, until he pours the last of his mother's ashes into the wind, and his dad sets a hand on his shoulder.

"Rest well, Mags," Dad says.

"I'm proud of you," Yates says softly, slipping his fingers into Connor's hand. Connor knows that he means *I'm proud of you for being brave. For letting your mother rest,* and those words don't come from his mentor, but his lover and best friend. "She'll be watching you from the heavens."

Yates looks up at the sky, his eyes solemn. Connor realizes that the wizard sees his own teacher in the clouds. Realizes that Yates must remember Quagmuth a lot. So he wraps his arm around Yates' waist, pulling him close. "You did well," Connor says. "Be proud of yourself."

The wizard blinks rapidly. "Thank you."

To the side, Connor's dad watches them warmly, his gaze understanding. "Lunch is on me," he says. "Grilled steak sandwiches sound good to both of you?"

Connor nods. Yates smiles, and the three of them head down the cliffs, a sea breeze blowing gently behind them.

HE MARRIES Yates on his twenty-fourth birthday.

In the same church where his father remarried a year ago, Connor looks down the aisle with his dad, to where Yates waits with Sheila. Around them, his fisherman friends watch patiently, and so do Yates' regular customers from around town. The church is large enough for a hundred, the pews barely filled, but all Connor can see is the man at the end of the burgundy carpet. Yates beams at him.

Connor can't help grinning back. They've been living together for a year, cooking, doing repairs, building a larger garden. This is just another milestone in their lives.

He's never seen Yates in a suit, though. It fits the sleek lines of the wizard's body, hugging his arms and legs. Across the church, Yates' eyes flicker down Connor's own suit, his shirt the same one he wore a year ago. Their gazes meet. Connor looks at the man he'll call his husband, and his heart misses a beat. He wonders if Yates is thinking the exact same thing.

"C'mon, stop staring and start walking," his dad says from the corner of his mouth.

He realizes then that he needs to move, that everyone in the church is watching him ogle the wizard. Connor blushes, hating the heat that creeps up his face. Yates' grin widens. Connor walks.

"Trying to kill the carpet?" Dad asks. "Quit stomping."

Connor *hates* blushing. "Just walking heavily."

They make it down the aisle with the carpet intact. Closer to Yates, Connor realizes that the wizard is pressing his lips together, quivering as he tries to stifle his laughter. "Shut up," he mutters, wishing they were getting married in his father's backyard instead, where there isn't anyone else watching him blush.

"I didn't say anything," Yates says. He can't stop beaming, though. "You're adorable when you're flustered."

"That's not making it better," Connor hisses. Feet away, the pastor watches in bewilderment, his eyes bouncing between them.

"He definitely doesn't do this in bed," Yates whispers at all of them. Sheila snorts. Connor wants to hide his face.

"Gods' sakes. Stop glaring," his dad says, nudging him. "This is your wedding."

It brings Connor sharply back to why they're here. Why Yates is standing before him, dressed up in a suit, their rings sitting on a silver tray in Sheila's hands. Yates' grin fades to a soft smile, and Connor's mouth twitches.

He doesn't hear the long, rambling speech the pastor gives. Instead, he looks at Yates' profile, the point of his nose, the pull of his lips, the way he stands still, leaning in until his shoulder nudges Connor's arm. It feels like everything in the last decade has led up to this.

"You may exchange your rings," the pastor

says.

They take the wedding bands from Sheila. Yates' ring glints between Connor's fingers, smooth on the outside, engraved lightly with protective runes on the inside. Those rings have been a constant reminder of *them* for a year now.

"You're certain about this?" Yates murmurs when he takes Connor's hand. Their fingers tangle, warm and firm, and Connor holds him tight.

"Yeah." He's never been surer in his life.

Yates' thumb brushes across his hand, his mouth a half-smile. "Still?"

"Always," Connor whispers.

Yates blushes. When he slides the ring onto Connor's finger, it pulses with magic, a warm, comforting assurance that makes Connor grin. He saturates Yates' ring with his own magic, takes Yates' hand in his own, and fits the ring onto his finger. Yates' eyes shine, joy radiant on his face.

Connor leans in and presses a kiss to his lips. Yates is his husband. They're married, two parts of a whole, and it feels the same as before except Yates is *his*.

"Thank you," Yates whispers against his lips, leaning in so his body fits against Connor's. "For accepting me. For everything."

"I love you," Connor says, holding him close. Yates will always be his best friend and lover. Will always be someone by his side. "That won't change."

And as Yates cups his face and kisses him harder, Connor knows that his wizard loves him, too.

ABOUT THE AUTHOR

Anna has been scribbling since she was fourteen. She has a soft spot for dorky guys who are perfect for each other, and she's a huge fan of stories with drama, angst and bittersweet tension. And pretty words.

She is currently living on the west coast of the US with her husband. She also collects tiny glass globes and glass atlases, massive stacks of notebooks and paper, and is on a never-ending hunt for state quarters missing from her collection.

Printed in Great Britain
by Amazon